The Heir of Woodmyst

THE WOODMYST CHRONICLES BOOK III

Robert E Kreig

WHITEKEEP BOOKS

THE HEIR OF WOODMYST

For James, my brother.

THE FROZEN WASTE

THE CORE LANDS

WINTERMARSH

IRONFIELDS

ERIMOOR

BLACKROCK HAVEN

WHITEKEEP

BLACKSHORE

THE CANYONS OF TERIXITH

LIGHTHOUSE

REDLOCH

MALLOWHILL

THE SEA OF SOLACE

STRONGHOLDT

MELAMWED

THE PILLARS OF MOHAA

CLEARFOE

HAVENCREST

KALISARD

OAKREACH

BROODNESS

NEWHOLT

MEADOWMOOR

WINTERSPRING

THE HEADWATERS

WOODMYST

OSTFORD

DELLMOOR

OLDCASTLE

GRASSREACH

PRYHOLT

BELBURN

GREYROSE

LUNKHUL FOREST

DWEAGAN

BARROWFIELD

THE SEA OF LUNKHUL

REDEDGE

LINPORT

BUTTEREDGE

SYVIEW

ROSSFORD

FREYMOOR

BELMORE

THE WESTERN SEA

THE EASTERN SEA

N
W E
S

Prologue

Slinking as low to the ground as she could, keeping as quiet as was ever possible, she moved rapidly, stealthily, through the undergrowth to avoid the enemy. Her thick white robe was weighing heavy from the moisture collected from the snow as she passed beneath a low limb or through a thick brush.

Turning, she saw her lair, her provisional home, billowing smoke through its roof. All of her supplies were there. The materials she needed to create her warriors were burning away to ash.

Hastily, she made her way towards the coast, hugging the ground where the mountain met the forest floor. The steep incline to the left was a guide towards the sea. Her only chance, her only option, was to clamber over the outstretched arm of the mountain that bordered these lands from the realm where the Sovereign dwelt.

As she breached the tree line, she saw a fire burning in the distance to her right. Two men sat by the flickering light, staring into the hearth as they talked.

They were too far away for her to hear their words.

She felt too weak to manipulate them, to destroy them.

Besides, she had what she needed.

Ivo had given her that.

Staying as close as she could to the steep rocky face of the elevation, adorned with snow, she moved silently towards the east. Leaving the men by the fire behind her, she noticed something else to her right.

A campsite.

Several tents formed a circle around a smouldering hearth. Grouped together in a tight mob were several horses.

She considered whether to venture over and slay the beasts. It would slow the travellers' pursuit and give her the advantage again. Pulling her dagger from her belt, twisting it in her grasp, she wrestled with the idea.

No, she thought. She returned her energy to flee.

The northern lands are full of strange creatures. If the weather doesn't slow them, the inhabitants will.

She moved to a place where the land almost met the sea. Enormous waves crashed against the jagged rocks at the end of the point, sending a fine spray into the air and over her face.

The wind was stronger here, colder.

She wrapped her cloak around her tightly as she scrambled over the rocks. They were slippery in places and her hand needed to leave the warmth of her clothing to steady her climbing.

It took some time, more time than she had planned for. She needed arduous climbing and careful navigation to reach the far side of the rocky protrusion.

Upon reaching the level ground on the other side of the rocky mound, she fixed her coverings before moving onwards. Her footfalls were clearly marking the snow behind her, but her concern was elsewhere.

With her eyes darting to the left and scanning the forest at the foot of the range, she kept watching for movement. She moved her hood to listen for sounds, training her hearing to focus past the whistling wind.

A glance towards the sky revealed the clouds parting ways to expose the bright stars that dotted the expanse like countless fires in the far distance. The moon sent a silver glow across the open ground, blanketed in white.

She blended in, camouflaged to her environment.

Her clothing and her surroundings matched well and apart from her footprints; she was difficult to see at a distance. She believed she would be safe from her enemy.

The creatures of these lands, however, were another problem altogether.

They hunted by scent, not sight.

One on its own would be easy for her to handle. She would have power over it.

But they hunted in packs and were extremely territorial.

People from these lands only ever travelled in large, well-armed groups, in case they happened upon such creatures. Usually, large numbers and loud noise were enough to deter an attack. However, there was no guarantee that this was always the case. During winter, when game was low and hunger was rife, the creatures became more daring.

Her eyes scanned the dark shadows beneath the trees. She willed herself to move faster, keeping close to the shore.

Her journey, she gauged, would be at least two days.

Two days of watching the west, fleeing the south and moving to the north.

She gave thought to the horses back in the camp on the other side of the encroaching mountain behind her. Her first thought was to destroy them, to slow her enemy down, but she didn't consider taking one for herself.

Not until now.

It was too late to turn back.

They are probably gathering now; she thought. *They may be on their way to find me.*

She returned her thoughts to the path ahead.

If she could get to the river by the end of the next day, she would have made substantial ground.

Get to the river and you're halfway home.

Raising her hands to her mouth, she breathed upon them to heat her fingers a little before returning them beneath her cloak and wrapping her arms around herself tightly.

She walked on, briskly, swiftly across the snow.

Get to the river.

Get home.

One

The survivors carried two bodies precariously through the forest and back to the two awaiting men at the edge of the open ground. The looks that fell upon their faces were of extreme dismay, particularly when they saw the still body of their beloved captain. Both rose to their feet, either out of respect or shock. The wounded man, pierced through his thigh during the battle with the dead, forgot about his pain momentarily as he limped over to the bearers of his commander.

"What happened?" he asked, his stomach tying itself in knots as he wondered if he truly wanted to know the answer to his question.

"It was the witch," Jeremy replied, aiding some men with the transport of the captain. "She was his daughter."

"No." The man shook his head and crumpled to the snow, as the throbbing ache in his leg returned. "Not Sumaiyya?"

"It would appear so," Jeremy said as they rested the bodies on the ground. "She stabbed him in the back as they embraced."

Tarkin looked at peace, partly because they had laid him face-up, obscuring his wounds against the ground. Ivo, however, was naked apart from the bearskin Tomas had thrown around him as they carried him away from the burning keep. The covering had slipped open to reveal the gaping hole in his chest.

"What happened to him?" the other man asked.

"The witch happened," David snarled.

Oliver and Simon raced off towards the camp as the men stared disbelievingly at the bodies.

"Where are they going?" the wounded man questioned.

"To get two horses and canvas sheets," Jeremy informed him. "We need to get both of them away from here, and we need more wood to build two large fires."

The men looked at one another. They understood.

Their captain and the man from Woodmyst were to be burned.

"We'll get some wood," the injured man grunted as he tried to get back upon his feet.

"You'll stay right there," Karlena said, crouching by his side to check his wound. "It needs stitching."

"We'll need to get him back to camp first," Jeremy told her.

"Aye, Captain," she replied.

Captain, he thought. *I don't think I will ever get used to that.*

The nine remaining able crewmen of the *Adelandria* gathered as much dry wood as they could. They used their swords afterwards to chop lower limbs from the pines at the edge of the tree line, adding to the wood they collected. A sizable stack of timber piled near the hearth the two men had set earlier in order to burn the body parts of the dead they had fought against earlier in the night.

Oliver and Simon returned on foot, leading two steeds by the reins, each trailing a canvas sheet behind it like a wheelless cart. Long ropes tethered the canvas sheets to the horse's bridles.

The bodies of Captain Tarkin and Ivo were placed carefully on one canvas sheet, side by side, as some of the wood was loaded upon the other. The kindling was too much to take on the first trip.

After unloading near the shoreline, they made two more trips to transport the rest of the wood.

The men busied themselves with building two pyres, stacking the wood high and spaced well enough to allow the flow of air through the timber. Smaller kindling went near the bottom of the masses on the western side, away from the effects of the onshore winds.

The Erilian women, Rhydra, Sharek and Akasati, prepared the captain's body, doting over him lovingly as they shed many tears, mourning their loss. They undressed him to clean his skin using cloths and warm water from a pot on the hot coals of the campfire.

Emily felt a little embarrassed at being left to prepare Ivo for the ceremony. She wiped the marks from smoke and battle from his face. Karlena and Rhyodia placed their attention on the rest of his body. If they felt uneasy about having their hands upon him, they didn't show it.

They washed the blood from Ivo's chest, and Tarkin's back before dressing both men. The women outfitted the captain in the attire he had worn for the duration of their journey, except for his spyglass, which they put aside for his successor. Emily and Akasati found bits and pieces of clothing articles in Ivo's tent and hoped that, if he wasn't the true owner of the items, the real titleholders wouldn't mind.

An Erilian dagger split one of the canvas sheets in two. Sharek divided the cloth evenly before laying the pieces flat on the ground.

Together, the women lifted Captain Tarkin onto one piece of canvas before moving Ivo onto the other. The canvas sheets were then wrapped around the bodies and held in place with strips of twine.

"Now," Akasati said to the injured man who had been watching the whole affair from beside the fire, "let's see if we can mend that leg of yours."

***

The departed comrades lay upon the large wooden piles near the shoreline. From the sparks Jeremy produced when he rapidly scraped his two small flint rocks together, the tinder ignited at the base of the wooden piles.

Tomas crouched by the other man, giving a soft blow upon the glimmers to entice the timber to ignite. Before long, the pyres were both ablaze.

The travellers watched in silence as their two friends burned away into oblivion and the sun peeked its head over the horizon. Some shed tears, while others thought of fond memories. Then there were those who silently fed their hatred and wished to exact revenge upon the witch who had taken so many of them.

All mourned in their own way.

When the bodies had all but burned away and the pyre collapsed, thoughts returned to their current plight and what was to be done now.

"Shouldn't someone say some words?" David asked Oliver quietly, hoping no one else heard him.

"Words to who?" Simon questioned.

"I don't know." David shrugged. "Maybe the gods?"

"There are no gods," Tomas grunted. "There never were."

Emily put an arm around him, soothing his temperament.

He turned to face the woods to the west, where he could still see smoke billowing from the base of the giant mountain. The keep wasn't visible from the beach, but it still burned, and that made him feel a tiny sense of satisfaction.

A place that contained such evil as it did should not remain. He was glad to see the dark smoke rising from it. The world, as far as he was concerned, was far better without such places.

"I can't speak for everyone here," Tomas put in. "I don't want to assume what any of you would want to do. The choice is yours to make.

"I plan to continue north for two reasons. First, to finish what I set out to do, and that is to bring Emily's people home. Second, I want to kill the bitch who did this to my friends." He pointed into the pyre as he scanned the faces of the men and women before him.

"I'll say the same as Tomas." Jeremy raised his voice for all to hear. "Captain Tarkin named me his successor, but I will not use the position of commander to order any of you to accompany me further than this. I will join Tomas and help him on his quest, but my intent is to complete what the captain originally set out to do. His mission was, and still is, to destroy the Sovereign.

"Join me if you wish and we will see this through one way or another," he said. "Or return south to Oakbeach and wait for me there."

The gathering was silent for what seemed an eternity.

Eventually, Oliver broke the meeting by walking away back towards camp.

"You're leaving?" David called after him.

"Yes," he called back, continuing his pace. "I'm leaving here to go there." He pointed to the campsite. "And then I'm going to prepare my horse to leave there and go after that bitch in white."

David felt a lump grow in his throat as a great smile stretched over his face. "Wait for me," he said, and raced after his friend.

The men and women silently agreed; the mission was worth it.

"Captain," Akasati said from Jeremy's side.

He turned to see her holding Tarkin's spyglass folded closed in her hand.

"I believe this is yours."

"Thank you, Akasati," he said, taking in a deep breath before reaching for the object. He took it carefully, as if it was some sacred object, and held it in his fingers as he scrutinised the casing.

The brass finish glistened in the morning sun's rays, shining into his eyes as he remembered the kindness his captain had shown him. He could only hope to be a fraction of what his commander had been.

Tears welled in his eyes as he tucked the spyglass into his pocket. Akasati put her arms around him, a gesture of condolence. He returned the gesture and gave her a gentle squeeze.

***

The travellers packed tents and loaded horses as they prepared to get underway. The eleven unmanned horses shared the weight of equipment and supplies. This also allowed certain articles to be moved from the riders' mounts and loaded onto the pack animals, thus easing the strain all around. Most riders freed themselves from their bedrolls.

With the travellers ready, Tomas gave the order to move out. Their first obstacle was the rocky mound that stretched from the giant mountain, across the plain and into the sea.

It reminded Emily of a tree root that breached the ground, twisting from the base of the plant to a point where it disappeared beneath the surface. Only, it wasn't a tree. It was a mountain that stretched so high that it pierced the clouds above.

As they drove the horses from the campsite towards the coast, the riders veered towards the base of the elevation. Eventually, they came close enough to observe the surface of the stony ground rising steeply to their left.

In places, the mound appeared smooth and passable. They sent a couple of riders to investigate, always returning with the same response. The covering snow was deceiving them.

The white blanket had filled with holes and crevasses along the dark stretch of stone. The riders would have surely lost their horses had they attempted to cross in any of these places.

Eventually, the only place to cross was near the water's edge, where the waves crashed violently against the jagged rocks. Each man dismounted his charger and walked ahead of their beasts, leading them carefully across the slippery terrain.

The smell of salt was thick as a fine mist of water continuously smeared the sides of their faces. Most of the troop members had tried to cover their skin by pulling their hoods low over their brows. The attempt to keep dry was in vain. Strong onshore wind wafted the tiny droplets of water under their cowls, leaving them just as wet as they would have been if they had left their coverings dangling from the back of their necks.

Precariously, cautiously, the travellers navigated through small gullies and miniature peaks, trying their best to not slip, fall or ultimately break any bones. Both man and beast made several close calls. On most occasions, trust between the two species saved their necks. Riders would be careful not to lead their steeds into a dangerous situation whilst horses would dig their hooves in as handlers slipped and fell, holding onto the reins as their only hope of survival.

The wounded man had the worst experience during this part of the journey. He had to stick to riding on horseback, as his leg wasn't ready to travel so far without resting often. He followed closely behind Oliver, keeping his steed on the same path trodden by the other. Oliver kept his eye on the young man as they progressed across the stony land.

"What's your name?" Oliver asked him as he viewed the level ground ahead of them. He saw a bit of a drop before him that others in front had taken in order to get to the open ground beyond. "If we're going to be travelling together, I should at least know your name."

"Baldwyn," the injured man replied. "Baldwyn Palmer."

"Well, Baldwyn Palmer. I'm Oliver Weston."

"I know who you are, sir," Baldwyn said.

"I'm no sir," the other said, laughing. "Just call me Oliver."

"I apologise." The injured man smiled. "It's a habit. I just about call everyone sir."

"Even the Erilian women?"

"Yes, sir." Baldwyn laughed.

"Steep decline coming up and then we're done," Oliver warned the other. "Let me take my horse down first and that way you can see where to go. I'll wait for you at the bottom."

It wasn't a long descent, only the equivalent of a few paces, but it was sheer.

Careful placement of his feet, and an overly cautious horse, made the first few steps slow. The beast became more confident after seeing Oliver go before it.

No sooner were all four legs on the section of steep decline, than they slid all the way to the bottom. As the ground rapidly came towards him, Oliver scooted to the left and timed it to land with his right foot ahead of the other. He continued running ahead a little to allow his horse to correct itself on the level ground.

The horse ran forward a little way. Oliver extended the reins to allow the steed some slack. It reeled around him, slowing its pace before moving to his side, where it nuzzled against his chest. With a smile, he stroked the golden steed on the muzzle and rewarded with a gentle nicker.

"See," Oliver called to Baldwyn, still sitting on his horse above. "Easy."

"Didn't look easy," the younger man replied.

"Just dig your heels in and go for it."

The young man shook his head, not to disagree with Oliver's advice, but more to shake the doubts from his own head.

His leg throbbed a little. He believed he could feel each of the tiny little holes that Karlena had made with her stitching. Hoping he wouldn't fall and tear her fine work open, he kicked with his heels.

The horse lurched forward and trotted down the embankment.

It slipped a little here and there, but for the most part, it kept control all the way down.

The horse reached the level ground safely and slowed its pace as Baldwyn brought the steed back around to Oliver's position.

"See?" The man from Woodmyst smiled as he mounted his animal. "Easy."

Baldwyn nodded, breathing hard as his heart continued to pound in his ears.

"Easy," he breathed.

Two

The troop regrouped on the northern edge of the rocky barrier that so definitively separated the southern lands from those they were in now. The men checked the horses and each other for scratches and wounds, as so many had minor slips over the damp rocks. Apart from Baldwyn's wounds, sustained the night before, no other injuries had occurred.

Twenty-one men and forty horses mustered on the snow to continue their journey. Tomas gave the call, and all riders set upon their quest.

"It feels different here," Simon remarked as they rode.

He looked about the surrounding expanse. Behind was the giant mountain that towered over everything like a menacing behemoth, ready to crush everything in its path. Before them was a seemingly endless stretch of snow. To their right, the sounds of thunderous ocean waves crashed upon the black rocks that lined the sea. To their left, a thick forest of pine trees, draped in white, stretched into the mountains beyond.

Visually, it appeared very similar to the region they had already passed through, but his stomach was tight and the hairs on the back of his neck stood more on end with each crunching step that his steed made in the snow.

"What do you mean?" David asked, riding at his side.

"I don't know," Simon replied. "It's as if we're being watched."

"Perhaps the witch is still with us," the other suggested. "Maybe she's watching from the trees."

He shook his head. "I don't think so."

David gave him a quizzical look. "How could you know?"

"I don't," Simon replied. "But there are tracks ahead of us."

"What?" Tomas said, suddenly tuning into the conversation. "Tracks? What tracks?"

"Right there," Simon pointed. "They go straight on."

"How could I not have seen them?" Tomas said to Emily by his side.

"You have a lot on your mind," she suggested. "We all do."

"I only just noticed them, myself," Simon admitted.

Jeremy retrieved the spyglass from his pocket as he pulled his horse to a stop. He lifted the lens to his eye as he extended the tube and peered in the direction where the footsteps led.

Moving the small telescope to the left, then the right, he could find nothing. The horizon was a hazy white through the view, making everything blend together.

"I can't see anything," he informed them as he folded the telescope before placing it back into his pocket. "Everything looks the same. White."

"That won't help us," Tomas told him. "The bitch is wearing white."

"Do you think she changes colours with the seasons?" Oliver quipped. "Perhaps green in summer and orange during the autumn."

"She'll be wearing red when I run her through with my sword and stain her pretty white frocks with her own blood," Karlena snarled.

"We need to get to her first," Tomas said, urging his brown mare forward.

The troop followed as David reached over to clip Oliver across the ear. "You idiot."

***

The higher the sun lifted into the sky, the more the sky cleared of clouds and the less the wind blew from the east. The path became more and more perceptible as the glowing orb illuminated the way before them more and more. The riders now saw their path wasn't merely a flat, continuous surface. There were small hills and shallow dales for as far as they could see.

Imprints in the snow from the fleeing witch were now so discernible that Simon believed that a newborn child could follow them. Still, he was instructed to use his tracking skills and lead the troop.

The clear impression of her left boot followed by a fair stretch of untouched snow before the print of her right boot told him she was moving swiftly; perhaps running at a rapid pace. How she could maintain the speed to produce tracks such as these was beyond Simon's comprehension.

She is a witch; he thought. *Maybe she is using her magic.*

The overbearing sense that someone or something was watching from the woods still perplexed him. He kept glancing off in the direction of the pine trees far to his left, only to see a quiet forest nestled peacefully beneath the mountains.

He wondered if his mind was simply playing tricks on him.

After the past few nights, the troop had experienced little rest and were all feeling the effects of over-tiredness. The witch had kept them on edge for most of the journey, stealing members of their company away to be used for her ill will, and sending horrific straw men to attack them from the darkness of the woods.

With such constant terrors to contend with, it was no wonder he felt a sense of paranoia.

He turned to see Tomas riding tall in his saddle, talking to Emily some distance behind him. It was too far to hear what they were saying.

Others behind them were looking this way or that, and a couple even slept as their horses did the work, oblivious to any trouble that was nearby. If there were any.

He returned his attention to the footfalls in the snow. They continued to be spaced apart at a regular distance, implying that she was moving with speed.

She must be using her powers to move so rapidly, he surmised again. *Nothing can move like this. It's unnatural.*

With his eyes switching between the imprints on the surface and the trees far to his left, Simon rode with a consistent sense of unease. He wiped his eyes and yawned, wishing for some time in his bedroll. He envied the bastards riding at the back of the mob, who were stealing a few moments of sleep as they rode.

Why do I need to be the designated tracker?

A half-wit could do this.

***

Tomas surmised it was time for them to stop for the day. The sun had arced across the sky and made her descent towards the mountain peaks. He directed the team a little farther to the west, bringing them to a place about halfway between the tree line and the shore.

The sound of the waves breaking upon the stony beach resonated from the shore to where they gathered. The smell of salt was still thick in his nostrils. He didn't believe he could ever get used to it.

"We'll camp here tonight," he informed the riders as he dismounted his mare. "We will need wood and water."

"The men can get the wood," Jeremy said loudly so that all could hear. "The rest of us will set up our tents."

"We'll unload the horses first," Tomas instructed. "Then we'll take a canvas sheet and one steed to help bring the firewood back to camp."

Before long, they had erected tents and put in place a makeshift yard for the horses. The women of Erilia worked fast and accurately. They moved their belongings into the tent that they once shared with their beloved Captain Tarkin. They shed some more tears as they considered that this would be their first night without him.

Emily moved both Tomas' and her equipment into their shelter and set up the bedrolls to prepare for the night. She then took several pots and packed them full of snow.

The men rummaged through the forest, gathering as much dry wood as they could find. It was a near impossible task, as the snow had blanketed everything.

They placed smaller pieces upon the canvas sheet attached to the horse waiting at the edge of the tree line. The men also gathered three large, long logs that had fallen in the woods, as was becoming tradition each night, so that they could have something to sit upon near the fire.

With the logs and the kindling, the load was too heavy for the steed to cart, so they split the cargo into two freights. The horse took the firewood in the first as the men carried one log upon their shoulders. After unloading, they returned to place another log on the canvas sheet, once again carrying the other to the campsite.

All the while, Simon still had the sense that something was nearby. Something with malicious intention. Something that watched malignantly.

The fire was set and the pots of snow soon melted over the flames as the sun veiled itself behind the jagged mountain ridge. Handfuls of dried oats fed the animals while the riders heated a pot of porridge.

Before darkness had swallowed the sky entirely, several men had retired to their tents. Others, including the three Simon had seen sleeping through the day, remained wide awake and talked by the light of the fire.

"You men," said Jeremy, from his place on a log beside Tomas and Emily, "are on watch until I relieve you."

"Aye, sir," they chorused as Jeremy rose to his feet.

"Wake me when it's your shift," Tomas said to him. "I'll join you on the watch."

"That would be much appreciated." Jeremy placed his hand on the other's shoulder. "But for now, I must get some sleep."

Tomas looked across the flames to Simon, who sat upright, sleeping with a bowl of porridge in his lap and a closed hand holding a spoon to his mouth.

"Looks like you're not the only one," he said with a smile.

Jeremy followed his friend's gaze and chuckled quietly before moving away towards his tent.

David, sitting beside the sleeping man, eyed Tomas quizzically. Tomas nodded towards Simon, urging the other to look at his neighbour.

"Oh bloody heck," David groaned, removing the bowl and spoon from Simon and placing them onto the snow at his feet. Simon made a chewing motion, lifting his heavy eyelids drunkenly.

"I was eating that," he protested.

"No, you weren't," David said as he lifted him by the arm to his feet. "It's time for sleep."

"There's something out there," Simon slurred as the other led him away. "Something watching."

"You let us worry about that," David replied, dismissing the words.

Tomas watched the two men disappear into their tent and felt his eyes weighing heavily as well.

"I am also going to bed," he told everyone as he rose to his feet. "Anyone not on watch may want to consider doing the same. Today was a long day."

***

Sleep came easily. He didn't even notice when Emily came in to lie beside him, but there she was. Her head was upon his shoulder and her arm was over his body. She was on her belly and somehow, his arm had made its way around her and rested upon her back.

"Tomas," a whispering voice called.

"Yeah," he replied. Emily stirred beside him but remained asleep.

"Jeremy," the other identified himself. "I'm about to go on watch. Are you still coming or would you prefer to sleep?"

"I'm coming," Tomas replied, removing himself from Emily's grasp as delicately as he could. "And I would like to keep sleeping."

He quickly dressed and exited the tent.

Walking beside Jeremy, he buckled his sword to his waist as they approached the fire together.

"You are a heavy sleeper," Jeremy told him. "I was about to leave you to your dreams and do the watch on my own."

"How long were you there?"

"I'm not sure," he replied. "But I called your name maybe five or six times."

"I must've needed the rest." Tomas cocked his head, frowning.

The three men on watch rose to their feet as the two commanders approached.

"Sirs," they chorused.

"We mixed a brew of tea in this pot, if you're interested," one man informed them as he pointed to a small iron container steaming at the edge of the coals.

"Most definitely," Tomas replied, stooping to retrieve a cup from the ground.

"Anything?" Jeremy asked the watchmen.

"Nothing, Captain," another man reported. "Some noises from the woods, but we think it was probably just snow dropping from the branches to the ground."

"It wasn't like that racket we heard when the straw men came for us," another put in. "It was quieter, if you get what I'm saying."

"Lumps of snow falling onto the ground." Tomas nodded as he lifted the cup to his lips. "Nothing to worry about."

"Thank you, gentlemen," Jeremy said. "Try to get some rest."

"Aye, sir," they replied before moving away to their tent.

When they had gone, both men sat by the hearth.

"Do you think the noise they heard was only snow hitting the ground?" Jeremy asked Tomas.

As if to answer his question, a dull thud resonated from the forest.

"Trees surround Woodmyst," Tomas replied. "That was the sound of a branch dropping snow upon the ground. I believe our witch has continued north. We have nothing to fear from her and her scarecrows for the time being. Relax and have some tea."

Jeremy peered towards the dark woods and nodded as he heard another soft thud.

Tomas cocked his ear in the noise's direction, keeping his composure calm for the sake of his friend.

The captain poured himself a cup of steaming brew. He took a sip and let out a loud, exhaling breath. "Oh, that's good," he said.

Tomas replied with a smile as another soft thud echoed from the shadows.

The man from Woodmyst felt the hairs on the back of his neck rising as an icy chill ran down his spine.

Simon was right.

Something watched.

Three

Setting off early in the morning, well before the sun had risen above the horizon, the troop continued northward. The ship they had originally set out to pursue was well beyond reach. They had no hope of seeing the vessel again until they reached the place where its commander weighed anchor.

Their new target was the witch that had escaped them during their skirmish at the keep on the southern side of the divide. Her footfalls were easy enough to follow during the previous day.

Today, however, proved more difficult.

Strong wind to the north and light snow from some smaller clouds had filled the imprints. The ground appeared clean, untouched, and empty.

"There's nothing left to track," Simon informed the others as he crouched on the ground.

"We can only hope she has continued to the north."

"She will have," Karlena said assuredly.

"How do you know she hasn't avoided us and hidden herself in the forest?" Oliver questioned.

Simon glared at the trees as the hairs on the back of his neck stood on end again. Tomas noticed his friend's reaction. He felt a gnawing unease in the back of his mind. Something was out there, but he didn't believe it to be the woman in white.

"We continue north," Tomas instructed. "Even if she has doubled back, the ship has not. We set out originally on a rescue mission. We continue with that in mind."

The company pressed on, maintaining their course ever northward.

A thin layer of cloud had collected above the sea and slowly drifted towards the land. At first, the vapours appeared harmless as they grew closer and closer to the shore.

By midmorning, Jeremy felt some apprehensions towards the weather. The clouds had grown thick and deepened in colour. Some places in the mists appeared green, showing a heavy load of moisture carried within the wisps.

"We're in for snow," Jeremy called, "or hail."

Tomas peered towards the clouds and saw the threat that had the captain concerned.

"We can tolerate snow," Tomas replied, "as long as the wind holds."

"And if it doesn't?" David asked.

"It may force us to set up camp again," he reluctantly informed his friend.

"Not even midday yet," David growled.

"Do you think this is her doing?" Emily questioned, remembering a terrible snowstorm just a few days before where two men went missing.

"I can't be certain." Tomas kept his eyes on the encroaching clouds. "In any case, we can expect a slower journey than we planned for."

Sure enough, snow fell.

Light flakes sprinkled towards the ground without presenting a hindrance for the travellers. The steeds occasionally stuck out their tongues to lick the white specks that tickled their noses.

Emily, riding on Tomas' left, giggled at the sight of the horses wrapping their tongues over their muzzles. Tomas smiled as he watched her, engrossed and intoxicated.

She noticed his stare and smiled cheekily. He felt his cheeks burning as he blushed. The change in his complexion made her giggle again.

Something moved in the distance.

He focused his eyes to see past her and to the forest across the open land.

Pulling his mare to a complete stop, he squinted towards the trees. The other riders yanked back on their reins, moving their attention from Tomas to where he was gazing.

They saw nothing.

"What is it?" Jeremy asked.

"Something in the trees," he replied. "It was fast."

"What did it look like?"

"I'm not sure," he answered. "I was too busy looking at Emily."

"Young love," David quipped, nudging Oliver to the arm with his elbow.

"Shhh," Oliver hissed.

"It wasn't just one," Simon put in. "There was a pack of creatures."

"Not the witch?" Karlena pressed.

Simon shook his head slowly. "Not any scarecrows or dead men, either. They were big and dark. Maybe the size of a horse."

"Could they have been horses?" David asked. "Maybe a wild herd?"

"No," Tomas assured him. "These things didn't move like horses. They moved more like predators."

They fixed all eyes upon the pine trees clustered at the foot of the mountains. There was nothing to be seen, but they knew not to disregard the words of the two men of Woodmyst. If they said something was there, then something was there.

"It appears you were right, Simon," Baldwyn, the injured man, said from his side. "Something *is* watching us."

✳✳✳

The wind picked up momentum and blew the intensifying snow across their path at an angle almost parallel to the horizon. Emily felt the build-up of white powder attaching itself to the side of her hood as they pressed on.

The horses had lowered their heads and turned their faces away from the onslaught. Their caparisons flapped wildly, catching the wind like sails between their legs and almost tripping them over.

Tomas made the call he wished was unnecessary.

"Halt," he called. "We set up camp here."

The men and women worked hastily to erect two tents across from each other and a small yard for the steeds. There was no chance of making a functional fire in the current conditions, so they opted to huddle together inside the two shelters and keep warm using their own body heat.

Peering through the tent flaps occasionally, the travellers saw no reprieve in the weather. They made a unanimous decision to use the time to rest.

What else was there to do?

Gathering most of the men into one tent and the women into the other, except for Tomas, Jeremy and David, the troop tried to make the best of the situation by telling jokes or taking time to rest their eyes.

"I don't understand why you ordered me to join you in this tent," David said.

"Because you're too big to fit over here," Oliver called out from the other shelter, "you big bastard."

"When this storm is over, I'm going to ram my sword up your arse."

"Promises, promises!" Oliver laughed.

They left bedrolls bundled and equipment laid upon the ground by the two erected tents. The company simply lay down upon the canvas flooring and slept if they could, or tried to sleep if they couldn't.

The wind built to a deafening howl as heavy snow relentlessly beat against the side of the shelters, preventing most of the campers from reaching any meaningful level of respite. Some of the hardened crewmen of the *Adelandria* drifted off without a moment of hesitation.

"How can they do that?" Simon asked Baldwyn.

The injured man pointed to his ears and shook his head. The noise of the storm too loud to hear the question.

Simon dismissed the question by waving his hand and lying down on his side.

Several hours had passed, and the sun had crossed to the other side of the sky before the storm eased her wrath.

A gentle drift fell from above with barely a breeze behind it.

Tomas opened his eyes. He must have fallen to sleep at some stage.

The sound of a horse snorting brought him back to reality and caused him almost to leap to his feet. He ventured out through the tent flaps to see the other tent partially covered in snow. Turning towards the shelter that he had emerged from, he saw the same had happened to it as well.

An enormous pile of snow extended from the peak of the roofs, covering the eastern walls of the canvas covers and all of their equipment left there after unloading the horses. From the animals' point of view, the shelters probably resembled two mounds of snow positioned side by side.

The steeds huddled together. Their backs partially laden with white powder that had collected upon their caparisons during the storm. Tomas conducted a quick count and saw none went missing during the blizzard, but there was a sense of fear in them as he approached.

His brown mare stepped forward, allowing him to rub her muzzle. She gave a soft nicker, which seemed to calm the nerves of the other horses nearby.

"It's over now," he told her. "Everything is fine."

She nuzzled him as Emily moved to his side.

"How are they?" she asked him as she reached to pat another horse, reaching its nose towards her.

"A little skittish," he replied. "But all right."

"The sun is getting low," she said.

"We'll need to set up camp here." He sounded disappointed.

"We'll get there," she assured him, wrapping her arms around him. "I know we will."

***

After clearing the snow from the sides of the tents and retrieving their supplies, the travellers set up their camp in a more traditional circular organisation. They gathered wood from the forest once again and lit the campfire.

It was just another regular evening on their journey.

The moon made her presence known as she lifted her full face above the horizon. The sun was still descending beyond the mountains, placing the company in the in-between moment where dusk turned to night.

Emily snuggled against Tomas as they sat upon a log, gazing towards the silver orb rising from the ocean. For a fleeting moment, there was no mission, no other men or women around them, and no need to be concerned about what may watch them from the trees.

This was just the two of them, sitting by the fire.

Tomas hoped that when this was all over, when they finally returned to Woodmyst, Emily and he could do this very thing every night. Just sit together and watch the stars wink to life one by one.

He wrapped his arm around her shoulders and gently squeezed her into his chest. She tilted her head onto his shoulder and closed her eyes.

Her thoughts suddenly returned to the night when she escaped the marauders. She recalled her sister's face, full of fear, as she cowered beneath other women chained nearby. When the thin, greasy man pulled her by her hair away from her little sister flashed through her mind. She remembered the scarred man removing her mother's head from her shoulders as she was being dragged away.

Her eyes filled with tears as she recollected deciding to leave her sister behind. She knew she didn't have any other choice at the time, but now Joanne was alone.

All alone.

"What's the matter?" Tomas asked softly.

"I miss my sister," she replied. "I left her with those animals."

"We'll get her back," he told her. "I promise."

***

The boards creaked loudly and the loose chains hanging on the walls chimed as the ship rose and fell methodically upon the waves. The smell of salt, sweat and defecation filled the iron cages where the women were held.

Several of the prisoners prayed silently for safe passage as they felt the sea rise and fall beneath them. Others wept, believing hope was lost when raiders took them from their home.

Subjected to living conditions not fit for animals and to regular abuse from the ship's crew, those who still held some faith desired only one of two things. To be rescued or to die.

The sound of an unlocking door caused all to become alarmed, peering through the darkness towards the source of the sound.

The door opened with a loud rusty screech and a thud as it hit the adjacent wall.

The women, tethered with chains, and the children huddled together, pressed themselves as far as they could against the walls to the rear of the cages.

Now they silently hoped to be spared from the crew's exploitation and cruelty. Now they secretly hoped the person beside them would be chosen instead.

Heavy footfalls of the large scarred man entered the room, accompanied by the softer padding of a young red-haired girl.

He held her by her hair, steering her before him by pulling her this way and that until he positioned her in front of her cage. Using the keys dangling from his belt, he unlocked the cage that held six other occupants. They were all as young as she was and all knew her predicament from their own experiences.

He pushed her hard, back into the pen. She stumbled and crashed into the other girls, who all gave an involuntary cry.

"Shut your faces," he barked as he slammed the cage door shut with a clang.

After locking it, he glared at the group of girls. His eyes were hungry.

He turned back towards the main door and closed it behind him. They listened to his heavy steps climbing the steps to the upper decks.

The girls broke down and cried, all wrapping their arms around the auburn lass.

"Gwendra, hear my prayers," whispered one of the weeping women in a pen near to them. "Protect these ones who have had their innocence stolen. Bring us salvation or bring us Grolle. We cannot endure this any longer."

Four

A soft whistle called across the plain as the wind swept from the beach and over the snow-covered land towards the dark forest. With it came a deep chill that Tomas could feel from beneath the thick coverings of his bedding. Emily pressed up against his side again, only this time she buried her head beneath the blankets and shivered slightly as she slumbered.

Tomas considered putting his boots back on for extra warmth. He only hesitated, as he knew it would be uncomfortable for both Emily and himself.

He reached for his bearskin cloak and draped it over the bed. She stirred and grumbled an indiscernible protest.

As quickly as he could, he placed the covers back over the two of them and snuggled against her, hoping that with the layers on top of them and their body heat, they could rest with some ease.

A tiny part of him felt sorrow for the night's watchmen. He pictured David, Oliver and Simon sitting as close to the fire as they could, possibly with their bearskin robes held tightly around them and their hoods pulled low over their faces. It was what he would do if he was stuck outside in such conditions.

His gladness for being inside his tent this night overshadowed the tiny part of him that expressed compassion for his friends. His night shift was during the previous evening with the new captain of the *Adelandria*, Jeremy.

Neither had a decent night's sleep since they set out from Oakbeach. With constant disturbances each night from terrifying noises that eventually culminated in attacks from straw men and dead crewmen, it was perplexing to ponder how any of the travellers could still think straight.

Tomas felt tired of travelling and sore from fighting. He missed his sister, Linet, and his best friend, Lor. He wondered what the two were up to in his absence. Recalling his last day with them, when they announced their plans to wed, he wished he could be back with them to share their happiness more extensively than he did.

If only for an hour or two.

He wanted so much to introduce them to Emily and let all those who close to him in Woodmyst know he had finally found her. He had finally found the one with whom he wanted to spend the rest of his life.

The wind striking the canvas shelter brought him back to reality.

The mission came to the foremost part of his thoughts. He remembered the promise that he had made to Antony Grenefeld, the lone surviving man from the attack upon Emily's village. He had promised Antony, Emily's father, to find his daughters and bring them back.

So far, he had found one and had fallen madly and deeply in love with her. The other was still being held captive by the enemy. He could return home only once he had her, Joanne, in his and Emily's possession.

Until then, Woodmyst and all the things he longed for would need to remain a fond memory and a hopeful dream.

A gentle sigh surged from his throat as he tried to smooth out the lumps in the bedding with his shoulders. Emily protested with a quiet grumble.

He missed his bed.

***

She pressed on, pushing her way through the chill wind towards the north. She pulled her hood low to her brow and her cloak held tightly around her chest, covering bloodstains soaking through the front of her clothing.

Ivo's blood.

She considered her victim momentarily and was thankful for his contribution. His innocence and naivety lured him to impending doom. *It was a shame,* she considered, *as he was such a nice young man.*

But it was necessary.

His seed and his blood were necessary.

Did it work?

Is this why I feel weak?

Each step she took was substantially smaller than the gait she had exercised throughout the day. Believing she had made substantial ground, she pondered taking a rest.

But where?

She had no tent and knew of no shelter in the region she traversed. Her only choice was to move.

She willed herself to continue and placed what energy she could muster into keeping herself warm and alive.

The moon was full and illuminated the path before her in a silver radiance. The land to the north appeared clear and clean, swept spotless by a white blanket.

She took comfort in her surroundings, knowing that she, being covered from head to toe in white, would be difficult to see in such an environment. Particularly from a distance.

If her pursuers had risked travelling at night, there was no chance they could find her. Their only guarantee that they were indeed on the right track would be her boot prints in the snow behind her.

The wind, to her advantage, took care of that, covering the imprints with loose powder it picked up as it blew across the surface.

While the company behind her provided a tiny and constant itch in the back of her mind, her primary concern was in the woods to her left.

The knowledge of the creatures that dwelt there brought fear with it. She was not one to fear much, usually being the one to deliver trepidation, but the things that lived beneath the trees made her terrified.

This was another reason for not wanting to stop and take a rest. Onwards she moved.

The wind pushed her from the right, veering her away from the coast. She constantly corrected her trajectory, not wanting to venture any closer to the tree line than was absolutely necessary.

If Ivo's contribution had worked, she needed to be careful. Her life was more valuable than it had ever been.

She focused her energy into surviving, moving, and making it to her destination.

She did not want to disappoint the Sovereign.

***

"Tomas, wake up," Emily called as she shook the man from his slumber.

"What's the matter?" he asked, sitting up. He did not know for how long he had been asleep, but it must have been for a while. He felt refreshed and ready to take on the world.

"David has been calling for you," Emily replied. "I don't know why."

Tomas strapped his boots to his feet and grabbed his sheath and sword. Emily was close behind him. They wrapped their cloaks around themselves and entered the inhospitable environment outside their tent.

It was brisk.

Tomas felt a sudden chill bite deep into his flesh as he approached the fire where the other men of Woodmyst gathered. They faced towards the woods with their backs to the flames.

"What is it?" Tomas asked as he drew near to them.

"We have company," Oliver replied, rubbing his gloved hands together and pointing with his golden brow towards the trees.

Tomas came alongside of him and peered into the direction the other gesture towards. He saw nothing but dark shadows beneath the pines.

"What hour is it?"

"Not sure," David answered. "Almost dawn. The stars are starting to snuff out near the horizon."

"Why are you still here?" Tomas gave the three men a confused look. "You were meant to be relieved around midnight."

"We sent the others back to bed," David told him.

"*You* sent them back to bed," Simon corrected him.

"Well..." David smiled bashfully. "They were tired and cold. We were awake and ready."

"Cold will do that to a man," Simon informed them. "That and make him piss a lot."

Oliver chuckled quietly.

"Who is out there?" Emily asked, bringing the conversation back to the original subject.

"Not who," Simon replied. "What."

"The creatures?" Tomas stared into the shadows beneath the snow-covered trees. They reminded him of silver arrow tips at their distance. Countless arrow tips all lined up in rows and columns like an army at the base of the mountains.

"I think so," the other replied. "We heard them running at first. Then they started calling to each other."

"Calling?" Tomas furrowed his brow. "What do you mean call—"

"Shhh," Simon interjected, as he held up his hand. He then pointed to a section of the tree line to the left of their view.

Tomas could make out the faint sound of raspy screeches, similar to those of certain types of birds, only deeper in pitch. The noise was quite alarming and caused his heart to pound a little faster.

"What was that?" Emily's voice shook.

Another replied with a call from the section of woods directly west of them. Simon pointed towards the origin of the sound.

Within moments, the call from the left repeated, followed by two deep, guttural coughs.

"Give it a few minutes and it will start up again," Oliver told them.

"How long has this been going on?" Tomas asked.

"That was number eight of the cycle," David said. "They're talking to each other."

"It would appear so," Tomas replied. He turned to the east and saw the unmistakable purple glow of light appearing on the horizon.

"What should we do?" David asked.

"Wake the captain and tell him what you have told me," Tomas replied. "Then pack everything ready to leave. As soon as we have finished breakfast, we move out."

"What of the creatures?" Simon queried, concern resonating from his voice.

"We can't go in there after them," Tomas informed him. "We need to wait until they come for us. Until then, we remain vigilant and continue with our mission."

**

They bundled the tents and packed equipment. After a quick breakfast of porridge and tea, the company set out once again.

With the news of the creatures' activities in the woods on the travellers' thoughts, all eyes scanned the tree line continuously as they moved. They were yet to see the beasts clearly, but men often made reports of consistent movement from beneath the pines as they rode.

"We are being shadowed," Karlena remarked.

"They've marked us," Akasati replied.

"Why would they do that?" Emily asked. Until the night of the raid upon her village, she had never experienced such terrors and fear. This was all new to her, and she needed information and answers to make sense of the situation.

"They're hunting us," Karlena told her. "Perhaps we ventured into their territory and they see us as a threat. Perhaps they're just hungry and see us as an easy meal. Maybe both."

A flash of grey moved quickly through a wide space between the pines. It was sudden, like a flash, and it caused Emily to gasp.

"Tomas!" A shudder moved along her spine as she turned to face him. He was riding to her right, between her and the sea. The Erilian women had positioned themselves on her left.

"I saw it," he told her. "Do you want to ride on the other side of me?"

She saw only a long stretch of land before the fluidity of the sea beyond him. At least he offered some protection for her on that side. The five Erilian warriors stood between the creatures and her position, and she knew Tomas would be there in an instant if he needed to be.

"No," she replied. "I'm all right."

He nodded reassuringly and patted her on the thigh.

The creatures, the company's shadows, continued to call with screeches and coughs from various locations from within the woods. Quick glances of the beasts moving through the forest set Emily further at unease, but she kept a stern countenance as she rode on.

Tomas noticed her overcompensation towards her fear. His concern was now for her state of wellbeing more than her safety.

"They're just animals," he told her. "They just do what animals do. I will protect you. I won't let them hurt you."

"I know," she said. "But what if they hurt you?"

"Then you will protect me," he smiled.

She grinned.

"I saw the way you are with a sword," he remarked. "Much scarier than any beast in the woods."

She snickered delightfully.

Tomas saw Karlena riding on the other side of Emily, grinning as she listened to the conversation.

"It's all right to have some fear," he added in a more serious tone. "It keeps us aware. It helps us to remember we are worth fighting for.

It reminds us we are alive. We just can't dwell upon it and let it have control."

She nodded.

***

The pursuers tailed the riders and their steeds to the west.

As they raced through the underbrush and navigated through the maze of trees, they watched, listened, and smelled their prey riding near to the water.

Screeching, coughing, calling to one another, they mustered their numbers, preparing for the hunt.

This was their land, and there were many strangers upon it.

A feast of this size was vastly overdue.

Five

"You know," said one crewman, leading two pack horses as he rode his own steed, "I believe that I'm the only one among us who suffered at the hand of the Sovereign but didn't lose any person who he loved."

"That's a nasty thing to say about your family," Simon replied.

"There's more to this story," Baldwyn put in as he rubbed his aching leg. "Jeff's tale is interesting."

"I lived alone on a tiny farm right by the sea," the man continued. "Far away from most people. My closest neighbour was almost a day's ride away."

"That's because you stink so bad that they forced you away," another laughed.

"No," Jeff replied. "It was my father's land and both he and my mother died there. It was a place of fond memories. I loved that place. It was my home. Still is.

"There was a stream not too far from the hut, just tucked neatly in a thicket. You couldn't see it from the house. Couldn't hear it either. If you weren't familiar with the land, you wouldn't know the stream was right there.

"I used to hitch the cart to my horse to fill the buckets and water skins from the stream. From the place where I collected the water, I could see the farm and keep an eye on my livestock and crops."

"What did you grow?" David asked.

"I grew wheat and corn mostly," Jeff replied. "Some other plants, fruits and vegetables, depending upon the season. I had some goats and a few cows. Not much. Enough to be content."

David nodded. It sounded nice, a little like home.

"One day, a black ship anchored just off the coast," the man continued. "I was collecting water and watched some men row a small boat from the ship to the beach just down from my house. I considered going out to greet them, but the sight of swords and axes gave me the impression that they weren't there to be friends.

"They entered my home and set it on fire before slaughtering my livestock and burning my crops. They took a couple of goats and left.

"I waited near the stream until the ship had vanished from view before I returned to the hut. All I could do was watch it burn to the ground, and it burned well into the night.

"The next day, when the flames had died, I rummaged through the ashes and found my box of silver coins hidden under the stonework of my fireplace. I had been collecting the wealth for quite a few seasons from selling my excess harvest. I never had need to spend any of it, as I had everything I needed on the farm. I owed no man anything. The land was mine, the crops were mine, and the livestock was mine.

"They took everything I owned from me in that one moment." He took a deep breath.

"I took my coins and drove my horse and cart to town," Jeff said. "I sold the horse and cart for a couple of pieces of silver. I then brought an old sword from the blacksmiths and went to the local tavern to spend the rest of what little wealth I had left.

"I told everyone my story of how the big black ship sent some men to burn my home. For three or four days I sat at the bar, taking time out only to sleep in some barn or to piss in the street. My story must have spread around the town pretty quickly because Captain Tarkin found me in the tavern, drunk out of my mind.

"He put me in a room and cleaned me up," Jeff told them. "He waited until I had sobered before asking me to join him on the *Adelandria*. I told him I had never been on a ship before in my life. He told me he would teach me what needed to be done. Then he told me he intended to find the black ship that destroyed my life and make it pay.

"I didn't hesitate. I joined the crew that day. For five years I've been a crewmember and I am so glad to be this close to seeing the captain's mission fulfilled."

"I would hate to think what they might have done to you had you come out of the trees to greet them," another man said. "I too came from a farm. We didn't live by the water's edge, but we lived by the edge of a fishing village that the men of a black ship visited.

"I don't know if the Sovereign was among them, but they were taking women and young girls. It seemed to me that they were being selective about whom to take captive and who to kill. I saw them slaughter quite a few younglings as I raced home from the town square. Girls and boys both.

"Five of them had beaten me to my home and had my mother and father bound and gagged before the house. They strapped me to a fence post and made me watch as they tortured my father by cutting pieces from his arms and legs until he bled out.

"All the while, they laughed and laughed as he screamed through the cloth they had stuffed in his mouth. My mother cried, and I was helpless.

"After they had their fun with my father, they turned their attention to my mother. They tied her hands to another fencepost near me and bound her feet to a horse. They made the horse pull and pull."

He closed his eyes and cried.

"It's all right, Gustav," Baldwyn told him.

"No," the other replied. "I need to say it."

Baldwyn nodded. He understood. Sometimes it felt better to get everything out than it did to hold it in.

"They tore my mother in two. The horse pulled away, dragging her lower half behind it, stretching her insides across the ground. Even then, she still looked at me. Her eyes were still looking at me for a long time before they closed.

"And those animals kept laughing."

"I was next," Gustav continued. "They turned their blades towards me, but a loud horn blew from the centre of town. And do you know what they did before leaving? They waved and smiled like we were old friends playing some sick game.

"I struggled for hours to get free. I buried my mother and father side by side. I burnt the house to the ground because I knew I couldn't stay there, and I could never return.

"Unlike you, Jeff," Gustav said, "I sought Captain Tarkin out. I asked questions about the black ship and the men on board. I heard the name *Sovereign* mentioned many times, whispered in fear mostly, and followed that trail to another name; Tarkin of the *Adelandria*. I heard this Tarkin was hunting the Sovereign, and I wanted to join with him. I found the *Adelandria* moored in Dweagan and offered my services to the first mate, Jeremy Schoenbach.

"Now, my captain," Gustav said proudly.

"What of you?" Tomas asked the captain. "Why did you join the crew of the *Adelandria*?"

"My reason was Meaghan," he replied. "She was the love of my life and there will never be another to replace her. In my eyes, she and I were husband and wife and will remain so until I depart from this world."

"What happened to her?" Emily asked, suddenly feeling insensitive after speaking her words. "I'm sorry. Don't answer that."

"It's all right," he told her. "I would not be honouring her if I didn't tell others about her.

The Sovereign took her from me because she was simply there.

"She lived in a villa near to mine and we visited one another almost every night. We considered moving into either one or the other together to publicise our relationship, but everyone knew. It was no secret. Truth be told, we kind of enjoyed the sneaking around and found it exciting. The play definitely helped with the romance," he smiled.

"I brought her flowers most every day and she would put them in a vase by the window," he continued. "I would usually steal them from an old woman's yard on the corner nearby. She used to catch me once in a while and spit some unenthusiastic obscenities. I always had the feeling she loved the idea that someone was taking her flowers for something useful. She would occasionally shuffle along the courtyard between the villas and comment to some passer-by about the lovely flowers in Meaghan's window." His countenance suddenly changed, his smile transforming into pursed lips.

"When they came, they killed her first," he said. "Hers was the first villa that they reached when they left the docks. They attacked other parts of the town, but our villas were our world. We all knew each other well. So, well that I could call the people who lived there my family.

"I didn't find out about Sasha, the old woman, until the next day. But she would have been the first. They peeled her skin from her flesh. I couldn't find any vital wounds to say she suffered a merciful death. Just that she suffered."

"They skinned her alive?" Emily looked as if she was going to be ill.

Jeremy nodded. "Several of the people living near her tried to hide. They heard her screams and those of others in neighbouring sections of our village. Not all were very good at hiding.

"The Prophets of the Sovereign, as they are known, made their way from villa to villa. They killed the men and you can only guess what they did to the women before torturing them and taking their lives also.

"I made it to Meaghan's villa and hid with her in the back room, beneath her bed. It was a heavy, oak structure and took significant effort to move.

"They broke her door down and came straight to our location. They lifted the bed with ease.

"One man," Jeremy told them. "One man with a scar across his face stood in the room."

"The Sovereign?" Tomas asked.

"Captain Tarkin believed so," he replied. "All I know is that he is strong. To flip that heavy oak bed onto its side was unnatural.

"He picked me up with one hand and slid his dagger deep into my face." Jeremy pointed to the mark that ran down his cheek with his finger. "He gave me this as a reminder. I could feel the point of his blade digging into my gums and scraping across my teeth."

"Oh, my." Emily shook her head.

"After that, he threw me into the wall. Not just at it, but he tossed me so hard, with one hand, so that I was actually planted into the wall above where the bed used to sit. I blacked out and didn't see what he had done to Meaghan.

"He must have thought that I was dead," Jeremy continued, "because I woke up sitting inside the wall. I had a few large splinters sticking out of me from the timber beams and wooden panelling, but I could move.

"My face hurt more than the rest of me, but my thoughts were on Meaghan. I set out to find her, but couldn't see her anywhere in the villa. I went into the courtyard and was stopped by one woman who hid successfully. She was distraught after what had happened, and could see that I was intent on finding my Meaghan. But she wouldn't let me go, holding onto my arm, until she tended to my wounds.

"After she removed the wood from my body, she stitched up my face," he told them. "It was while she was doing this that an elder came to our courtyard. He told us that the black ship was gone and that Meaghan had been found.

"I wanted to go to her and see her, but he urged me to stay where I was." Jeremy paused to take a breath. "He told me that the other elders were still piecing her together to prepare for her burial."

Emily lifted her hand to her mouth. Karlena, who had heard the story before, wept silently at her side.

"She was so beautiful." Jeremy allowed a tear to run down his scarred cheek. "So beautiful. They took turns with her in the town square. When they were done, they dismembered her at every joint. Their fun was over. They broke their toy so that no one else could enjoy it."

The riders were silent.

There was nothing they could say.

Jeremy wiped his cheeks and stared towards the north with steel eyes. "I want to kill them all."

"They only attack places by the coast," Oliver said after a while.

"What?" Tomas asked, surprised by the comment.

"The Prophets of the Sovereign," he replied. "They only attack villages and towns near the coast."

"Easier for the ships to get to," Baldwyn suggested.

"That doesn't explain why they attacked Emily's village," Tomas put in.

"Were you born there?" Jeremy asked her, a spark emerging in his thoughts.

"No," she replied. "It was a new settlement. We only arrived there during the spring."

"Where were you originally from?"

"Clearspring. It's a village south of Morport."

"Morport is a trade centre," the captain informed the group. "Ships from all lands visit there."

"But why would they travel so far inland when there are more than enough women and young girls and resources on the coast?" David asked, knowing his question was a tad insensitive.

"I've been thinking about this for some time," Jeremy answered. "Captain Tarkin once told me that his daughter was *special*. I brushed it off as something any loving father might say about his daughter. But after our encounters with Sumaiyya, and after seeing what she is capable of, I think our old captain may have meant something much more significant when he called her *special*."

He directed his attention back to Emily. "Did all the people of your village in the mountains come from Clearspring?"

"No, we came from many places. Why?"

"Did all the families have daughters or were there some that only had sons?"

"Daughters." She furrowed her brow. "All of them."

"Did you or your sister ever show special capabilities?" he pressed.

"Special capabilities? I don't know what you—"

"What are you alleging?" Tomas asked, irritated by Jeremy's interrogation of Emily.

"Please bear with me. I think I've figured out what type of people the Sovereign targets."

"I remember a butterfly," Emily said. It was such a peculiar statement that all ears and eyes couldn't resist falling upon her. "Back when we lived in Clearspring. My mother was taking Joanne and me for a walk through a small wooded area. Joanne was still tiny and was learning to walk.

"She fell down on the grass, and usually she would laugh, but this one time she cried. She was holding a butterfly in her hand. It had died.

"She held it up by a wing. My mother tried to tell her it was all right, but she kept crying.

"I don't know why, but I put my hands around hers, enclosing the butterfly within. When I let go, the butterfly flew away."

"That's it," Jeremy nodded. "That's why he came for you."

"Because she brought a butterfly back to life?" David quizzed.

"Because either Emily of her sister possesses power," Jeremy explained. "Perhaps they both do."

"But that was so long ago. And only my mother knew. Not even Joanne knows that story. She was too young."

"Somehow, the Sovereign knows," the captain told her. "He knew about Sumaiyya and he came for her. He knew about either your or your sister's ability and came for you too. He's drawn to power."

"And you think that's why my father moved us away from the coast?"

"I think people are afraid of what they don't understand," he replied. "The knowledge of the Sovereign may have been a factor for your relocation. But I think it is more to do with the reaction of the everyday people.

"Think about it. What images enter your mind when I say the word, *witch?*

"I don't think any person riding these horses would have originally pictured a voluptuous blonde girl dressed in white. Would they?

"By the same measure, I don't think most people would think of a kind-hearted red-headed lass, either.

"What they would imagine is what they believed was hidden behind the skin and outer shell that looks like a woman. They would see darkness, evil, and something that must be destroyed.

"You would need to ask your father, but I believe he moved you to keep you safe. And I think all the other fathers of your new home did the same for their daughters. My guess is that they made some agreement to take all of you to a place as far away from anybody as was possible."

She pondered that for a long moment as they rode on.

"But how did he find them so far from the coast?" Tomas finally asked. "The Sovereign, I mean."

"That I can't be sure of," Jeremy admitted. "I don't profess to know about mystical things. I'm just a man. Perhaps he is drawn to such power. Perhaps he can find it like a dog finds a scent. Who knows?"

"It doesn't matter," Karlena said. "He found them. And now, we go to kill him."

To her, it was that simple.

Six

"Heave to," a loud voice barked from above their heads.

The sound of heavy footfalls rushing back and forth on the upper decks reverberated around them as the constant swish of water breaking against the hull filled their ears.

Something was happening outside, and they were curious and frightened at what it could be.

Huddling closer together, the seven girls locked together in a tiny cage held each other tightly. Soft cries emitted from each of them as they felt the ship slow its pace.

The women and other girls locked in the pens around the deck prayed and wept as the fear of not knowing what awaited them hit them suddenly and forcefully. Subjected to the worst atrocities on the ship that they could imagine, they had spared little thought about what their destiny at the end of their voyage. Until now.

"Anchor aweigh," the commander called in his deep, gruff voice. The sheer sound of it caused all the young women to shudder.

Every time he called, their muscles tensed and their stomachs turned. They felt his horrible, hot breath on their skin and his sweat clinging to their flesh.

Stained is how they felt. *Stained* with his essence.

"Take it in," he ordered as the vessel continued to slow its speed. "Steady."

The ship slowed to a crawl and felt as if it was sitting stable. A new order here and there from the scarred man let the women know they were still moving.

"Ahoy," a man on deck called.

"Ahoy," came a reply from the outside of the vessel.

"Make a line," shouted another voice.

The prisoners heard some further shuffling as the scarred man called again, "Furl the sails and drop anchor."

"Welcome home, ya bastards," shouted a man from off the ship somewhere. The crew gave a cheer.

Joanne had never felt so scared in her life. After making it through days of abusive torture, she was now in the monster's homeland who captained the ship.

What other terrible things did they have planned for her?

She sobbed profusely as footsteps made their way across the upper decks towards the door to their prison. With a loud click, the lock was unfastened, and the door opened to allow the light of day to spill into the room.

"Shyah," called a man, "smells like death."

"None of them are dead," replied the scarred man. "I can assure you of that."

"I hope you didn't destroy the young ones." The other chuckled. "They're required for service."

Service?

Joanne felt a sharp stabbing fear pierce her heart.

What could he mean by service?

"I know the ways better than you," the scarred man retorted. "Remember who you're talking to."

"I'm sorry," the other replied. "I'm sorry. I'll take the first lot to the dock. The wagon is waiting at the end."

"Good," he grunted before turning away and disappearing to the upper decks.

"Right, ladies," the newcomer said as he unlocked the cage with the seven young girls inside. "You will come quietly or else feel the sting of my lash." He patted a whip coiled upon his hip.

The girls cowered as he opened the gate and stepped to the side.

"Up the stairs until you get to the gangplank," he ordered. "Go."

The girls moved slowly, shoulders hunched and little steps, afraid they were going to get struck no matter what they did.

"Come on," he yelled. "Quickly, quickly. I don't have all day."

They moved a little more hastily once they exited the dark room. The scent of fresh air and baking bread filled Joanne's nostrils. It was far more inviting than she imagined it would be.

The girls climbed the steps to the upper deck, where they saw a wide plank stretching from the edge of the platform downwards to a neat dock to which they moored the ship.

"Down the plank and to the right," the man commanded them.

The girls walked carefully along the steep gangplank from the ship to the dock. The sensation was strange and their legs and heads didn't feel right.

Joanne looked towards her left where she saw a large open door to the cargo hold on the side of the ship. Some men, using horses that were stowed in this sector of the ship, lowered a cage to the surface of the wharf by rolling it down a shallow ramp.

She remembered being transported in the vehicle before her cell upon the ship. Squeezed together with other prisoners from her village and livestock; goats and pigs thrown on top of them, they had travelled over the mountains to the coast in the east. Now, they had come north.

She wondered if this was just another stop before they were to be moved on further. She wondered if they were to be put back into the tiny wagon and taken across the mountains to some other place.

At the far end of the dock, she saw a market with a few stores and people milling about. There were lots of men making up the crowd. She couldn't see any women at all.

What a strange town, she thought. *Only men, no women to be seen.*

Perhaps the women are inside with the children.

Then she thought of something terrible.

She wondered if they had brought the captives on the ship to this port to be used by the men in this place, just as they had been by the men on the ship.

Perhaps we are to be sold to these men to be their slaves.

Frantically, she searched for an opening, a chance to make a break for it.

The man with the whip was busy looking at something on the deck of the black ship. The other men continued with their work unloading vessel.

Without a second look back, she sprinted as fast as she could towards the marketplace. Her stained dress, smelling of waste, flapped behind loudly as she bolted as fast as she could.

"Stop her," a man on the ship called.

She was so near to the end of the pier when she glimpsed the scarred man to her left. He was running to cut her path off at the end of the timber walkway.

It was amazing how fast such a large man could be.

But she was faster.

She angled towards the right of the dock and hit the ground at the end with an invigorating strength. It was as if she wanted to be faster, so she was.

His hand almost caught the hem of her dress as she raced past him and into the market. The scarred man snarled and gave chase.

Joanne ducked between the crowded people, under tables and through the narrowest of paths to slow the large pursuer down. Checking over her shoulder, she could see him right behind her, barging others out of his way and shouting for them to move.

Too busy with watching her pursuer, she ran straight into a well-dressed woman standing in the middle of the street. Joanne fell backwards onto her backside into the slushy snow and mud.

Her eyes moved from the ground, following the furry black hem of a regal gown that ran along the edge of the slender garment. Predominantly green with gold trimmings, the gown appeared thick and warm.

At its top was a hood with the same black fur hemming its edge. Beneath the hood, Joanne could see red lips and a pointed chin. Shadow obscured the rest of the woman's face.

Perhaps it was her thin frame, but Joanne believed her the tallest woman that she had ever seen. She was so stricken by the sight of the lady that she didn't even notice the scarred man behind her until his hand was wrapping her hand into his fist.

She gave a loud scream when he tugged, pulling her to her feet. He gave a wry smile as he lowered his mouth towards her ear.

"Perhaps," he breathed over her, "I will keep you an extra night to teach you some manners."

Joanne continued to stare at the woman in green. The scarred man noticed that her attention was elsewhere and followed her gaze.

Upon seeing the tall woman in the majestic robe, he let Joanne's hair free.

"Mistress." He bowed his head respectfully.

She simply cocked her head slightly to one side. He stepped away, backing off.

The woman stretched her hand out to Joanne, offering it in a friendly gesture. A closed-lip smile spread across the woman's face.

Not knowing what else to do or where else to go, Joanne placed her hand into the lady's palm. She knew that if she was to reject the woman's offer, the scarred man would have her in moments. Joanne didn't want to ever return to that ship.

The tall woman gently pulled the Joanne to her side and returned her gaze to the scarred man, the smile now gone.

Her other hand extended and gave a dismissing wave to the man.

"Yes, Mistress," he replied, bowing again before returning to the ship.

The woman led Joanne by the hand to a covered wagon nearby. It was large and black, with gold adornment around the windows and panels.

A large white horse wearing a black bridle and blinkers, tethered to the vehicle, stomped its feet impatiently as it waited for the passengers to step on board.

The driver, a well-dressed elderly man, held the door open. The lady directed the young girl to step inside.

Upon seeing the interior of the carriage, she felt completely out of place. Mauve cushioning covered the seats and walls. She was in raggedy, filth-stained clothes inside such a clean, special space.

I don't deserve to be here; she thought. Crying, she stood in the middle of the carriage, not knowing what else to do.

The woman stepped inside and sat upon the soft seats, reaching out to Joanne and pulling her towards her chest.

"No," Joanne protested, pulling away. "I'm filthy and smelly. I shouldn't be here."

The woman cocked her head slightly and smiled sweetly, wrapping her arms around the girl and drawing her into her bosom.

"It's all right," she said, her voice warm and soft. "You're safe with me."

Uncontrollable tears burst from Joanne's eyes as she let herself go. She didn't know this woman, but she heard her words and believed them.

***

Sumaiyya's pace slowed, and she found it more difficult to focus. Occasionally, her mind wandered. She continuously worried about how close her pursuers were.

With the advantage of horses, her hunters wouldn't tire as quickly as she. They could ride all day and make substantial ground as she continued to press on, day and night.

Her strength was growing dim, and she wasn't sure how much longer she could go without needing rest.

In her weakened state, memories of her father flooded back. Her childhood was a merry time and her father had always shown her love and affection. A deep guilt swept over her as she remembered plunging her blade into his back over and over.

Why did I do that?

She shook the thought away.

There was no time for feeling sorrow.

There was no need to feel remorse.

Her goal was to survive and get back to her home. She *was* important to the Sovereign. Her gift from Ivo had made her an integral part of the destiny of the world.

A river ran across her path in front of her. It was usually wide throughout the warmer seasons. During the winter, snow drifts built up thickly on each bank.

It appeared as only a mere bubbling brook on the surface, but she knew better. It flowed rapidly and deeply beneath the white surface.

The snow and ice at the edges were thin. Treading carefully, Sumaiyya pressed with her feet to test the strength of the ice. She moved as far as she could to the edge of the build-up before leaping as hard as possible.

Landing on the other side as light-footedly as she might manage, she felt the surface give way beneath her weight. She stepped onto solid ground just in time, as the collected ice and snow broke away from the edge and rode the water flow downstream.

This gave her an idea.

Staring at the stream, drawing from a power deep inside, she caused a deep chill breeze to sweep over the exposed river. Before her eyes, ice built up on the water, appearing as a solid surface from where she stood all the way to where the river disappeared into the woods to the west. With a quick movement of her hands, a thin layer of snow covered the ice, disguising the hidden river as part of the ground.

Content with her effort, feeling depleted from the experience, she turned and continued towards the north.

The sun was creeping towards the mountains again. She needed to make more ground before nightfall.

Her stomach felt empty and her legs and feet ached.

With luck, she thought, *I will make the outpost by morning.*

***

The screeching and coughing barks of the creatures had been silent for several hours. A few men risked travelling closer to the woods to see if they could view the creatures or hear their calls. They reported no sign of the shadowing pack.

Tomas and Jeremy agreed they needed to rest for the night and set up camp with the men of Woodmyst and the Erilian warriors while the crewmen of the *Adelandria* gathered firewood.

Jeremy ordered extra kindling to set smaller fires around the edge of the camp. He hoped that fire might be a deterrent to wild creatures, assuring them of some element of safety for the night ahead.

The men penned the horses beside the tents, forming part of the circle with the other campers instead of being positioned away from the shelters. With the larger hearth in the centre of the tight circle of tents and several smaller ones burning around the outside, the travellers set to eating and relaxing.

The sun sank below the mountains and darkness fell over the land.

Conversations switched between places where the *Adelandria* had been to what her history entailed.

"So, she was a merchant ship?" David asked.

"What merchant ship has cannons?" Simon grunted.

"Our merchant ship," Jeremy replied. "There are pirates and un-friendly folk out there. Sometimes, the only message they understand comes from cannon fire."

"Were you on her from the beginning with Tarkin?" Emily asked.

"No," the captain answered. "Captain Tarkin gained the *Adelandria* a short time after those bastards took his family from him. He originally worked as a merchant marine commander for a shipping company on another vessel.

"When they killed his wife and son," Jeremy explained, "and you know what happened to his daughter, he left his employment and used his life savings to buy the biggest and strongest ship he could afford."

"The *Adelandria*," Karlena breathed.

"Aye," Jeremy replied. "The *Adelandria*. Some crewmen that worked with him in the merchant marines went with him at first. When the money dried up, and that happened a lot quicker than he had planned, they left him and returned to the company.

"His entire focus, an obsession really, was to find the Sovereign. But with no crew, he was stuck high and dry.

"So, the situation forced him to take a few jobs as a merchant marine and used the work to find other people like himself; victims of the Sovereign.

"That's when he found me," Jeremy told them. "We got a small crew, some of which are still here, and we did a few jobs to build up our stores. When the supplies were full, we went hunting. When they were low, we would find some work for the ship and her crew.

"It's how you found us at Oakbeach. We brought supplies up from the southern ports and spent the winter there. Our next voyage was to be north when the spring melted winter away, but you came along and made the journey more immediate." The captain smiled. "And here we are."

Screeching resonated from the dark woods.

"And there they are," David quipped as he turned his head towards the sounds.

"I guess we'll find out if this plan of yours works, Captain," Tomas said.

"All we need to do is keep the fires burning," he replied. "I think it will keep the animals away. Most things are afraid of fire."

"Most things," Oliver replied, thinking about the dragons that destroyed his village when he was a lad.

The other men of Woodmyst looked to him understandingly.

"Most things," Tomas nodded.

Seven

Tomas had a restless sleep. The sounds of vicious callings from beyond the circle of tents had woken him from time to time during the night. His eyes weighed a little heavily as he woke one more time.

It was still dark outside, but the chirps of small birds fluttering nearby informed him that the sun was on its way. He got up and had some tea, but Emily's arm across him felt unusually heavy and caused him to reconsider.

He was comfortable. As was she.

Her slumber had been deep and unbroken, and he could tell from her breathing that she wasn't ready to be woken. He closed his eyes again, but could not drift back into slumber.

Carefully, he pried her arm from his chest and placed it beside her body. As quietly as he could, he sat up and slipped his boots on before standing to place the covers back over her.

Before leaving the tent, he wrapped his bearskin cloak around him. He was glad to have it as light snow fell across the plain.

Four men sat by the fire. He knew them as Lon, Calvin and, the two storytellers from the previous day, Jeff and Gustav. They had a pot of water steaming on the coals, and Gustav started preparing a cup for Tomas as he made his way towards them.

"Morning, gentlemen," Tomas said, sitting next to Gustav.

"Morning, sir," they replied. Gustav dipped the cup into the hot water and dropped some tea leaves into the cup.

"Here, sir," he said, handing the cup over.

"Tomas," the other replied. "And thank you."

"Habit, sir," Gustav stated. "Hard to break."

Tomas nodded. He didn't quite understand the protocol of shipmen, but he appreciated the manners and respect.

He sipped at the cup and almost spat it back into the cup. It hadn't mixed yet.

"I should let this rest a little longer," Tomas said, nursing the cup in his hands. "Tell me of your watch."

"The beasts came close," Lon told him. "One of them circled the entire camp and stood far behind the horses for a while. My guess is that it was considering taking a horse."

"They kept calling one another all night," Jeff put in.

"So, I heard," Tomas agreed.

"One or two from the forest would make that weird cry." Jeff pointed to the area he had heard the noise come from. "Then the ones near to us would call back. I don't know how any of you could have slept through it."

"Neither do I," yawned Tomas.

"They've been quiet for a long time now," Calvin said. "Do you think they've gone?"

"Not bloody likely," Gustav replied.

"They're still watching us," Tomas told him. "They will attack eventually. Their basic need to feed will overcome their caution. That they ventured so close to the camp tells me they are getting more courageous. We need to be ready."

"What do we do?" Calvin asked.

"Let's prepare breakfast for everyone," Tomas smiled.

***

With their stomachs filled with porridge and bread, the company set off once again when the sky was a light blue, but the sun was still hiding below the sea. Her rays struck them momentarily as she crept over the horizon, poking holes in the cloud cover once in a while to let them know she was there.

The snow from the previous night and early morning had covered any trail left by the woman in white. Their only guide to lead them on was the expanse of land between the forest and the shore that stretched on and on.

A chill wind blew up from the beach and across their path, kicking up a fine dust of frost and snow like a mist that wafted across the surface towards the trees.

Tomas surmised that if the creatures were still shadowing them, and he believed they were, then the scent of the horse would surely fill their noses thanks to the onshore breeze. He hoped the beasts may have gone elsewhere to sleep after their raucous performance during the night, but he knew better than to hope.

Movement in the trees drew his attention now and then. But no sooner did his eyes focus upon the trees and what lay beneath them than the objects had vanished. He thought that perhaps his lack of sleep, because of the constant calls of the creatures hunting them, was playing tricks on his mind.

He closed his eyes, just to rest his burning eyelids for a moment. Others around him were watching the trees, and his mare knew how to walk without his assistance.

Tomas.

He heard a woman's voice calling.

Tomas.

He turned his head, peering about for the owner of the voice. It sounded familiar, a long-lost memory.

Tomas.

He was alone on the plain. His friends nowhere to be seen. The crew of the *Adelandria* were missing. His beloved Emily was not by his side.

Tomas.

One rider, a woman cloaked from head to foot in white, mounted upon a silver steed, approached from his left. She drew nearer and nearer, right to his side. Tomas wanted to strike her down, move away, anything; but he could not move. He tried to read her features, but her hood obscured her features.

Tomas.

Her voice struck a chord within.

She lowered her hood.

"Tomas," she said with a smile. His mother. Catherine.

"Mother," he gasped.

Her smile changed. The corners of her mouth twisted and split open. The flesh of her cheeks cracked and ripped apart.

"Tomas," she hissed as blisters formed on her skin. Her eyes melted in their sockets as fire engulfed her face.

"Tomas."

His eyes flashed open as he took a deep breath.

"Tomas." He turned to his left, hoping never to see that image again. Emily was there. "Are you all right?"

"I didn't sleep well," he told her. "I just dreamt about my mother."

"Not a pleasant dream," she said. "It didn't sound like a pleasant reunion."

"I made a noise?"

"You were groaning," she replied, "softly. I don't think anyone else heard."

"It was horrible," he told her. "But it was so real."

"Was she a beautiful woman?"

"Yes," he said. *But not in this dream.* "But not as beautiful as you."

She smiled.

"The dragon burnt her alive," he said. "I just left her in the Great Hall so I could be with this old nag." He reached down to pat the brown mare on the neck. He shook his head and felt a tear tickle his cheek. "Why did I do that?"

"It's not your fault," Emily assured him. "You were a child."

"I should have known better," he said. "I was the son of a councilman. I should have acted more like it."

"You were the son of a councilman," she said. "But you were not a councilman yourself. You were a boy that loved horses. You're still a boy who loves horses. I'm sure your mother would understand and tell you so herself if she could."

"I saw her melting," he said. "Maybe that's how she looked when the dragon fire smothered her. Maybe she was telling me what she thought of me."

"It was a silly dream." Emily shook her head. "You're tired and your mind needs rest. You've been carrying an incredible load inside your head since you told my father that you would come find my sister and me."

Tomas frowned and nodded slightly.

"Tomas," Simon said softly from his other side. "I have been listening. I apologise for doing so, but I need to tell you one thing. I was in the Great Hall with my mother during the attack. You forget we were all taken, all the children. They took us to that cave where they were holding you. There were no younglings in the Great Hall when the dragon attacked. They spared us.

"If you were there," he continued. "If you had stayed, they would have taken you as well. There was nothing any of us could do. None of us were there.

"Your mother's death and my mother's death were sad tragedies that we had no control over," Simon finished.

"You're right," he said.

The image of his mother, burned and blistered, scarred his mind.

His eyes wanted to close again, but he fought the urge.

There wasn't any part of him that wanted to see that horrifying vision again.

***

A slight and gradual depression in the land brought them low to the horizon. The view of the path ahead was obscured by the gentle upward slope ahead of them. They were making their way through a wide vale that funnelled the wind from the sea.

The ferocity of the breeze intensified, almost to gale force conditions. The horses leant into the blast to keep their balance and continue. They, as well as their riders, wanted to be out of the valley as quickly as they possible.

"Stay close," Jeremy yelled over the roaring wind. The riders clustered together tightly as they pressed onwards towards the northern slope.

A thin haze flew by them at an intense speed, obscuring an unobstructed view of their surroundings. They could still see the contour of the land and the trees to the west, but it was as if someone had placed a sheer white veil over everything.

Many grey blobs appeared at the edge of the trees and fanned out, both left and right. They moved rapidly along each of the ridges that hemmed the valley floor.

Tomas wasn't sure if his mind was playing tricks again as he watched the grey figures moving.

"Simon," he called. "Do you see?"

"Yes," the other replied as he squinted, peering towards the southwestern and northwestern ends of the slopes. "We are about to be attacked."

"The bastards were waiting for us to get to this spot," David grumbled.

"Well," Oliver said, frowning. "They know it's a good place to ambush someone."

"How many do you see?" Jeremy asked.

"Perhaps twenty," Simon replied. "Maybe more."

Tomas pulled his sword as his view of the creatures became clearer as they drew closer and closer.

The creatures reminded him of hounds. They ran similarly, but their size was much larger than any dog that he had seen.

The creatures bore box-shaped heads with a wide mouth that bared sharp teeth longer than a man's fingers. Grey, furry flanks with thicker patches around the shoulders rustled in the breeze as they sped towards the riders.

Tomas kicked hard and sent his mare sprinting towards the closest creature on the northern ridge.

His sword was pointed forwards, along the right shoulder of his steed. Pointing it upwards a little, he gauged the distance and speed of the oncoming attacker, preparing himself for the strike.

The beast snarled as it drew nearer, thick saliva spilling from the corners of its mouth.

It leapt into the air; mouth wide open with an intent to sink its teeth into the mare's neck.

The mare ignored the danger, trusting her handler and continuing to race forwards.

Tomas thrust his blade forwards and struck the monster in the roof of its mouth.

The tip of the sword pierced the skin and bone just behind the creature's teeth.

It screeched a cry of pain and recoiled, pulling Tomas, who was still holding his sword, clear off the mare's back.

Tomas landed face first in the snow, empty-handed. His sword was still sticking out of the beast's mouth. It was continuing to make whimpers and screeching cries as it tried to pry the sharp object out with its paws.

Pulling his dagger from his belt, and while the animal was too engaged in its own self-preservation, Tomas attacked. He plunged his dagger deep into the creature's eye.

It howled, pulling its head away from the man.

A part of Tomas felt sorry for the creature as he reached for the hilt of his sword that still protruded from the wide, tooth-filled mouth. The animals were only doing what instinct told them to do.

Hunt and eat.

But Tomas didn't intend to become fodder for any creature, no matter how hungry it was or how sorry he felt about it.

He pulled with all of his might and retrieved his blade from the animal. Instantly, he dug the blade into the creature's neck and twisted the hilt.

A spray of blood hit the snow as he pulled the sword out of the wound. The giant beast moved away, snarling at Tomas, knowing it lost the fight.

It lay on its side, watching him with its one good eye as it bled out upon the snow.

Tomas turned to see the other men and women engaged in similar battles.

More creatures descended the slopes towards them as he looked for Emily. She was fighting on the ground with the Erilian warriors and had helped take down one monster.

They were now engaged in defending the horses from another two beasts. It was then that Tomas saw the tactic that the creatures were using. The fight was a distraction. The steeds were the target.

"Protect the horses," Tomas called. He turned towards his own brown mare and ran towards her.

He needed to get back to the group as quickly as he could, as most of the fighters spread thin. Gaps that were too wide had formed, and the hungry predators noticed.

Grabbing the reins, Tomas moved to the left side of the mare and placed his foot in the stirrup, preparing to hoist himself into the saddle.

Suddenly, the mare jolted forward.

One creature had approached from behind her, out of both her and Tomas' vision.

It knocked her upon her left side, pinning Tomas' leg. His sword flew from his hand and went skirting across the ground to his right. Too far to reach.

The beast had its teeth buried deep into the mare's neck.

She gargled as the predator shook its head from side to side, tearing the wound open wider and wider.

Thick, dark blood gushed over the creature's lips as it held the mare in place.

"No," Tomas breathed, a lump forming in his throat.

She slowed her breathing and relaxed her tense muscles as her life extinguished.

"No!" Tomas wept as he watched his most loyal friend leave him forever.

The large predator dragged the mare towards the northern ridge, removing the horse from Tomas. It continued to pull its prey away, ignoring the man on the ground, taking what it had come for.

He sat there in the snow, watching the creature drag his mare away. His eyes filled with tears.

Looking around, he could see several other horses from the pack being taken as well.

The gaps between the fighters weren't closed in time. The hunters took many steeds.

Tomas clenched his teeth and felt his face growing hot.

He reached for his sword and picked himself up from the ground.

The beast continued to drag the mare up the slope of the northern ridge. Mustering all of his strength, anger and frustration, Tomas raced across the snow towards the beast.

The creature didn't see him coming; too absorbed in moving its kill. Tomas came to its side and plunged his blade deep into the flesh behind its left forelimb.

The monster let go of the mare instantly, giving a loud roar as Tomas pulled the sword from the wound.

"Come on," Tomas urged the creature.

It turned and swiped at the man with its right paw. Long, sharp claws extended from the appendage and swished through the air near Tomas' stomach.

He lunged with his blade and struck the beast deep into the neck just behind the jaw.

The creature hissed as a spray of blood jetted from the wound.

Tomas didn't feel sorrow for the beast this time around. He felt angry.

Something told him that feeling this way was wrong. That this creature, like the others, was only behaving as creatures do.

But it killed my horse.

He cut it deeply, and he knew he had to put it out of its misery.

It slumped onto the ground, continuing to use what energy it had left to hiss at him.

With a great blow, Tomas stuck his blade deep into the creature's skull.

It closed its eyes.

Turning to his mare, he kneeled beside her and cried as he rubbed her cheek.

She was gone, looking back at him with a dark, lifeless stare.

Eight

A large fire burned at the end of the cavernous room. Joanne, dressed in scarlet, sat in a deep chair by the hearth, staring into the flames to keep warm. She wondered how she came to be in such a situation where she was being taken care of so well, protected behind great stone walls and ever under the watchful eye of the woman in green.

She gave a sideways glance towards the man standing against the wall like a soldier to her side as she thought about her arrival at the castle.

Directed to a room deep in the structure's belly, she believed her destination was another prison cell, or a cage such as the one into which they had placed her in onboard the ship.

Instead, she was taken to an enormous white room filled with humidity and warmth. In the centre of the area was a wide pool carved into stone and filled with steaming water.

Large, polished marble columns stretched from floor to ceiling in six places around the water's edge. They were so wide that she didn't believe she could reach her arms half-way around if she tried.

Upon each of the marble pillars facing the water, bright lanterns hung upon hooks. The white tiling beneath the surface of the water and around the edges of the pool reflected the light in all directions, cancelling out many of the shadows behind the large supporting columns.

In the centre of the far wall were two levers, one directly above the other.

High upon the wall near the ceiling was a long iron tube that stretched over the water, ending above the middle of the pool.

White tiles hemmed the edge of the pool, extending from water's edge to the walls.

Beneath the water's surface, five wide steps that lined the pool on all sides. Joanne could see they weren't simply there to walk down to the base of the structure, but could be used to sit on. She wondered how many she could move down, remaining on her backside, before the water was over her head.

Positioned against the walls on either side of the room were young men. She counted eight.

They were shirtless and stood with their backs to the wall, straight and tall, with their hands behind them. Like soldiers.

They looked a little older than her sister, but not much. Perhaps seventeen. Maybe a little older or younger.

She felt intimidated by them. Their muscular forms frightened her and after her experience on the ship, she wondered if she could ever trust men again.

"This is the bath," the hooded woman in green told her. "Take off your clothes."

Joanne hesitated, moving her eyes across the eight men standing around the pool.

"They won't touch you," the woman said. "They won't even look. Not unless you want them to."

Joanne furrowed her brow, confused.

"They serve me," the woman informed the girl. "And they now serve you."

The woman lowered her hood to reveal dark red hair set into a long plait that disappeared beneath her cloak.

Two men quickly moved to her side to relieve her of the garment. One man folded it and draped it over a golden framed chair that sat near the entrance to the room.

The woman used another man as a balance to steady herself by placing a hand on his shoulder. She lifted her foot behind her by bending her knee so that the other man could unlace her boot and remove it from her foot. She repeated the manoeuvre for the removal of the other boot by switching hands. The men instinctively swapped their duties to see the task fulfilled.

With her bare feet on the tiles, the woman removed her green garments and let them drop onto the tiles. She was now standing naked in front of the eight men and an eleven-year-old girl. Her face didn't change expression as she kept her deep green eyes on Joanne.

The girl stared dumbfounded as the men backed away to their original places by the wall. The woman was truly beautiful. Joanne had never seen such splendour in a person before.

"Take off your clothes and join me," the woman commanded Joanne as she stepped into the water and descended the steps until she was chest high in the warm liquid. "Someone needs to wash you clean and I do not believe you will let one of these servants in the water to assist you. Hurry."

Joanne gave the men one more look before she removed her boots and dress. Using her arms and hands, she covered her privates, cowering as she hurried into the bath, dipping her body beneath the water as quickly as she could.

The woman pointed to one man, "Vessel." She then pointed to another, "Clothes."

With that, one man moved to the rear of the room, where a table sat against the wall. On the wall was a large pitcher made of bronze. He stepped into the bath in order to bring it to the woman.

Joanne, now beside the lady, tensed.

"No." The woman held her finger to the servant. She pushed with her feet and drifted across the water to the edge where the man waited. "Give it to me."

The other man gathered Joanne's garments from the floor and left the room.

"Where is he taking my clothes?" she whispered. Her voice bounced along the walls so loudly that she thought the world must have heard.

"He will destroy them in the fire," the woman replied.

"Then what will I wear?"

"I have new clothes," the other replied, "better clothes for you."

Better clothes? My mother made those for me. How could they be better?

"Tilt you head back," the woman ordered as she filled the pitcher with water from the bath. She then poured the contents over Joanne's hair as she raked through the tangled mop with her long fingernails. "There is so much silt in here. And your skin is covered in grime."

"I like your hair," Joanne said. "And skin. It's so clean. And red."

"My skin is red?" the woman asked as she drizzled more water over the girl's hair.

"No," she answered. "Your hair. I don't know many people with red hair, except for me and my sister."

"Your sister," the woman breathed, almost a sigh. "Do you think she is coming for you?"

"I don't know." Joanne frowned and thought about the night when the scarred man killed her mother. "No. She ran away and left me."

"Then I will take care of you," the woman told her. "I can't replace your mother or sister. But I will look after you as if you were my own. I promise."

After her bath, Joanne dressed in a thick white robe, handed to her by the lady. Two men clothed the woman in a white robe of her own.

Hand in hand, shadowed by one of the young men, Joanne and the woman walked up the wide stairwell that led to a sitting room. It was a large space with a grand fireplace at one end and an open archway at the other.

The fire was roaring and Joanne wanted to sit by its warmth, but the woman led her through the arch and into the large foyer of the building. Large wooden doors to the outside world stretched high and wide to her right and a grand stair to her left. Two corridors disappeared on either side of the stairwell, leading to the servant quarters and kitchen.

There was another open archway across the foyer from the sitting room. Inside was a large room with a high-backed chair elevated on a stone platform at the far end.

A throne.

The more Joanne saw, the more curious she became.

Was this lady a queen?

Still led by the hand, she mounted to a platform where the steps split into two staircases; one to the left and the other to the right.

"My quarters are to the left," the woman told her. "Yours are this way."

The two women, still followed by one servant, moved to the right and into a long and wide passage. Many doors lined either side corridor, spaced so far apart from each other that Joanne believed she could fit her family's hut between each of them twice over.

The hallway seemed to stretch on forever.

It had stone walls and a white rug that ran the entire length of the passageway. The carpet felt soft under her bare feet. She had never felt something so nice and wanted to walk on it forever.

She must be a queen, Joanne thought as she passed six doorways.

"Key," the woman commanded the servant.

He handed over an iron object to the woman, who unlocked a door on the left and pushed it open.

They stepped into a room that was about the size of Joanne's family's hut. It surprised her to see something so small, considering the size of the spaces between each of the doors along the hallway.

Still, it was bigger than the area that she had to share with Emily.

To the side was a bed that looked comfortable. A closet with wooden doors rested on the wall nearby. There were no windows, but after seeing the rest of the castle, Joanne figured there had to be some shortfalls. It was simple but sufficient, and a great deal more than she had ever had before.

The woman let go of Joanne's hand and stepped farther into the room towards another locked door against the far wall.

It seemed to be a strange place for a door.

Perhaps it's a storeroom, she thought.

The woman opened the door to expose a well-lit room that exuded luxury.

A large window was the first thing that Joanne saw. It stretched across the length of the wall and had white lace curtains hanging from rails above its frame. A broad balcony sat neatly outside the glass, over-looking an immense courtyard in the centre of the castle walls.

Snow and ice covered everything beyond, but the girl imagined it must look lovely in the warmer seasons.

To the left was a large four-poster bed adorned in thick white covers and white lace draping from the overhanging frame; too large for one girl. White rugs covered the floor from wall to wall.

Some deep cushioned seats were positioned around the room and a dressing table by the wall near the bed. It had a large looking glass on top with brushes and different coloured ribbons neatly laid out in rows on its surface. Red, yellow, blue, green, white and black.

Joanne moved to the middle of the room, following the woman inside. Her attention moved to another set of doors to the right of the area.

"These doors are your closets," the lady said, opening the doors to reveal different coloured dresses draped upon hangers; just like the ribbons. "These are your clothes. We can work out your colour later. You have boots of different sizes and in here is your privy." The woman opened a door to the far right on the wall.

"Privy?" Joanne asked. She had never heard of such a thing.

"Come see," the lady ordered.

Joanne stepped into the room to see a washbasin on a small waist-high cupboard by the door. On the far wall was a stone bench with a wooden seat in its centre. The wooden seat had a large hole in the centre that led to a deep hole.

She stuck her head over the hole and could see only darkness descending forever.

"What's it for?" Joanne asked.

"For those nasty times when you would usually go behind a tree," the woman answered. "This is a far more civilised approach to living. Rags are in the cupboard."

"Rags?"

"You can work out the functionality of this room in your own time," the woman replied. "For now, pick out something to wear and meet me in the kitchen as soon as you can. We will receive more young ladies to join us soon."

"More?"

"You'll see soon enough." The woman handed the key to Joanne. "This is yours. It opens both doors to this room. The outer room is your servant's quarters. He will be at your beck and call."

"He?" Joanne showed some trepidation as she took the key.

"He won't come in unless you allow him," she told the girl. "His task is to serve you. He will clean for you. He will set out your clothes for you. Cook for you, brush your hair. Whatever you want. He will do it."

"He won't come in?" Joanne asked timidly.

"Not unless you want him to," the woman answered. She turned her attention to the servant who was waiting in the front room and called to him, "Boy."

"Yes, Mistress," he answered.

Joanne measured the man with her eyes. His face was clean-shaven and dark hair cropped close to the scalp. He was tall, though not as tall as the woman, and broad-shouldered. His form was robust, like a warrior. But his eyes seemed both kind and sad.

"Come in here," the woman ordered.

Joanne's eyes widened.

"I can't, Mistress," he replied. "The young Miss hasn't willed it."

"What's your name?"

"Andris, Mistress. Am I to be punished?"

"No." She smiled as she kept her eyes on Joanne. "You responded correctly."

The woman turned towards the door, stopping at the entrance to speak to Joanne one last time.

"Get dressed and meet me in the kitchen," she said. "Andris will show you the way."

With that, she closed the door and left Joanne to explore her room.

***

Joanne sat by the fire with a red ribbon in her hair. The servants prepared lunch for the young girls, who were now under the protection of the woman in green. She remembered how the seven of them had been penned together on the ship, all similar in age.

They had subjected each of them to things that they couldn't have imagined before their treatment. Until this moment, their families protected them and knowledge of such behaviour as shown by the men of the black ship.

She was angry towards the men of the ship. She hated them.

The girls locked in the cage with her, she knew, hated those men as well.

How could they not?

But Joanne still wondered how this place, this castle, fitted into the scheme of things. The men of the ship had brought the girls to the castle and abused them during the journey.

The woman in green, however, showed only kindness.

Why would the men, who were so evil, bring the captive girls to one so kind?

Did she purchase us?

Were we sold as slaves?

Has she saved us from a far worse fate than we had on the black ship?

Joanne didn't understand.

She couldn't comprehend.

"Lunch is ready," the woman said from behind Joanne. "Come."

She rose from her chair and followed the woman in green with her own shadow, Andris, in tow.

Nine

"We have seven able horses left," Jeremy said to Tomas, who was crossing the plain back to the group dragging his saddle and bridle behind him. "Most were injured in the attack and are being put down as we speak."

Tomas turned to see some men holding steeds upon the ground. They had deep wounds from scratches and bites along their flanks. Other men plunged their swords into the poor animals' heads to give them a quick death.

It was heartbreaking.

"We pack what equipment is absolutely necessary onto the able horses then." Tomas frowned. "Leave the riding gear here. We'll travel on foot."

"It could be a long way," Jeremy said. He didn't know why the words came out of his mouth. It sounded silly.

"We've already come a long way," Tomas replied. "It makes no difference to me if you want to go on or not. I made a promise and I intend to keep it."

"Good enough," Jeremy said, patting the other on the shoulder. "I'm sorry about the mare, Tomas."

"So am I." He wiped his eyes. The horse had been a good friend to him since his childhood.

"Should we bury them?" the captain asked.

Tomas shook his head.

"Those things will just dig them back up to feed on them," he replied. "Leave them. Perhaps the sooner we can get moving, the more ground we can put between us and them. At least they will be occupied with something other than us for a while."

And that was the harsh reality of the situation.

It was about survival.

They quickly sorted through their equipment and discarded articles they didn't think they would need. They packed five tents and some bedding onto five horses. Cooking equipment and they loaded some more bedding onto David's draught horse. The seventh horse carried the injured Baldwyn Palmer. He also took two extra bed rolls, and his own, to help.

They left the spare canvas sheeting and tent poles that had been used to pen the horses on the snow and bedding and belongings of the men they had lost along the way.

The intention had been to take the lost men's equipment back to their homelands for family or close friends to receive. Sadly, with the loss of quite a large number of their horses, they could not carry the belongings.

Slinging their swords over their backs and water sacks to their hips, they set out once again. As they walked away, leading the horses towards the north, each of the travellers felt as if they were leaving a piece of themselves behind.

Emily wrapped her arm around Tomas' elbow and placed her head against his shoulder. He twisted out of her grasp.

She thought he was rejecting her until he wrapped his arm around her shoulders and kissed her forehead. Tears had run down her cheeks. She knew how fond Tomas was of his mare and that they had a long history. Her heart ached, and she wanted to say something, but the words wouldn't come.

"Funny," he said finally. She creased her brow. "Funny how I feel more for that damned horse than I did for Ivo."

"You loved the horse," she said. "You had loved it since you were a boy."

"Yes," he said. "I knew Ivo since I was a boy too."

"But you didn't love him," she told him. "The horse mattered more to you."

"I spent more time with that horse, that's for certain. More than I did with my sister. I spent nights sleeping in the stables by her side. I ate meals there and talked with her more than I did any man." He looked around at the other men of Woodmyst walking nearby.

"I know they called me names behind my back because of it. But I loved that horse. Until this journey, I didn't really know these men at all. All because I preferred the company of a stupid animal."

"She wasn't a stupid animal, Tomas," David put in as he led his giant steed. "She was smarter than a lot of men that I know. She wasn't a stupid horse. She wasn't even a good horse. She was a magnificent horse."

Tomas felt a lump in his throat. He swallowed hard to suppress his feelings, but it was too late. Tears streaked down his face.

Emily squeezed him around the waist as they continued to press northward on the plain.

***

Step after arduous step, the company moved on.

The sun was leaving its highest point in the sky and making its descent. There were a few more hours of travelling that the group wanted to make.

Several times, both Tomas and Jeremy asked if anyone wanted to take a rest. Apart from the necessary stop for relief, no one wanted to set up camp or even to sit for a spell. Instead, all travellers wanted to keep moving.

All understood that without their animals to bear them, their journey had become longer and more difficult.

Now, they needed to rely on their own strength. It was their own legs that would take their weight for the rest of their quest, not those of the horses they once rode.

The wind persisted in blowing across their path, lifting icy particles from the ground and flinging them towards the trekkers. Simon squinted into the snow and mist as biting pieces of frost pricked his face. He turned to see Baldwyn riding above the onslaught, oblivious to the plight of the people below him.

Feeling the urge to say something, Simon bit his tongue and pulled his hood farther over his face. He would not let petty envy get the better of him.

The sun continued to move on across the sky, veiled behind a thin layer of clouds that constantly dropped snow from the heavens. The ground cover reached almost to their knees, making each step an effort.

By mid-afternoon, the company grew tired. They were indeed very appreciative of the horses they once rode.

It was Tomas' guess that they hadn't even travelled a quarter of the distance that they would have with the animals. But they had to make do with what they had.

After a long march, they ventured onto the crest of a rise that overlooked another wide vale.

Cautiously, they moved towards the valley floor, peering towards the trees to see if the predators were there to meet them.

Baldwyn, seated in the best vantage point on top of his steed, made observations and reported nothing on the horizon or beneath the trees.

Keeping a steady pace, the troop moved across the plain.

David thought he heard a loud crack. It was difficult to be certain as the wind was blowing a gale and filled their ears with a constant drone and whistle as it swept across the valley.

"I'm not sure about this ground," he called as they continued forward, hearing the cracking again.

"I hear it," Simon called. "It's ice underneath us. Probably a river."

"Stop the horses," Tomas called to the others, leading the steeds. The men stood in place and waited for Tomas to give further instructions.

"Keep going, David," Emily called. "You're over the ice now. You need to move."

He didn't hesitate. He pulled his massive horse forward, hearing more cracking noises as he moved the beast on.

Only when David had reached the base of the next ridge, Tomas called the next horse over. He beckoned to Baldwyn to ride his steed a little to the left of David's path. His thought was to keep moving a little to the left for each horse so that it didn't tread upon ice that the previous steed had weakened.

Again, as Baldwyn rode slowly over the expanse, cracking resounded from beneath the snow. With him and his horse waiting beside David, Tomas called for the next.

Eventually, four horses stood on the northern side of the valley with their handlers. Two waited on the southern edge as they led the other across the icy section.

Cracking noises continued to resonate as Gustav led the horse over the area of concern.

"Come on," he urged the horse. "We're almost there."

The horse followed compliantly and wanted to be off the questionable ground as much as he.

A loud and deep crack erupted and water exploded from the ground as the ice gave way.

The horse fell into the water and smacked into the ice sheet that covered the river to the right, downstream.

Gustav was on safe ground and slid along the ground beside the river as the horse moved downstream.

The ice sheet covering the river broke away as the steed smashed into it, kicking with its forelimbs and tossing its head wildly.

Blood and water splashed onto the snowy banks as Tomas dived upon the reins, holding onto the leather straps with Gustav for all of his might.

The current was strong and gripped the animal strongly.

Emily sidled up to the men and clutched the reins as tightly as she could. She dug her heels into the snow and pushed with her legs, using all of her strength.

The horse stopped drifting downstream and floated in place. Its head lifted out of the water, it flared its nostrils and panted excitedly.

The Erilian women quickly made their way to the three, holding the reins. They took a piece of the strapping each and dug their heels in.

"Pull," Tomas called.

They pulled the horse towards the northern bank of the river.

"Pull," he called again. Others on foot made their way over the unbroken section of ice to offer help.

Eventually, they pulled the horse to the shore.

Several deep wounds from the sharp ice had perforated the beast's neck and front legs. The incident had broken and twisted one of its back limbs around. *Possibly from the initial fall through the ice,* Tomas thought.

Simon came running to the animal's side as Tomas crouched near its head and stroked its muzzle.

"It's all right," he whispered to the animal. The animal let out a nicker. He could hear a quiet gargling sound from inside the beast's throat.

Tomas looked at Simon and gave him a nod. The other closed his eyes and nodded reluctantly as he pulled his sword from his sheath.

***

With the supplies repacked upon the remaining six horses, the group set off again. Even with the sun getting lower in the sky, the travellers wanted to be as far away from the steed's remains as they could. They knew it would attract predators, and if they were nearby, another potential danger might ensue.

On they went.

With the wind's consistent beating against their right and the threat of attack from the left, the company grew increasingly tired both physically and mentally.

Everyone simply wanted to pitch tents and crawl into their bedding. They didn't want to sleep in case the creatures of the woods returned.

Worse yet, what if the white witch came back with her straw men?

The sun had descended beyond the mountain peaks, and Jeremy called for them to stop.

"We can't go much farther," he said. "We need to rest."

Tomas looked at the sky and saw the deepening change in colour. He nodded, agreeing with the captain.

They set up camp and collected wood.

There was neither sign nor sound of the predators, making the troop feel a little more at ease than they had been for most of the day.

They set fires around the circle of tents again with one in the centre of camp.

A few of the troop sat by the fire, cooking porridge and brewing tea. The rest had retired to their tents for the preference of bedrolls and shut eyes.

Oliver was the only man of Woodmyst to remain by the hearth. He was tired but had broken through some wall that wouldn't allow him to sleep. Instead, he ate and drank with Sharek the Erilian Warrior, Baldwyn, the injured crewman and two other seafarers.

The five had opted to stand watch for the first half of the night, intending to wake some poor soul after midnight to relieve them of duty.

They had been sitting and talking by the hearth for several hours. The stars weren't anywhere to be seen, but the moon was high and trying to force her silver light through the clouds.

"I don't think I can return to the ship," Sharek said suddenly.

All eyes moved to her.

"What do you mean?" Baldwyn asked. "You practically grew up on the *Adelandria*."

"But he's gone," she said. "He was everything on that ship that I ever needed. He was the *Adelandria*."

The others nodded, except for Oliver. He didn't understand what she meant. How could one man be the ship?

He let it go, knowing that it must be something only the crewmen of the *Adelandria* would understand.

"He was a grand captain," one of the other men said. "The best I've ever had the privilege to know."

"Aye," the others said.

"I haven't known many captains," Oliver told them. "But I will say that he was a respectable fellow. We venture little outside our own little world in Woodmyst and so trust is something that you need to earn with our people. Captain Tarkin was a person who had my trust almost from the moment I met him. He was a good man."

"Aye," the crewmen said again.

A long screech echoed across the valley from the west.

"Did you hear that?" Sharek got to her feet.

"It's far away," one man replied.

"If we can hear it," Oliver informed him, "then it's already too close."

David emerged from his tent, blade in hand and hood over his head.

The long screech resonated again from deep in the woods.

"So, they're back," he said.

Ten

Gripping her cloak around her tightly, her breath coming in short wheezes, Sumaiyya climbed a steep embankment that overlooked a small bay. Nestled comfortably on the southern edge of the inlet sat a large fort with a tall wooden tower.

She had reached the outpost.

It was dark, with few torches or lanterns alight. She wondered if it was still being manned or whether the inhabitants had abandoned the fort during the height of winter.

Behind the walls, she could see the snow-capped roofs of several small buildings. It was too far to observe if anyone was moving about. Not that it mattered.

Even if all inside were dead, she would at least have some shelter and surely be able to find something to eat.

She quickly descended the steep ridge towards the fort, almost falling as her legs turned to jelly and her body tilted too far forward. Correcting herself, she slowed her pace and mustered more self-control as she walked on.

It took some time, but she eventually reached a large wooden gate at the base of the tower. Two men, posted high above her, looked down upon her frame.

"Who goes there?" one man called.

She removed her hood to allow her blonde hair to wave in the breeze.

"It's the White Mistress," the other man called to someone inside the walls. "Open the gates."

A loud clunk resounded as the barricading beam across the gates lifted and slid to one side. The gates creaked and groaned, opening inwards to reveal a neat yard with buildings placed around the outside.

A scruffy man with a sword strapped to his back ran to her side and offered his hands to her.

"Mistress," he said. "Take my arm. Are you all right?"

"I'm being pursued," she said weakly.

The man looked back towards the ridge.

"They are a long way off," she informed him. "It will be some time before they reach this place."

"You're weak," he said, sounding shocked. "I thought nothing could drain you so."

"I've not rested," she replied.

"Come into the commander's hut and sit by the fire."

"Where is your commander?" she asked.

"In bed sleeping," the man answered.

"Wake him," she ordered.

"Wake the commander," he said to another standing nearby before turning his attention to another. "Close the gate."

As she leant against the man who aided her across the yard towards a building at the far end, the gates loudly creaked shut with a final thud. The barricade slid back into place before all eyes finally latched onto the woman in white.

He took her into the front room of the commander's hut, where a stove sat tucked into a corner with a crude wooden chair next to it. The only light in the hut was from the tiny flames emitting a faint glow through the grill of the stove. The scruffy man lowered Sumaiyya into the seat and opened the grill to stoke the fire.

All heard the commander groaning protests for being stirred from his slumber.

Sheepishly, the other guard, a young man not much older than Sumaiyya, appeared from a darkened doorway that led to the commander's bedroom.

"He told me I was to be drawn and quartered for waking him and for telling lies," the young man told her. The scruffy man placed a log onto the fire, swallowing hard.

"Does he make such threats often?" she asked the man by the stove.

"Yes, Mistress," he replied. "Although, he usually calms down after some time and reverts to the lash instead of such extreme measures."

She nodded as she took her gloves from her hands and stretched her fingers near the heat of the fire.

"Stand over there." She pointed to the door. "Both of you. And close the door."

The two guards complied immediately. They had heard stories of the white witch and were deeply afraid of her.

Stretching her hand towards the commander's bedroom door, she closed her eyes. She inhaled a deep breath and held it. As she opened her eyes again, the men stood back and felt their hearts skip a beat at what they saw.

Her piercing blue eyes had turned into two pools of empty blackness. It was as if nothing was there. Not just empty sockets, it was nothing.

The men had never felt such darkness, desolation, and evil. It surrounded them, filling the room.

She made a fist.

A loud thump thundered from the commander's bedroom as something hit the wall near the door from inside.

She opened her hand and closed it again.

THUMP!

A man called in pain beyond the open bedroom door.

She repeated the action again and again.

THUMP!
THUMP!

THUMP!

Each time, the cries of someone in pain grew louder and louder.

She opened her hand one more time and made a sweeping gesture to the floor by her feet.

The commander, half-naked and bleeding from head to toe, burst from the doorway and landed in a messy pile on the floor. He cried in agony as he moved his right hand to his left forearm where a clean white bone had broken and protruded through the skin.

"Do you know who I am?" the white witch asked, her voice steady and emotionless.

He opened his eyes, or at least tried to. Swollen and resembling a large red tomato, one eye remained closed shut.

"Yes," he replied as he peered with his good eye.

"Stand when you address me," she ordered.

"I think my leg is broken," he replied, slobbering and blubbering.

"Stand," she said again, motioning with her hand. He lifted into the air, both legs dangling from the ground. He cried in pain as his whole body moved from the twisted heap on the floor to the straight figure hanging in the middle of the room.

The two guards looked on, frightened. Their breathing became shallow and their bodies shook with fear.

"You have broken your leg," she said. "And your arm. You only have one good eye and you can't even stand to address me correctly. We have no use for you."

"No," he protested. But it was too late.

She squeezed her hand tightly, making a fist one last time.

The man's head and torso instantly caved in with a loud crunch as bones and joints crushed, spilling a mess of blood and tissue onto the floor beneath him.

Sumaiyya lowered her hand and relaxed, letting the body fall to the floor with a thud. Her eyes changed to their regular blue and her breathing returned to normal.

"I need to sleep," she said to the two guards as she stretched her fingers towards the heat of the flames. "Clean up his room and change the linen. I need something to eat and a horse prepared in the morning.

"And," she said finally, pointing to the commander's remains, "clean that filth up."

***

"We can't let them take the horses," Tomas called out.

The screeching and coughing calls of the creatures echoed from the forest and across the open ground towards the camp.

"I guess the other horses weren't enough for them," Baldwyn said as he sat upon his steed, sword in hand.

The other travellers stood on the ground, near the northern edge of the camp. The fires around the tents were blazing, and they had moved the horses into the middle of the circle.

"We fight until there are none left," Jeremy barked. "It's either them or us."

"Aye," came several calls as they prepared themselves for battle.

Suddenly, the calls stopped.

Silence.

"Get ready." Tomas tightened his grip on the hilt of his sword.

Their eyes scanned the tree line with intensity. The creatures were there, just out of view. The dark night obscured their forms beneath shadow.

The travellers heard their own hearts beating in their ears. Their breathing instinctively quickened and most were having trouble getting it under control.

Suddenly, the creatures burst from the woods.

Snow flew in all directions as they approached the camp at high velocity.

"Here they come," David called.

Akasati and Rhydra loaded arrows into their bows and took careful aim.

"I count twenty," one crewman called. "We outnumber them."

"They're bigger than us, you fool," Jeff Parish replied. "Not to mention stronger and faster."

The Erilian archers let their arrows fly.

The projectiles whistled through the air and found their targets true. The arrows hit two beasts through their eyes, the tips of the arrows planting themselves deep into the animal's heads. They crashed to the ground, flipping and flopping across the snow from the momentum and speed of their attack.

Eighteen more continued their assault, maintaining their speed, driven by instinct.

The two archers reloaded and took aim again as the predators reached a distance halfway between the tree line and the encampment.

With a loud whoosh, three arrows shot through the air.

Two more beasts crashed into the snow, sending up a cloud of white powder.

"One more," Tomas commanded them. "Quickly."

Their teeth bared and their long, grey tongues dangling from the sides of their enormous jaws, the creatures continued forward.

Thick drool foamed in the corners of their mouths as the scent of both horse and man filled their senses.

The women fired again.

Akasati hit her target, sending it into a tumbling mess.

Rhydra's arrow pierced the animal's shoulder and stuck deep. It wasn't enough to deter it.

"Here we go," David called as he stepped forward a few paces, swinging his sword in an upward arc.

His blade connected with one creature's chin, piercing both flesh and bone. The force of the strike caused the blade to continue into the roof of the animal's mouth.

It recoiled and fell onto the ground, pawing at its muzzle as blood spurted from its nose. David quickly plunged the point of his blade deep into the beast's skull. It stopped moving immediately, its limbs relaxed and its snarls and growls silenced.

David frowned.

Killing such a beast didn't give him any satisfaction. It wasn't like the hunt for the Qedia that he remembered from his boyhood. He remembered the tracking and manoeuvring they would use to corner the gigantic bird.

Even then, he felt some remorse for the fowl. At least they made a feast out of it.

These creatures were simply hungry and trying to survive.

So are we, he thought.

It was that simple.

Survival.

He returned his attention to the oncoming creatures.

Tomas had put one down with Emily's help, he with his sword, she with his dagger. Her abilities impressed David. She had proved her worth and more during their expedition.

Baldwyn poked his blade towards another that was trying to take his horse from under him. Every time the creature moved in with its jaws opened wide, the rider plunged his blade towards the predator's head. He made a few good hits, but not enough to dissuade the attacker.

David bolted over as quickly as he could. As the creature attacked Baldwyn and his horse, giving its full attention to its intended prey, David plunged his blade deep into its side.

It howled as it pulled away from the sword. Realising that it would not win this battle, the beast turned and moved away. A great trail of blood fell onto the snow as it headed slowly towards the forest.

There was no time to chase after it or see if it made it back to the shelter of the trees. Three other creatures continued to attack to his right, forcing their way past the blades to get to the steeds in the middle of the camp.

The Erilian warriors moved between the attacker and the six remaining steeds and fought hard to keep three beasts at bay.

With snapping teeth and deafening roars, swiping claws and loud screeches, the creatures pushed the Erilian women further into the camp.

Rhyodia ducked under the biting attack of one predator, plunging her blade deep into its neck, slicing to the side to open arteries and the wind passage.

It fell upon its side, writhing and snarling.

Another beast next to it seized the woman in its jaws and shook wildly, digging its teeth into her flesh.

She didn't have time to scream as the ferocity of the shaking broke her neck. Rhyodia was gone before she knew it.

Karlena screamed as the monster continued to shake her friend's body from side to side. Its teeth sawed through flesh and bone, causing her to fall back to the ground in two pieces.

Akasati and Sharek ran in to attack the beast, plunging their blades into its flesh over and over around its head and neck.

Karlena and Rhydra focused their attention on the other remaining predator.

Before long, all three creatures lied upon the snow side by side.

As others fought the remaining beasts, the Erilian women dropped their swords and fell upon their knees by their childhood friend's remains.

The troop finished the last remaining attackers off as the Erilian women wept uncontrollably.

David peered towards the trail of blood that led towards the forest. His foe, one of the attacking beasts, lay upon the snow at the end of the red track.

His heart felt heavy at the sight.

Giving a slight frown, he reflected on what had just happened.

After some time, he turned back towards the camp.

Eleven

"You look lovely," the woman in green told her.

Joanne wore a sapphire garment. She tied her auburn hair in a loose ponytail with a blue ribbon.

"Thank you, my lady," she replied shyly, eyeing the other girls around the table. All of them had shared the cage with her on the ship. They now all dressed in fine clothes of varying colours. One was in gold, another in scarlet, others in white, olive, lilac, and black.

A large fire was blazing in a deep fireplace at one end of the room. Two open doorways on either wall next to the hearth were the only ways in or out of the room.

"Yet I don't think this is your colour," the lady told her from her place at the head of the table. "I'm uncertain about any of you yet. Except you." She pointed to a dark-haired girl in scarlet, seated across the long table from Joanne. There was instant recognition between the two. The girl in scarlet's name was Tricia. She and Joanne were not only locked in the cell together on the black ship, but knew one another from their village in the mountains.

"That colour is yours," the woman continued. "You will be the Scarlet Miss."

Tricia was afraid and confused. She bowed her head reluctantly and whispered, "Thank you, my lady."

"Are you afraid of me?" the woman asked, her posture upright and her eyes boring into the child in red.

"Yes, my lady," she whimpered.

"We all are, my lady," Joanne told her quietly.

The woman in green moved her eyes slowly and deliberately across the table to the auburn-haired girl.

"You don't seem so afraid," she said.

"I am, my lady." Joanne looked at the table, avoiding the green stare of the lady at the end of the table.

"Yes, that is true," the woman acknowledged. "You are afraid but you don't fear me."

"You've only shown kindness," she replied. "Bet, we don't know you."

"I've shown kindness to you, yes. But it is only because it serves a purpose."

"Are we slaves?" asked a girl dressed in gold. The woman moved her gaze to the other girl. "My lady," she finished, lowering her eyes.

"That depends upon your point of view," the woman replied.

"You purchased us?" Joanne asked, looking directly at the woman in green.

"In a manner of speaking," the other replied.

"Are we to serve this Sovereign?" the auburn girl asked.

"You've heard of the Sovereign?"

"On the ship," the girl in gold replied. "The man with the scar said the name all the time."

"And what impression did you get from the discourse on the ship about the Sovereign?" the woman asked.

"That he is powerful," Joanne replied. "That he has killed and hurt many people. That he is a terrible force."

"Indeed," the woman replied. "The Sovereign is a terrible force. The answer is yes; you are to be trained in the service of the Sovereign."

"What kind of service?" the scarlet girl asked, her voice shaking and full of fear, remembering what black ship's captain did to her.

"You will never be subjected to the treatment that you received on the ship," the woman replied. "That, I promise you. Your service will be in positions of power. You will control men, as men control dogs."

She stretched her hand towards the cutlery on the table in front of Tricia. A spoon lifted from the table and flew at an incredible speed, right into her grasp.

"You will control many things in the name of the Sovereign," she told them before turning her attention to Joanne. "Pass me your fork."

Joanne reached out with her hand.

"No," the woman chided. "Try again."

Joanne moved her eyes between the silver object on the table to the woman at the end. She wasn't sure how to achieve what the lady required of her. Her eyes darted around the table to see all facing her way. The other girls appeared just as confused as she.

"Try," the woman repeated.

Her eyes darted to the spoon, to the fork, to her empty white porcelain plate.

How?

She stared at the fork.

How do I make you move?

Her entire attention focused on the silver object.

Move.

Her surroundings vanished from her mind. There were no girls in garments of varying colours. There were no men servants standing around the room. There was just the fork and the woman in green who required it.

Move.

The fork shuddered upon the table.

It slid a fraction towards the woman, shuddering, shuddering.

It made a loud tapping noise across the table as it inched slowly, slowly.

Suddenly, her concentration broken, the environment about her flooded back.

The faces of the others around the table expressed surprise and awe. Even the looks on the men behind the girls appeared shocked.

"Very good." The woman smiled. "No one has ever displayed such prowess in as little time. No one."

Breathing rapidly and feeling as if she had just run up a steep mountain and back down again, she turned to the lady seated at the end of the table.

"Who are you?" Joanne asked, her voice shaking. She furrowed her brow, confused, as a tear streamed over her cheek.

"Some call me the Green Mistress," she replied. "Most refer to me as *my lady*. But my real name is Yasmeen Svoboda.

"I was once like you. A little girl who didn't know what power she possessed until circumstance provided the opportunity to find out.

"But we can talk about that another time. For now, I think we should eat."

As she finished her words, a large metal tray on wheels, loaded with a breakfast of roasted pork, toast and boiled eggs, pushed through the open door to the right side of the fireplace by a man dressed in white.

The servants reached over the right shoulders of each of the diners and snaked around the table in a single line to retrieve their mistresses' meals.

Simultaneously, the servants placed the laden plates in front of the diners before stepping back to their places against the walls.

"Eat up," the woman commanded.

The girls watched how the Green Mistress used her cutlery and did their utmost to emulate her. Some were more successful than others. The distinction between those who were more successful was the number of times the silverware screeched across the porcelain surface of their plate.

***

The men carefully place Rhyodia on the wooden stack and set ablaze. It wasn't as grand a pyre as given to both Captain Tarkin and Ivo, but it was the best that the troop could do given the circumstances.

Her body wasn't prepared and cleaned, as was tradition, but most agreed that there was no way that the gods would reject her from the hereafter, as she was one of the bravest warriors that they had ever had the privilege to be associated with.

Emily and Karlena had dressed Rhyodia in her cloak and pulled her hood far over her face before the women placed her on top of the hearth. It only seemed fitting that the other females in the troop partake in some form of ceremony for the warrior. For any of the men to have touched her just didn't sit with any of them.

Jeremy said a prayer. Tomas tuned out and stared blankly into the flames. There had been too much loss on this journey. Way more than he had bargained for.

He couldn't imagine what their situation would have been if he had continued from Oakbeach without the crew of the *Adelandria*. Perhaps they would all be dead and unable to build a pyre for each other.

But then he wondered if the crew of the *Adelandria* were thinking how they may have ended up if they had decided not to join the expedition as well. Perhaps they would sit in James Halle's Inn, sipping on ale and telling raucous stories of their adventures around the coastal lands.

As Rhyodia burned, Karlena approached Emily, holding a curved sword in extended hands. Tears streamed down her face as she moved close to the auburn-haired girl.

"We agreed this sword should be yours," she sniffled. "Rhyodia would want it, and so do we. You are already one of us. A sister. Take this, use it and remember her."

Emily tried to swallow the lump in her throat as she took the sword with both hands, one upon the hilt, the other upon the blade.

Sharek followed Karlena with the sword's sheath and strap and buckled it carefully around Emily's waist.

"A sword is heavy to carry," she said. "You will need this also. Wear it, and remember her, sister."

Emily slid the sword into the sheath as tears welled in her eyes.

Rhydra approached with the leather quiver filled with arrows as Akasati followed with Rhyodia's bow.

"Load your bow with these, sister," Rhydra said, draping the quiver over Emily's shoulders.

"Aim and shoot true." Akasati placed the bow into her hands. She then placed her arms around the other and kissed her cheek. "Sister."

Emily couldn't contain her emotions any longer. Tears streamed down her face as she breathed in quick gasps. The other Erilian women closed their arms around her, together.

Tomas looked on with a lump in his throat.

He had never been so moved.

***

Sumaiyya woke refreshed and stretched her arms and legs as far as she could in the thin bed that once belonged to the commander of the outpost. She flung the covers away and instantly felt the morning chill against her skin.

Quickly, she dressed in her garments, still stained with Ivo's blood, before draping her thick cloak around her. With her boots on, she opened the door to the bedroom, allowing the light of the morning sun to creep into the darkened room.

A guard was still scrubbing the floor with warm water where the commander's remains once lay. He was having little luck removing the blood from the floorboards.

"Food and drink," she said as she stood in the doorway.

"Yes, Mistress." He rose to his feet. "We have little, so I prepared toast, but we have no butter. I have brewed some tea on the stove and there are some oats that I could mix into a porridge."

"It will do," she said, sitting in the chair by the stove.

The man busied himself serving the woman in white as she stared at the bloodstain and steaming water in the bucket nearby.

"How long have you been at this?"

"All night, Mistress," he answered as he handed her a mug of hot tea.

She sipped the steaming liquid slowly.

"I must have been exhausted," she told him. "It's a wonder that you didn't wake me up."

"I tried to keep the noise down as much as possible, Mistress," he replied.

"This is good," she said, holding the mug up.

"Thank you, Mistress." He bowed.

"My horse?" she asked after taking another sip.

"We have our best steed being prepared for you," he answered. "As soon as you are ready, we will saddle her and you can be on your way. Would you like any of the men to accompany you?"

"No," she replied. "You will need your men here. If my pursuers made it past the Rukyul, you will need all men here."

"You saw Rukyul, Mistress?"

"No," she answered. "If I had, in my condition, I don't think I would have made it this far."

The guard found that hard to believe, considering what she did to the commander during the night before. Then again, he didn't profess to understand anything to do with such things as mysticism. He quietly returned to stirring oats into boiling water, putting a spoonful of sugar into the mix as he moved the spoon around.

After she had eaten her fill, she stepped outside into the morning sun.

The clouds had cleared, and the bright rays from the glowing orb filled her with some warmth. Closing her eyes, she took a deep breath and smiled. She was ready to move on.

"This way, Mistress." The young guard that had served her breakfast pointed to a large building by the gates. She could tell from the small spillage of straw near its opening, and the ripe smell of horse manure, that he was leading her to the stables.

There were several pens with some horses along the right side of the structure.

Equipment such as ropes and harnesses, as well as different farming tools and implements, hung from nails on the left wall.

A large chestnut steed stood in the middle of the floor, having a saddle buckled in place. It looked like a powerful beast and she hoped it proved to be so as she intended to ride non-stop to Blackrock Haven, the port town north of the outpost.

"My apologies, Mistress." One of the stable hands lowered his head. "We have saddles suited to men only."

"I know how to ride," she said, rubbing the horse upon its muzzle.

"Of course, Mistress." He bowed lower.

She placed her foot into the stirrup and, to the men's surprise, hoisted herself into the saddle with ease.

"Open the gates," she commanded, urging the steed to amble out of the stables.

The young guard repeated the order, yelling at the men standing post near the giant wooden entrance.

With a loud clunk, they removed the barricade to open the gates inwards.

Sumaiyya kicked the horse gently in the flanks with her heels. It lunged forward and trotted through the open passage into the wild lands of the north. With haste, she pulled the horse to the right and kicked hard, sending the beast into a gallop.

The steed raced away, tossing the snow up in a flurry behind it.

With the wind in her ears, she didn't hear the gates shut behind her. She didn't look back to see the men on the tower watching her speed away.

The fort and its inhabitants had served their purpose.

They no longer mattered to her.

Ahead, only ahead was all there was.

For now.

Twelve

Twenty travellers and six horses trekked across the snow, leaving the smouldering ashes of the pyre behind them. Their hearts were heavy after losing Rhyodia, the Erilian warrior, and a loved crew-member of the *Adelandria*.

The sun shone brightly in a magnificent blue sky. The travellers took it as an omen that Grolle, the god of death accepted their lost friend, into the life after this.

All except Tomas, who kept his thoughts about the gods to himself.

Baldwyn continued to rub and scratch his thigh where the sword of an enemy soldier had pierced him some nights before. He remembered the face of his attacker, a dead man whom he knew from the ship upon which he served.

He wondered, if he lived to tell the tale, how he could convince people that this adventure ever took place. The truth, he thought, was harder to believe than some made up stories.

How would people comprehend attacks from straw men, dead men, and a white witch? Not to mention giant beasts and whatever lay in wait for them to the north.

"Does it hurt?" Karlena asked, referring to his leg.

"A little," he replied. "It feels better when I scratch it."

"Don't," she commanded. "The wound needs to close on its own. If it's itching, then that's a good sign. Don't scratch it."

"Can't help it," he replied. "Force of habit. If I have an itch, I've got to scratch it."

"I'll smack you in the gob if you make that wound worse, Baldwyn."

He didn't like the sound of that. He had seen Karlena smack others in the gob on the deck of the *Adelandria*. They usually went down like a sack of potatoes and didn't get back up for some time afterwards.

"I'll try," he promised her.

She shot him a sideways glance and continued to walk by his side as he rode.

They continued to walk on well into the afternoon without as much as a stop for relief. As they crossed another low-level plain that swept from the west to a long beach, Jeremy called for them to halt.

"Some of us need to have a rest," he told Tomas. The two had become so familiar with each other's words that the man from Wood-myst understood the captain needed to piss.

"All right," Tomas said to the captain, who wandered away a little distance to perform his bodily duties.

"Why are we stopped?" Simon asked their commander. The other men of Woodmyst and Emily gathered about.

"Piss stop," Tomas replied.

"May as well make the most of it," David replied, untying his cords.

"Not here," Emily objected. "Go down to the water's edge with the rest of them."

"Oh." David looked embarrassed. "Sorry." He turned and strode to-wards the seaside as the others gave a chuckle.

"It's disgusting." Emily screwed up her nose.

"Well," Tomas said, "while they relieve themselves, I'm going to take a walk to the top of that ridge and see what lies ahead. Do you want to come?"

"No," she replied.

"Okay." He looked surprised.

She frowned a little. "I need to piss too."

Simon laughed out loud.

"I'll come with you," he said to Tomas.

"I think I'll join you," Oliver added as he gave a chuckle.

"We'll meet you up there," Tomas told her before kissing her on the forehead.

The three men walked across the plain and up the steep embankment.

"I miss home," Oliver told the others.

"Aye," Simon replied. "You know what I miss the most about home right now?"

"What?" Tomas asked.

"Becka's gruel."

"You've got to be joking," Oliver replied. "You could have said the wide marsh to the south or the mountains to the north. You might have even mentioned your little hut with your nice bed and maybe even Agnes Fysher's tits. But no, you miss Becka's gruel?"

"I can't stand the bloody porridge anymore," he said. "Every day. Porridge, porridge, porridge."

"Do you miss Agnes Fysher's tits?" Tomas smiled as he directed his question to Oliver.

"Well..." he grinned. "They are quite..." He held his hands way out in front of his chest.

The other two men laughed as they neared the top of the ridge.

Tomas saw it first.

"Get down," he hissed.

The three men dropped into the snow.

Together, they crawled to the peak of the rise and peered over the edge.

The first object that came into view was the tower at the southern end of the compound. The entire structure, walls and buildings made of well-weathered timber nestled tightly against some dark rocks at the closest side of a narrow bay.

Even from their distance, they could see several men moving about inside the walls. Two men posted in the tower watched the ground in their general direction.

The glint of steel from the tower and upon the ground informed the men of Woodmyst, the inhabitants of the fort were well armed.

Tomas surmised someone, perhaps Sumaiyyah, informed the soldiers of the travellers' approach.

"The witch has been here," he told the others.

"Maybe she's still here," Simon suggested.

"Only one way to find out," Tomas replied.

"Should we attack now?" Oliver asked. "During daylight?"

"No," Tomas answered. "We should wait until dark and sneak over the wall where it meets the rocks there." Tomas pointed to a place where the wall ran past a mound of black stone that climbed partially up the wooden structure. "There's a structure just behind the wall where we can hide."

The others nodded.

"Back," Tomas ordered. The men crept down the embankment and out of view of the tower. When they believed they were safe from the tower guards' vision, they rose to their feet and walked back to the troop.

"I thought you were going to wait for us at the top," Emily said as the men drew near.

"Change of plans," Tomas explained as Jeremy approached. "There's a fort on the other side of the ridge. I suggest we wait here until nightfall and conduct a sneak attack."

"We can't go around?" Gustav asked.

"We will need to enter the woods to stay out of sight," Oliver answered. "We can't be sure we destroyed all of those creatures. They could be waiting for us in there."

"Even if we were able to go around," Tomas put in, "we would then have an enemy behind us and before us. We need to take them out of the picture before we move on."

Jeremy nodded. "You're right. We wait until nightfall and attack. What's the plan?"

Tomas explained his strategy to the men and women gathered about. When they believed they had worked out the kinks, they set up two shelters to wait in as the sun continued to lower towards the mountains.

They lit no fires, as they didn't want their position given away by plumes of smoke.

So, they waited.

And waited.

**

Four hours later, when the sun had gone down and they had packed the tents away, the troop readied itself for an attack on the fort.

Baldwyn and Gustav stayed back with the horses as the others made their way along the southern slope of the embankment towards the rocks near the edge of the water.

Waves crashed noisily on the black stone as Karlena and Akasati climbed to the top of the mound.

With careful aim, the two warriors flung arrows into the two men upon the tower, dropping them to the platform far above the yard below.

The rest of the company made their way along the side of the timber wall to where the rocks and wood were at their highest touching point. It was still higher than any of the men could reach.

Tomas and Simon boosted David, using their shoulders as a stand. He scrambled to the top and repositioned himself so his legs dangled inside the fort walls and his arms still outside.

It was a dangerous place to be. If any of the inhabitants were to see him, they would have an easy target to practise firing arrows into or throwing knives.

He reached with his long, powerful arms and hoisted the women one by one up to his face. They climbed over him and softly dropped onto the ground inside the fort and hid behind the building just inside the wall.

Tomas and Jeremy climbed up next and joined the women on the other side. Next came the other eight crewmen of the *Adelandria,* with Simon being the last man to clamber over.

David landed with a thud next to the others, rubbing his abdomen.

"That hurt my belly." He winced.

"Do you want me to kiss it better?" Simon offered.

"Bastard." David scowled.

"Shhh," Tomas hissed as he peered around the corner of the building they used for cover. He counted two men near the gates and one near the stables. Carefully, he peered around the yard for sight of any more guards and found none.

He pointed to the Erilian women and held up three fingers.

Akasati, Karlena and Rhydra complied by loading their bows and crouching by Tomas' side. He indicated where the men were and they took aim.

Together they fired.

Together, their targets hit the snow.

Tomas put a finger to his lips and signalled the troop to follow.

They moved into the yard and towards the barn, the only building with an open door.

A lone man, holding a bridle in his hand, stared dumbfound at the bodies on the ground outside the barn door. Tomas moved into his view and he suddenly realised the situation.

"Heh," he gasped, his eyes full of fear. "Heh. Help! HELP! HELP!"

His calls grew louder and louder. Tomas ran at the man and slid his dagger into the other's neck, silencing him.

"Get ready," Tomas called to the others as the man slid from the dagger's blade and onto the ground.

Several men came tearing out of the buildings, half dressed and with swords in their hands. Some wiped the sleep from their eyes as the troop took advantage of the situation.

Most of the fort's inhabitants didn't realise what had happened until they were on the ground spilling blood. Others instinctively blocked the blows of the travellers and fought back.

As the skirmish ensued, another twelve men, who had taken time to put some appropriate clothing on, bolted from the huts with swords held high. They now numbered eighteen. Far fewer than the company.

But they fought well.

The only advantage the troop had against their enemy was that the guards were tired and still half-asleep.

Swords clashed and iron struck iron, sending a loud ringing din across the yard of the outpost.

Parrying, thrusting, swinging and slashing. Tomas hacked his way through the yard to support Emily, who was still near the building they had hidden behind when they had first entered the fort.

When he had reached about halfway of the distance to her, he realised he hadn't any need to bother trying.

Emily was slashing her blade around her as if it were a part of her. She hit every target she intended to hit.

Her opponent blocked a few of her blows, but once she sliced his belly open, there was no hope for him.

She was quick.

She was accurate.

She was deadly.

The guard fell to the ground in a pile of his own mess.

She didn't stop to admire her work. Instead, she turned and plunged her blade into the neck of another guard engaged in battle with one crewman.

Before long, they covered the ground in the corpses of enemy guards.

They opened the gates and dragged the bodies outside.

"We need to burn them," Jeremy said.

"Agreed," Tomas replied. "If the white witch has been here, who knows what curse she may have put on this place. We don't need the dead to attack us again."

"We can use some of the straw from the stables to light them," Oliver suggested. "And then we can use the horses for the rest of our journey."

"See to it," Tomas said as he walked through the gates. "Burn the bodies out upon the open ground."

"Where are you going?" Emily asked.

"To get Baldwyn and the horses," he replied as he disappeared into the night.

David and Simon took the Erilian women through the buildings to seek any enemy guard who was hiding within.

The first structure, next to the stables, was a kitchen and mess hall. A large stove, set into the stone fireplace to the left, was still alight and sent radiant heat into the room. Once inside, the small group didn't want to leave.

One long table stretched across the other side of the room, from front to back, with some crude benches made from pine logs positioned nearby.

Simon checked the food stores around the room. He found a sack of potatoes, some flour, and a large sack of dried oats.

On a shelf above the fireplace sat a large tin canister. David lifted it down and opened the lid. A sweet, familiar smell filled his nostrils.

Tea.

"I'll be back for this," he said as he closed the lid and returned it to the shelf.

Back outside, they moved to the next building. Inside were eleven cots; six against the far wall and five near the wall adjoining to the door.

Carefully, the group moved through the room, checking under beds and lifting lumpy blankets to see if anyone hid beneath. Still, they found no one.

The next hut was the same. A bunk house with eleven beds, but no survivors.

The last structure they needed to search was the one they had hidden behind when they first climbed over the large timber barrier near the black rocks by the shore.

There was a stove in the centre of the left wall with a chair positioned nearby. A small table rested against the back wall of the room. An open door to their right led to a bedroom where the blankets laid tousled and unmade. They found none alive inside the hut, but thought the bloodstain inside in the middle of the floor near the stove was peculiar.

"No one scrapped in here," David said. "As far as I know, no one has been in here."

"The blood is not fresh," Karlena observed. "It's been spread, as though someone tried to clean it."

"They killed someone here," Sharek suggested.

"Maybe the witch?" Simon asked.

"No," came an answer by the door. They turned to see Emily standing there, peering at the dried stain. "She's still alive."

"How do you know?" David asked. "Did one of them tell you?"

"None of them had time to talk. We killed them all." She looked at the large bald man. "I can just tell. I don't know how. She was here, but now she is not."

"Emily's right," Karlena said. "She lives."

"She's continued north," Sharek nodded.

"Then we continue north," Akasati replied.

"Not tonight." Emily turned away and walked back through the door. "We stay here tonight."

"There's a bed in here," Karlena called after her. "Perhaps you and Tomas can—"

"I won't stay in there," she replied. "She slept in there."

David furrowed his brow and looked over at Simon for answers.

"I don't know how they know," he answered the silent question. "Maybe it's a woman thing."

Thirteen

The chestnut steed lowered its head to the ground as it staggered on in the chill night air. The white rider had fallen asleep and slid to the side of the saddle.

The shift in her weight caused her to snap back to reality. She corrected her posture and peered around her.

The forest sat nestled beneath the mountains to the west and the thunderous sound of waves crashing on rocks came from the east. The horse plodded forwards, heading slowly north.

She wasn't sure how far they had come and, even with the moon glowing in the sky, she didn't recognise her surroundings. All she had was the direction to travel and the knowledge that she hadn't reached her destination yet.

Blackrock Haven could be over the next rise for all she knew. At this pace, however, it could take half the night to reach within sight of it.

She dug her heels into the steed's flanks.

It lunged forward, but not at a rapid pace. It moved only slightly faster, trying its best to please its passenger.

She urged it to go faster by kicking again and again.

It tried.

It so desperately tried.

Dragging its hooves through the snow, it became sluggish again, its energy spent. Its legs started to cross one another as they wobbled back and forth like jelly.

Finally, after taking as many more steps as it could, it fell on its right side.

She lifted herself from the saddle before it hit the snow, landing upon her feet unharmed.

The horse looked up to her helplessly as she wrapped her cloak tightly around her chest. She shot a quick glance at the exhausted beast before turning away to continue trekking through the snow, leaving the beast to die a slow, painful death.

**

A great fire burned upon the shore of the bay. Several men stood nearby watching, including Oliver, who threw pieces of kindling on the flames every once in a while.

Tomas approached, trailing two pack horses behind him. Beside him sat Baldwyn atop of his steed and leading another three laden steeds.

"Good fire," Baldwyn said as he saw the shapes of men piled inside.

"We don't want them coming back while we sleep," Oliver replied.

"Aye," Baldwyn agreed. "That, we don't."

"Just stay until the flesh burns," Tomas told the men. "After that, I want everyone inside. We all need to rest."

They nodded, some replied with speech, all sounded drained.

Steering the horses towards the gates, Tomas and Baldwyn entered the fort. They moved directly towards the stables just beyond the gates.

Inside the building were two other men. They were assessing the state of the horses in the pens and checking the riding equipment that belonged to the guards at the outpost.

"Twenty-three horses," one man said to the newcomers as they led the pack horses in.

"If I help you down," Tomas said to Baldwyn, "can you stand on your own?"

"Yes," he replied. "And I can get up and down fine. It's just walking long distances that causes me grief."

"Good," the other said. "You can help unpack the horses."

"We've enough riding gear," the other man called over to them. "Saddles, bridles, blankets. No caparisons."

"We'll need to make do with what we have," Tomas replied. "Good work."

The men approached to help with unloading the pack animals before finding places for the six beasts in the pens. Some feed went into the troughs in each stall before the lanterns hanging upon the wall dimmed and the stable doors closed.

Emily was walking from the mess hall towards Tomas. She looked tired, but she also looked as if she wanted something.

"I need the tent," she told him. She offered a sheepish look.

He was tired and really didn't want to do anything else but sit, eat, then sleep.

Wrapping his arms around her, knowing that he would regret it later if he denied her request, he kissed her forehead.

"All right," he whispered into her ear.

"You don't want to know why?" she asked.

"Only if you want to tell me," he replied, holding her hand as they moved back towards the stable where they stored the equipment.

"She was here," Emily told him.

"I figured as much," he replied as he opened the doors.

The horses turned their faces towards the two figures in the entryway as moonlight filled the room.

"She slept in that building by the wall." She pointed towards the south-western corner of the yard.

"How could you know that?" Tomas asked as he lifted the tent roll from the floor. "Grab the bed rolls just there."

She moved past him and retrieved the two bedrolls.

"That's just it," she said, answering his question. "I don't know how I know. I just do. The Erilian women know it too."

"You think it might have something to do with this *power* that Jeremy was talking about?" he asked as they exited the stables. "The thing that attracted the Sovereign to you?"

"Perhaps." She frowned. "He destroyed their village just as he did mine."

"The Erilians?"

She nodded. "What if I'm realising my power?"

"What is it exactly?" he asked as he put the tent roll upon the ground to shut the stables' doors. "I mean, what is it you think you can do?"

"I'm not sure," she replied as they moved towards the middle of the yard.

Tomas dropped the roll onto the ground and pulled the cords binding it in place so that it opened. He rolled the canvas out on the ground, the tent poles neatly hidden within.

"Well," he said. "You know she was here and where she was. That means you are sensitive to others like you."

"She's nothing like me," Emily growled.

"I didn't mean it that way," he told her as he lifted one end of the tent into place. "I meant... Well, remember when we first met the Erilian women. You sensed something about them and they sensed something about you. None of you understood what that was, but you felt something.

"Perhaps you can tell when others with *powers* are nearby. Perhaps you can track them and find them."

"So..." She smiled. "I'm a hunting dog."

"I've seen you in action," he said, and chuckled. "You can certainly fight like a bitch."

She picked up a handful of snow and threw it at his head with a smile.

Pretty soon, they had the tent erected and the bedrolls laid out inside.

Tomas moved to the mess hall to grab something to eat. The other travellers sat around the tables either finishing their meals or sipping David's brew of tea.

"Cup?" the giant man called as his commander entered the room.

"Thank you, yes," he replied as he approached the stove. "What's for eating?"

"Well," Simon replied. "You can have bread. Toasted, if you like. Or you could try the delicacy of these lands, porridge."

"Anything but bloody porridge," Oliver said as he entered through the door.

"Agreed." Tomas nodded as he sat on a bench across from Jeremy.

"I see you set up your tent," the captain remarked to Tomas.

"It's personal," he replied as Emily sat by his side.

David, the designated cook for the night, placed a steaming cup in front of his friend.

"Mind," he said. "It's hot. Oliver? Cup?"

"Make it tall," the other replied before pointing a finger to the men who were out by the fire with him. "The same for my friends."

"Coming up."

After a hearty meal of dry toast and tea, Emily and Tomas returned to their tent to bed down for the night.

The men of the *Adelandria*, including Jeremy, took the bunkhouse nearest to the commander's hut. The Erilian women claimed the building between the men and the mess hall.

There were enough beds remaining in the second bunkhouse for the men of Woodmyst, and the Erilians suggested that the men use the cots for the night. Declining the offer, not feeling right about sharing the room with the women, the three men grabbed their bedrolls from the stables and slept on the floor of the mess hall instead.

They believed they had the better deal compared to the others. There was no fireplace in the tent, and no stove in the bunkhouses to warm the rooms. The kitchen inside the mess hall, however, was toasty and comfortable.

Two men stood watch upon the tower, changing shifts every three hours. They need not have bothered setting a guard, as the only intruder during the night was the chill wind that blew over the land from the sea.

***

With her hood pulled over her face, allowing her to see only her path directly before her, she trudged on. Her legs lifted high with each step as she pushed through the deep snow.

Her legs felt damp and her back was cold as the wind swept across the plain and towards the mountains. The first light of morning started creeping over the water, illuminating the world around her.

She still didn't know how far it was until she would reach her goal. The landscape looked the same as it did an hour ago, and the hour before that.

Bleak, white, void ground stretched on and on and on.

The sound of waves crashing upon the shore and the constant whistle of the gusting wind filled her ears as she pressed forward.

Rubbing her shoulders and her arms beneath her cloak, she thought about how the Green Mistress of Blackrock Haven might receive her.

Would she chastise her?

Would she punish her?

After all, she had failed.

The company of men that pursued her, as far as she knew, still followed.

She could feel something, like an irritating itch on the back of her neck that stretched down to the place between her shoulder blades. It was something she couldn't satisfy, no matter how hard she tried.

Something that told her of a pursuing power.

At first, she thought the source of the power might belong to one man. A particular man from Woodmyst came to mind.

But her thoughts returned to the red-headed girl. The one with his stink upon her.

She was his, and he was hers.

It made her feel ill.

She was intended for something more.

She was meant to belong to the Sovereign.

Her hatred for the man festered and bubbled.

What was his name?

She willed death towards him but felt a blockage. There was something that prevented her from getting through.

Tomas, she suddenly remembered. *His name is Tomas.*

She pictured his head caved in, as she had done to the commander at the outpost. Her thoughts, the picture inside her head, didn't eventuate any further than simply being that. A picture in her head.

Why?

She scowled as she trudged on.

Why can't I get to him?

Suddenly, she saw the red-haired girl again.

Her.

Some kind of protection enveloped him. Some type of power shielded him from her will.

That protection, that power, came from her.

And there are others among them, she thought.

She could sense that, too.

The red girl wasn't the only one with *power*. She wasn't the only one to shield this *Tomas*.

What made him so special to them?

The woman in white shook her head. She didn't understand.

No one had never taught this kind of power to her.

She grasped the concept of the red-haired girl's connection to the man. They were together. They were one.

The others, however, were not one with him. Yet they shielded him as if he was.

It made little sense.

Why should they care what happens to him?

Why should they care for him at all?

She trudged up an embankment, shaking the thought from her mind.

If she couldn't get to him, she should place her energy on herself.

Reaching the top of the rise, she was overcome with a deep sense of relief.

Farther along the coast, still a fair distance away, sat the port town of Blackrock Haven.

She could see the wharves stretching from the land's edge and over the water. A tall black ship was sitting alongside one of the wooden causeways. Nearby were many buildings and houses nestled and gathered neatly around the port.

Behind them, on the far side of the town, towering above it all, stood a castle. The sight of its high stone walls, grey and bleak, made her heart skip. A broad smile spread across her face as she started forward for the last stretch of her long journey.

She was almost home.

Fourteen

Making her way closer to the shoreline, she made her way as quickly as she could to the wharf where the tall black ship was moored. She hated the sight of the vessel, remembering the voyage she took beneath its decks, from her homeland to this very port.

She despised the captain, a large specimen of filth with a scar that stretched across his face. She remembered his face close to hers, the stench of his sweat and his large, groping hands.

She would like to see his scar open and his head tear in two.

Her ability would allow her to do it.

But it wasn't the will of the Sovereign.

The brute had a place in the scheme of things. A reason for being.

But as soon as that reason became moot, as soon as his place wasn't needed, she would be ready to act.

Oh, how she would be ready.

There was no sign of any movement in the village except for a few men milling about on the wharves. Too early and too cold for most people to be out of bed, she surmised.

She made her way to a set of stairs at the end of the wooden walkway, where she ascended them to the platform leading to the ship. One man saw her approaching and mistook her for an ordinary woman from the town.

"Well," he said in an overconfident tone, "hullo love. Come for a piece of a well-hung sailo—" Suddenly, he convulsed as his spine snapped near his shoulders. He fell hard against the planks, spitting blood as he writhed in agony.

"Mistress." Another man bowed, ignoring the twisting mess of a man on the walkway nearby. "How can I be of service?"

She eyed him for some time. His broad shoulders and scruffy looks gave her an appetite for more than food.

"Find me a place to rest my legs," she commanded.

"There is an inn nearby," replied the man, pointing to a quaint building that looked like any ordinary house. "They have food and a fire. Would that suit, Mistress?"

She peered at the building with distaste.

"It will do," she replied. "Take me there."

"Yes, Mistress." The man led the way to a set of stairs that descended back to the street level.

"Mistress?" a man called from behind her.

She turned to see the scarred man running along the pier towards her. He passed the dying man on the wharf without as much as a glance before pulling to a stop at the top of the stairs, smiling at her.

"Mistress, you are here?" He reached out his hand to her.

"Don't touch me, scum," she spat.

He recoiled, his countenance changing immediately. He quickly bowed his head, remembering his place.

"My apologies, Mistress," he said. "How may I serve?"

"Race ahead and find the innkeeper," she commanded. "I need food, a room, and fresh clothing. I cannot go to her like this."

"Of course, Mistress." He bowed again and raced past her to the inn across the street, where he started thumping on the door.

"What of me, Mistress?" the man from the wharf asked. "Do you still require my service?"

"Yes," she replied, moving her eyes over his body. "I have something in mind that involves you. Now, lead the way."

The inn door opened to reveal an overweight man wearing his night clothes. "Are you aware of what time it is?"

"The White Mistress requires your service," the scarred man informed him.

"The White Mistress," the man gasped. "Of course. Of course."

He opened the door wide and let the three others into his establishment. There was a fire smouldering in the corner and a few tables and chairs about the room.

"How may I serve?" he asked.

"The Mistress requires food and clothing," replied the scarred man.

"And a bed," she interjected.

"And a bed," the scarred man repeated.

"Of course," the man nodded. "Ah, let me stoke the fire for you and I'll get right on it, my lady."

"Will that be all, Mistress?" the scarred man asked.

"No," she said as she sat in a deep chair by the fireplace. "Send some men towards the south. There are people pursuing me. I want them destroyed."

"But you are the White Mistress," he replied, furrowing his brow. He pointed towards the misshapen man lying dead on the jetty. "Surely you could just…"

She shot him a look. He closed his mouth and bowed before leaving the inn. Before, he too, became a twisted mess upon the floor.

"I must apologise, Mistress," the innkeeper said. "The only clothing I have that could fit you belonged to my wife. She was a tad bigger than you and her garments are nowhere near as fine as yours."

His eyes appeared suddenly sad, as if a painful memory returned briefly.

"We'll make do," she replied as the warmth of the flames swept over her. "I will return them once I have gained more suitable clothing."

"You are indeed kind, Mistress." The innkeeper rose to his feet. "I will fix you the best breakfast we have. No. I will make it even better. It is such an honour to have you with us."

The innkeeper moved through a doorway to the side of the room in a fluster, leaving the white witch and the wharves man in the room alone. She kept gazing at him as he stood a little away from her.

"Am I to remain standing here, Mistress?" he asked finally.

"Yes," she replied. "So shut up and just stay there looking pretty."

***

"Should we torch it?" Oliver asked as they rode out through the gates and back into the open lands of the north.

"No," Simon shouted. "What if we need to come back this way? We will at least have a roof over our heads and some stoves to keep us warm."

"What bloody stoves?" Gustav called back. "It was freezing in those bunkhouses. Aren't no stoves in there."

"Still," Simon said to the other, "you had a roof over your head and didn't need to pitch a tent for the night."

"Aye," Gustav admitted. "That was one benefit. But then, we didn't have time to cuddle either."

The men laughed as the last of them moved out of the compound.

"Should we shut the gate, at least?" Jeremy called.

"Too much of a hassle," Tomas replied. "Some poor soul will need to climb the fence to get back out."

"Fair call," David nodded, remembering the last poor soul that had to climb the fence in order to get them all in.

With fresh horses and new riding equipment, some men constantly repositioned themselves on their saddles, as they simply didn't feel right to sit in. Tomas was especially finding the ride difficult. His horse, a large black gelding, not only had an uncomfortable saddle, but the beast moved differently to his beloved mare.

He tried to find a spot that felt correct but could never quite get it right. Besides that, he had to do most of the work with the reins, as his horse had no idea where they were going. The brown mare would have figured out its handler's intentions by now and reacted accordingly.

This thing is brainless, he thought as he wrestled the beast towards the north.

Eventually, the other horses gathered around and steered the gelding like a mob. It soon realised the direction they were heading and gladly joined the others in moving northwards.

They travelled at a steady walking pace to conserve the horses' energy as they pushed their legs through the thick, frosty ground cover. Idle talk started amongst the men as the sun rose above the water, sending her bright rays across the white surface of the surrounding land.

"I wonder why we haven't seen any more straw men," one crewman said.

"You're mad, Lon," answered another. "I'm bloody glad we haven't seen any more straw men."

"Here, here," called another.

"No, I just mean, ever since what happened back at that keep, they seemed to have just stopped," Lon elaborated.

"Maybe the bitch ran out of straw," Calvin quipped.

"I think she might be hurt," Jeremy suggested. "Or she's been weakened."

"From what?" David asked, uncertain how a witch can be weakened.

"I'm not sure," he answered. "But something happened in that keep before we arrived. Something that Ivo was a part of."

"You think it involved Ivo with that woman?" Oliver's voice sounded angry.

"No," Jeremy replied. "Of course not. He was used. Manipulated. She made him do something. I think that after she escaped, something changed in her."

"Or something grows in her," Karlena said.

The troop fell silent and moved their eyes upon her.

She looked around to see them all looking at her.

"Oh, come on..." She slumped her shoulders. "Don't tell me you didn't consider this. He was naked on the ground when you found him. They weren't eating a baked dinner."

"So, you think she is carrying Ivo's child?" David cocked his head and squinted his face.

"She said something about his seed," Emily replied.

"Yes." Oliver nodded. "And then she said something about blood."

"Well, what do you expect?" Sharek added. "The girl is not right in the head. She murdered her own father."

"And she will pay for that," Akasati said coldly.

"So," Lon, riding upon his steed behind them, joined back into the conversation, "if I am hearing you right; the white witch, who is Captain Tarkin's daughter, humped with Ivo, against his will of course, which made her pregnant before she killed Captain Tarkin and escaped your fury. Right?"

"Right," Gustav replied.

"This is so muddled up," Lon said, shaking his head. "None of that explains why we haven't seen any bloody straw men."

***

Sitting in front of the looking glass, wearing black, the only colour that seemed to feel right, Joanne brushed her hair straight back over her shoulders. She placed the brush upon the dresser and tied a long, black lace ribbon into her hair, making a long ponytail that started at the crown of her head and trailed to between her shoulder blades.

She traced the ends of the ribbon over her shoulders before reaching for her black cloak. She stood and drew the cloak over her shoulders and lifted the hood over her head.

Looking at herself in the mirror, she silently admitted that it not only felt right, it looked right.

She moved her eyes to the brush and focused her energy on it.

It rattled.

It shuddered.

It slowly lifted from the surface, just fractionally.

KNOCK!
KNOCK!
KNOCK!

Her head snapped to around to face the door.

"Miss, are you awake?" Andris' voice sounded through the wooden barrier.

"I am," she replied.

"My apologies for disturbing you," he said. "The Mistress wishes for you to be present in the throne room."

Joanne turned to see the brush sitting comfortably on the dresser where it was sitting only moments ago. She felt as if she was going to cry as she thought about this *power* that she had just learned about. All she wanted to do was go home and forget about this place.

"I'm coming," she answered.

Swallowing her sadness and putting on a façade of strength, she turned towards the door and opened it to see Andris dressed in formal attire, waiting for her. He poked his right elbow out, offering his arm to her.

"Miss." He bowed his head.

She entered his quarters and took his arm. He reached with his free hand and closed her chamber door, locking it with his key. Together they entered the wide corridor, where again he closed and locked the door.

The other six girls were also entering the corridor, dressed in their brightly coloured garments. Only Joanne had dressed in black and donned a hooded cloak.

She didn't know why she had worn the covering. It just seemed right.

They descended the stairs to the bottom and turned left, entering through the open archway to a room where a large, high-backed chair sat atop of a stone platform. Seated upon the chair was the woman in green, Yasmeen Svoboda. She too, had worn her cloak, concealing her features beneath her own hood.

She followed Joanne as her servant led her to a cushioned seat against the left side wall of the room. The young girl counted the seats that lined the wall. There were eight on each side.

They placed Joanne in the seat closest to the Green Mistress. Next to her was a golden-haired girl wearing jade. Beside her was another in lilac, then another in gold.

Directly across from her, the first seat remained empty. They gave the second to Tricia, who wore scarlet, the next seat to the one dressed in lilac, and finally, the last to the girl in white.

Joanne wondered why the first seat on the other side of the room to her remained empty. Or perhaps she should be more concerned with why she sat in the first seat on her side of the room.

The Green Mistress was still looking at her.

Had Andris made a mistake by placing her in the wrong chair?

Perhaps she was meant to be sitting in the jade girl's seat and everyone else should be down in one place.

She looked up to the Mistress, maintaining her composure.

The green hooded woman nodded to Joanne before turning her gaze to the arch from where they had entered.

Two men, armed with swords in sheaths, stood by either side of the entrance. With a wave of the lady's hand, the two men left the room and moved to the main doors of the foyer.

"You will need to remain silent and simply observe," Andris whispered into Joanne's ear. "No matter what you see, control your emotions."

He corrected his posture and stood tall on her right with his back to the wall.

"I have some business to attend to," the Green Mistress announced. "When we have finished here, we will enjoy breakfast."

Scuffling emitted from the foyer, causing all the girls to move their eyes towards the intruding noises.

"Please," a man's voice begged. "I won't do so again. You could just let me go."

The two guards dragged a beaten man past the girls and along the stone floor to the base of the throne's platform. They threw him onto the ground and stepped back.

Blood spilled from the man's mouth, nose, and ears and he emitted a revolting stench that reminded Joanne of the swine pen in her village.

"This is the man who was caught stealing from the town's stores," a guard informed the Green Mistress. "We have held him in the cells for three days, as you commanded. He claims that his family was hungry, and that they had run out of their own supplies. A crime of desperation is what he calls it, Mistress."

She waved her hand dexterously, gracefully, gesturing for the man to make his plea. His eyes widened as his mouth opened, rising to his knees and clutching his hands together.

"Please forgive me, Mistress," he begged. "It was a stupid thing to do. We are hungry. Starving. We have nothing of our own and I didn't know what else to—"

Suddenly, the man's head imploded.

Two girls gave involuntary squeals whilst others gasped at the sight.

The man's body remained rigid, up on its knees, hands still clutched together before it, with a mess of flesh and bone resting upon its shoulders.

Joanne breathed heavily and rapidly.

Her heart pounded so strongly in her chest that she thought it was going to burst through her rib cage.

She moved her eyes away from the man's remains to the woman in green seated upon the throne.

The woman stretched her arm towards the man, her fist clenched tightly at its end.

She relaxed her fist.

The man fell to the floor.

After a moment's silence, the Green Mistress looked around the room to each of the girls, deliberately, as if reading their expressions.

"This is the power that lives in each of you," she said. "You will learn to harness it. You will become powerful like me, and they will all fear you."

Joanne couldn't take her eyes away from the man on the floor. She had never seen such a thing before.

She hoped she would never have to see such a thing again.

"Breakfast will be served in the dining room," the woman told them.

"Mistress," another guard said from the door. "There is someone to see you."

"An uninvited guest," she replied. "See this person in."

Joanne hoped this would not be a repeat of what she just witnessed. She watched the archway as the guard led a man along the centre of the room towards the platform.

Every young girl in the room tensed as they recognised the figure that approached the Mistress. His bulky frame and his salty, sickening stench. Most of all, the one thing that made him stand out above all was the scar that stretched across his face.

If she could crush a man's head, she would do it for this one. She would do it a thousand times over.

She deepened her breath and controlled her emotions as the man moved past her. He paused at the feet of the dead man lying on the floor and bent his knee.

"Mistress," he started. "Forgive me for the intrusion. I have news."

"A moment," she commanded, holding a finger up to the scarred one. "Ladies, wait for me in the dining room."

Andris responded to the instruction immediately and offered his hand to Joanne. She took it, allowing him to escort her out of the room. They followed the other girls and their escorts through the arch and down the corridor immediately to their right.

Soon after, the girls were seated around the long table with their manservants standing behind them, waiting for the Green Mistress to arrive. A loud silence filled the dining room as they all gave mind to the horrific scene that they had witnessed in the throne room.

Joanne looked at an empty glass on the table before her. Her throat was dry, and she felt completely uncomfortable. Finally, her needs got the better of her and she turned her hooded head to the side slightly.

"Andris," she called softly. She reached for the glass, but he beat her to it.

"Of course, Miss," he replied, taking her cup to a pitcher placed on a table near the fireplace. He filled it with water and returned it to her as hastily as he could. She swallowed it down in a few large gulps and replaced the glass on the table.

She returned her hands to her lap as the Green Mistress entered the room with her own servant in tow.

"Good news ladies," she said as she moved around the table. Passing by, she brushed her hand over Joanne's shoulders. The girl felt a chill sensation run down her spine. "We will be having a visitor," the woman finished as the servant moved her seat out for her.

She removed the hood from her head and gave a slight smile before moving her gaze to Joanne. Joanne lowered her hood from her crown.

"The White Mistress will join us before nightfall," the woman announced.

The White Mistress?

Who was this White Mistress?

We have the Green Mistress and now a White Mistress, Joanne thought.

How many are there?

Fifteen

She dressed in the rags left for her by the innkeeper. The frocks, in her mind, were those worn by peasants and people of a lesser stature than she. Uneven patchwork and crooked stitching zigzagged across the material with obvious mismatching patterns and tones.

Dressed in a dull brown and cream array, she felt dirty, disgusting and repulsed. It made her feel itchy and uncomfortable.

She combed her fingernails through her hair, wishing for a looking glass to at least see her face. She assumed that she still wore the marks of soot and frostbite upon her cheeks.

Although, she reflected, she couldn't look too much of a mess. The man, snoring in the small bed that she had just climbed out of, performed to her liking. He told her she was beautiful.

Why would he lie to her?

She opened the door and walked along the hallway back to the room with the fireplace where she had been seated earlier. Returning to the chair, she positioned herself by the hearth to soak in its warmth.

"I trust you feel refreshed, Mistress?" the innkeeper asked as he wiped a table down.

"As good as can be expected." She stared into the flames.

"And the clothes?" he questioned. "They fit well?"

"They will suffice," she replied.

"Would you like some refreshments?" He stood up straight, twisting the cloth between his fingers nervously. "We have warm cider, or ale."

"Wine?" She lifted an eyebrow without taking her gaze from the flickering light.

"Sorry, Mistress," he replied. "They took all the wine to the castle for the lady in green."

She nodded and smiled.

Of course, it is.

"Ale," she ordered.

"Yes, Mistress," he replied, disappearing through the door that led to the bedrooms.

She took some deep breaths and closed her eyes as the heat of the fire flowed through her skin, muscles, and bones. She absorbed it, drew energy from it as she placed her hand upon her belly.

Ivo.

Her eyes opened.

She didn't understand why his name came back to her so suddenly.

Could it be that a part of him had stayed with her?

Perhaps her mind was a little mixed up.

She had just experienced a journey that had drained her of almost every ounce of the power that she possessed.

More rest, she thought. *I need more rest.*

The man brought back a tall clay mug with a frothy substance inside.

"Here you are, Mistress," he said and handed the mug over to her.

She took a big swig and wiped the froth from her lips with the back of her sleeve. It was good.

A smile spread upon her face as she rested her head against the back of the seat.

"Would there be anything else, Mistress?"

"Yes," she replied. "Wake my guest and tell him to dress. I would like for him to find me suitable transport to the castle. It's time I should go home."

***

Riding through the snow became an arduous task. Even though they were moving at a slow pace, the horses were using a great deal of energy to lift their legs high enough to step over the soft ground cover before planting their hooves back into the deep snow.

Shaking his head, Oliver thought that the new steeds would be used to such conditions considering that they came from these lands. Their behaviour, however, told him otherwise. They fretted and snorted their protests as the men drove them through the wet substance that covered the ground.

Perhaps they had been in the warmth of the stables for far too long.

The ground continued to rise and fall, presenting steep ridges and gentle rises that always extended towards the sea, ending in jagged black rocks where the waves crashed violently. Large sprays of white foam exploded into the air as thunderous roars emitted from the collision of water against stone.

As they crossed another wide valley, they spied a gaggle of black birds squabbling upon the ground in the near distance. Something lying half covered in the snow had their attention.

The riders drew closer to the birds. Some of them fluttered away, landing a short distance from their object of interest. Others stayed, braving the threat of men, and squawked defiantly as the horses stamped their hooves, crunching the snow loudly beneath their weight.

In the snow lay the remains of a steed. It was missing portions of its flesh because of the feasting of the crows, but all could see clearly that it was equipped with riding gear. The black leather strapping and saddle looked similar to that worn by many of their fresh horses.

"Do you think this steed came from the outpost?" Baldwyn asked.

"Possible," Jeremy replied. "It wears the same kit as these."

"Perhaps the white witch rode this one," Gustav suggested.

"She rode it until it couldn't go any further." Oliver frowned. "How could anyone do that?"

"She's desperate," Tomas replied, peering at the remains. A crow bounced back across the snow towards it. It dug its sharp beak into the flesh around the animal's cheek and started tearing a strip of meat to eat.

"Get out of it!" Oliver waved his arm towards the bird.

It fluttered away a little, looking at the man upon the horse sideways before hopping back towards its feast.

"Let it go," Tomas told him. "The bird's probably starving. It can't hurt the horse any more than it already has been."

"Poor thing," Emily said.

"For those of you who don't understand," said Jeremy as he looked at the other seafarers. "This is why we rest the horses."

They pressed on, riding over the next ridge and the next. The sun climbed higher and higher into the morning sky as they progressed northward.

"She would be on foot now," Jeremy said to Tomas. "This would slow her down."

"I'm not so certain," he replied. "Remember how fast it appeared she had moved when we first found her tracks. She has abilities to do things that mere men like us do not. I don't plan to underestimate her potential in anything. I half expect her to fly."

Jeremy looked at Tomas quizzically. He measured the man to see if he was joking and could clearly see that he was not.

Perhaps he was right.

Perhaps they shouldn't place limits upon their enemy.

After all, she had made straw come to life. She had raised the dead to fight in her place. She had seduced a young man who knew her to be the enemy into fulfilling her will. On top of that, she had tricked his captain, his dearest friend, into believing that she was still his loving daughter, only to plunge her dagger into him over and over.

He swallowed hard, trying to push the lump in his throat away.

Tomas was right.

They couldn't underestimate Sumaiyya's abilities.

None of them truly knew what she was capable of.

Upon reaching the top of a steep ridge, Tomas pulled his black gelding to a complete stop. It shook its mane wildly, protesting the action of having its head yanked backwards.

The other riders pulled alongside and looked to him to clarify why they had stopped.

"What is it?" Jeremy asked from his side.

Tomas pointed with his chin, keeping his eyes fixed upon the ridge at the far side of the valley they were yet to cross.

Jeremy squinted. The elevation was far away. A careful scan of the higher land revealed five black dots side by side at the crest.

He pulled the spyglass from his pocket and extended it. Finding the dark objects in the lenses, he saw five riders looking towards them.

"Scouts," the captain informed them.

"Well." David grimaced. "That doesn't sound too good. Does it?"

"Could be just doing surveillance," Karlena suggested.

"Which means they will report our position," Simon put in.

"Should we give chase?" Oliver asked.

"No," Tomas replied. "By the time we get our horses halfway across the plain, they will be long gone."

"What if they bring an entire army down upon us?" Jeff Parish questioned.

"Then we fight until the last," Jeremy told him. "We can't escape this anyhow. We're heading north. They are north of us. We will eventually have to fight them."

He lifted the spyglass to his eye again. The riders were turning their horses and slowly riding away from them.

"They are leaving," he told them.

"We'll see them again," Tomas replied, urging his steed forward.

They descended the ridge and started crossing the valley floor. Emily pulled to Tomas' side and rode in silence for a short distance before speaking.

"Do you think they may have an army waiting for us?" she asked him.

He sensed the worry in her voice and thought hard about how to respond.

"I don't know," he replied. "It could just be five men on horseback. They could ride back to wherever they came from to tell others we are coming. In any case, I don't think they will cook a feast for us and will welcome us with open arms."

"What if..." She paused and looked at the horizon ahead of them. "What if we die out here?"

She hadn't really thought about the possibility that all of them could perish. But that was the reality.

With so many of their comrades lost along the way, she still believed that they had the upper hand.

Until now.

They were getting close to their goal. She could feel it.

And now, when their aim was so near, she was nervous. Knots formed in her stomach and every time she gave her thoughts to it, she felt as if she might be ill.

"Well," Tomas began. He paused suddenly to consider her question. He thought about lying to her, telling her that everything was going to be fine; that they would find her sister and the other women. That they would rescue every single one of them without casualties. They would destroy enemies, and return to his homeland with every one of their company alongside. Both she and he would settle down together, have a proper ceremony to recognise their unity and to appease their family and friends' desire for weddings. Children would eventually come along as they lived a quiet life of farming and fishing.

But he couldn't tell her that.

He simply didn't know what the outcome was going to be.

"If we are to die," he told her. "I want to be by your side, forever."

She smiled and reached her hand across to his.

"I love you, Emily Grenefeld," he told her for the first time, hoping it wouldn't be the last.

She let a tear fall over her cheek as a broad smile grew upon her radiant face.

"I love you, Tomas Warde."

Riding behind them upon his giant draught horse, a lump forming in his throat, David wiped a tear away.

"You are a soft one." Simon smiled. "Like a little kitty cat."

"Better than being a scruffy-looking mongrel dog, like you," he said, and smiled.

"Wuff, wuff," the other replied.

They reached a distance about halfway across the plain when the five riders returned.

They sat atop of the ridge to the north, spaced far apart from one another.

"They're back," Oliver called.

All eyes moved to the crest of the elevation.

They pulled their horses to a complete stop and peered at the enemy scouts.

More riders appeared along the ridge, ascending from the other side.

A long line of thirty darkly clad men glared down upon the company of travellers.

Tomas scratched his scruffy chin as he counted them.

The enemy riders pulled their swords from their sheaths slung over their backs.

"I guess we're in for it now," David called.

"Any words of encouragement, Captain?" Tomas called.

"Don't let any live," Jeremy commanded those around him. "And most importantly, don't get killed."

The dark riders lunged down the crest of the ridge at a rapid pace.

Snow flew into the air around the horses in a flurry.

Tomas pulled his sword from his sheath upon his back.

"I don't intend to wait until they get to me," he yelled as he kicked his heels into the gelding's sides.

The horse took off at an immense speed, Tomas holding his sword high.

"There he goes again," Oliver said, pulling his own blade free and chasing off after his commander.

Within an instant, they released the packhorses, and followed hard after Tomas.

The enemy reached the valley floor and targeted Tomas, the closest of the travellers.

Nearer and nearer, they drew.

Faster and faster, the gelding bolted.

Tomas lifted his feet from the stirrups and placed them onto the saddle, squatting as he rode towards the dark riders.

He could see their faces and chose a target. An older man than the others with a greying beard.

Tomas assumed the man to be the commander.

He veered the horse towards the grey man.

Closer and closer.

Faster and faster.

When there were only a few paces left between the grey man's horse and the black gelding, Tomas pushed with his legs as hard as he could.

He flung himself into the air and placed both hands around the hilt of his sword over his head, pointing the blade towards the grey man.

"What the blazes is he doing?" Oliver called.

His commander was flying, sword in his hands, directly towards the enemy.

Sixteen

The grey man's eyes grew wide. He had seen nothing like this before. A man was coming straight towards him, in the air.

In the air.

There was no time to react. No time to even cry out.

He plunged the sword deep into the grey man's face, knocking him from his horse and onto the soft snow below.

Tomas toppled over, ripping the sword from the man's head as he rolled onto his side.

Quickly, he lifted himself to his feet, ready for the next foe.

Most of the enemy riders continued towards the oncoming travellers. Two slowed their pace and turned their attention upon Tomas.

Seeing their comrade spilling blood upon the snow seemed to infuriate them as they charged towards the man from Woodmyst.

Tomas dug his heels into the ground and held his sword, ready to attack.

The dark riders swung their blades downwards towards him.

He crouched, dropping into the snow below their reach. With a quick stab to the left, he dipped his blade into the ribs of the horse on his right. Swinging the sword around, he struck a deep gash into the rump of the horse on his left.

The first horse dropped into the snow, sending her rider flying over the steed's head and into the snow. The second horse kicked with its hind legs, the rider falling to the side on the ground.

Tomas ran towards the second rider, the closest to him. Before the man could get back to his feet, Tomas stuck him through the gut and turned his attention to the first who had tumbled into the snow beside his dying horse.

The rider was now on his feet, sword in hand, expressing rage at what had happened to him. He ran towards Tomas, roaring in anger.

Ready for the attack, Tomas blocked the rider's blow with his blade. The enemy rider chopped madly with his blade, trying to knock the sword from Tomas' hands.

The sound of sword against sword rang across the vast expanse of the valley as others engaged in battles of their own nearby. Tomas, however, wanted this one to be over quickly so he could assist his companions.

As the enemy rider continued to hack at Tomas with his blade, the man from Woodmyst lunged forward, kicking with the sole of his boot, connecting with the other's knee.

A loud crack resounded from the man's leg before a gut-wrenching cry bellowed from his lips.

The leg was bent in the wrong direction, causing the man to fall to the ground.

Seizing the opportunity, Tomas swung his blade towards the fallen man.

The man raised his blade with both hands in desperation, blocking Tomas' blow.

Tomas tried again from a different angle, but his opponent blocked him again and again.

With his boot, Tomas stomped as hard as he could into the man's crotch.

He screamed a blood-curdling cry.

Tomas then brought his boot upon the broken limb.

It was too much for the man to handle. He dropped his sword into the snow beside him.

Tomas pushed his blade deep into the man's chest and held it there until his adversary stopped moving.

Using his boot again, placing it onto the man's torso, he pushed with his leg to retrieve his blade from the body.

The battle was underway behind him. He looked around for a place to join his friends and could see no one else had yet vanquished an enemy soldier.

The closest skirmish to him was Baldwyn's. From horseback, both he and an enemy rider exchanged blows with their swords.

The clanging of their blades was reminiscent of a tolling bell with a rapid rhythm.

Tomas made his way across the snow towards them. He observed as Baldwyn swung high, then low with his sword, blocked by the enemy each time. Likewise, when the dark rider was on the offensive, Baldwyn prevented any connection being made to his flesh.

It was a fight that could simply go on and on until one or the other eventually grew too tired to continue. Tomas felt that by assisting Baldwyn and putting the other rider on the ground for good, he and the crewman would be free to engage other enemy soldiers and assist their friends.

Baldwyn reached behind his back with one hand as he blocked another barrage of blows from his foe.

Tomas drew closer from behind the dark rider. Neither man on horseback could see him approaching, as they were both too engrossed in their fight.

Lifting his blade above his head, Tomas readied himself to plunge his blade into the enemy rider.

Suddenly the man fell from his horse in a convulsing heap upon the ground at Tomas' feet.

A dagger stuck from the man's neck, just below his ear.

"Lucky I had that on me." Baldwyn smiled.

Tomas bent and retrieved the blade from the dead man, wiping the blood from the blade onto the dark clothes of the rider. He handed the dagger back to Baldwyn.

"Thank you," he replied, taking it and returning it to his belt. He gave a quick glance around him. "Better get back into it I suppose."

With that, he trotted off towards another skirmish on the plain.

Tomas, still standing in the snow, looked for Emily.

She was a part of a tight circle formed with the other women of the company. The Erilian warriors. The *sisters*.

Surrounded by several men on the ground, the *sisters* fought with passion, precision, and fluidity. They kept the enemy soldiers at bay during the squabble. None could get close enough to any of the women without receiving a cut on an arm or a scratch across the face.

The amount of blood from tiny wounds over their bodies made Tomas believe the men would bleed out from the small wounds received from the curved Erilian blades.

A man lunged towards Emily with his blade thrusting towards her.

Tomas felt his heart stop as he feared the worse. In his mind, he saw the blade entering her stomach.

Instead, she twisted her body, spinning around the blade.

As she did so, she swung her sword fluidly with a move from the wrist so that it pointed out behind her.

The blade slipped into the man's ribs. His momentum from lunging pushed him along, the sword right up to the hilt.

He bumped against Emily's back as he dropped his sword.

She pulled her sword from her enemy as she swung back around to face her next assailant.

The man fell to the ground, his mouth wide open in a shocked and silent cry.

Emily's attention fell directly upon another man who tried to seize the chance to attack while she was engaged in killing the first enemy soldier. His attempt was in vain.

She continued to spin on her heels, lifting the sword in a rising spiral. The blade slid through the attacker's neck as easily as if passing through water. Sharek, standing near to Emily, swung her blade in a downward strike, slicing through the man's thigh.

He was still falling to the snow in three pieces as they turned their attention to yet another foe.

Tomas was awestruck. He could watch the Erilians in action all day.

More so, he could observe Emily and her technique forever.

She had learned so much in so little time. It was almost as if she had been using a blade since birth.

His memory flashed back to several nights before, when they were camping in a clearing and she was training with the Erilian warriors using tent poles instead of steel.

Now, here she was, in an actual battle and winning.

She didn't need his help.

He needed hers.

Peering around, he found David, Simon, and Oliver in a tight circle of their own. The men were fighting back-to-back, surrounded and outnumbered by dark-clad warriors. Tomas ran across the snow towards his friends as fast as he could.

A rider on horseback galloped towards him from his right. He saw the horse growing larger and larger in his side vision.

Ducking low, he swiped at the beast's forelimb and sent it catapulting into the snow with a loud crunch. The rider landed spreadeagled beside the steed.

Tomas started towards him as he lifted himself from the ground, retrieving his blade from beside him.

The man hacked in a downward swing towards Tomas.

Stepping to the side of the blow, Tomas chopped into the flank of the man, as if with an axe into a tree.

The blade stuck deep.

Falling to his knees, the man glared at Tomas as he dropped his sword into the snow.

Tomas' blade stuck well into the man's side, just below the ribcage. He pulled, but it didn't budge.

The man pulled his dagger from his belt as blood trickled from his lips.

"I'm taking you with me," he gurgled, raising the small blade in his hand.

Tomas kicked with the sole of his boot, connecting with the man's face. The dark rider gasped loudly, falling to his side and opening the wound slightly as he did so.

The sword came loose as Tomas gave a tremendous tug. He was about to finish the enemy soldier off with a final blow, but saw it was too late.

The man lay silently on the snow; the gaping wound to his side spilling a tremendous amount of blood over the white surface.

Tomas left the man to breathe his last as he returned his attention to his friends, still fighting together a short distance away.

Too engaged in confronting the three men of Woodmyst, the enemy soldiers didn't see Tomas approaching from behind them.

With a quick thrust, he pierced one man through the back, the tip of the blade breaking out through the opponent's chest.

He retrieved his sword and swung it at another to the now fallen man's left.

The other, now aware of Tomas' presence, blocked the strike with his own blade.

As Tomas engaged his new foe, the other three men of Woodmyst branched out a little way to squabble with their opponents a little more freely.

A small distance away, across the valley, Baldwyn joined with the other men of the *Adelandria* who were engaged in battle with several other soldiers. All had moved onto the ground to take swipes at each other, leaving their horses to run freely around the valley.

Baldwyn noticed the steeds seemed to have congregated near the pack horses in the centre of the expanse. Their heads looked back and forth at the battle transpiring nearby.

He surmised that, in their minds, it was a silly exchange that made no sense. Men killing men.

Returning his thoughts to the conflict, he urged his steed forward with ferocity, barging a few enemy warriors onto the ground.

They were too far for him to reach from atop of the saddle, and his horse didn't have the sense to crush them with her hooves.

"Get them," he called to his fellow crewmen.

A few, not currently engaged in a fight, slipped in and plunged their swords into the toppled men.

The enemy's numbers were thinning rapidly.

Jeremy, tussling with two swordsmen, silently prayed for someone to offer help.

A quick glance around told him that everyone had their own battles to deal with, meaning his prayers would go unanswered.

He was going to have to do this on his own, or die trying.

Each time he dissuaded one warrior, perhaps knocking him off his feet or forcing the blade from his hands, the other would step in to take his place.

The captain was feeling weary, as this was how it had been for him since the skirmish began.

With a block and then a parry, he survived a strike to the face and neck.

Seeing a chance as the attacking foe recoiled his sword, preparing for another strike,

Jeremy lowered the tip of his blade and thrust forward.

The long sword in the captain's hands plunged into the other man's chest.

Remembering that the other man, picking his weapon up from the snow, was still nearby,

Jeremy pulled his sword from his current opponent and swung his blade across the man.

The sword slid deep across the other's belly, spilling its contents onto the ground.

As the man slumped to the ground, his entrails slapping against the snow noisily, the captain turned towards the other warrior.

The man stared at the remains of his comrade lying on the ground before turning his fear-filled eyes upon the captain.

Without warning, the man turned and ran across the snow away from the battle, towards the north.

Jeremy shook his head in disbelief as he watched the other running away.

He glanced around him to see the battle was all but over. Apart from the man racing away towards the ridge, there was one other soldier being treated to the hospitality of Erilian women.

"Akasati," Jeremy called.

"Aye, Captain," she replied as Sharek plunged her blade into the last enemy warrior still fighting on the battlefield.

"Arrow." He pointed to the man running away across the valley.

"Aye, Captain," she repeated in a tone that told him she understood the command.

Tomas sheathed his sword as he watched the woman load an arrow onto the bowstring.

"You might want to see this, gentlemen," he said to his men.

"Absolutely." David smiled.

She tilted her aim high as the runner reached the base of the ridge. Taking a deep breath, she loosed the arrow.

The runner breathed rapidly, heavily, wheezing as he used both arms and legs to clamber up the embankment. All his comrades had fallen upon the snow behind him and not one of them had bled a drop.

In desperation, he needed to get back to Blackrock Haven. He needed to inform his commander of what had happened.

The White Mistress needed to be warned.

The Green Mistress must be told.

Frantically, clambering, crawling, he scrambled up the steep embankment.

Just get to the top and run.

A sharp whistle broke through the air, louder, louder.

The arrow pierced through the back of his skull and through his forehead.

Watching as a few tiny drops of blood fell upon the snow before him, before his world turned black.

"Amazing." David shook his head, looking on in wonder. "Bloody amazing."

Seventeen

Seated about the sitting room, the girls in varying-coloured garments waited quietly, shyly, for their visitor to arrive. Bright rays of light beamed through three tall arched windows onto a large green rug that filled most of the floor.

A great fire roared in the fireplace. The woman in green sat in a deep-cushioned chair, facing it, with her back to the girls seated about the room.

Joanne sat in a high-backed chair in front of the middle window, her hood pulled back over her head as she stared at her shadow on the sitting room rug. Andris stood beside her, his shadow standing tall and strong beside her.

By putting the cover of her cloak over her, she blocked her view of most of the other girls in the room, avoiding eye contact with them. Most of all, however, she shut the muscular shape of Andris from her eyes.

She liked him. He was handsome, and she felt things for him she didn't quite understand. She shouldn't understand at all. It made her feel uncomfortable and curious all at the same time.

Returning her attention to the rug, she traced the floral design around the edges with her eyes. Roses set upon vines of thorns twisted along the hem in golden embroidery.

It was quite beautiful. Like much of the belongings in the castle, it all seemed a little too much.

So much wealth.

So much expense.

People were starving around the lands, and here lay a piece of carpet that, if sold, could have fed her village for a year. Perhaps more.

Instead, it remained on a stone floor while men tried to steal from the village stores to feed their families.

She couldn't get the image of the man's head being crushed upon the throne room floor. She shot a quick look through the archway at the end of the room. She could see through the foyer and into the throne room beyond.

The servants had cleaned the mess up, as if the incident had never happened.

What will happen to that man's family now?

Her eyes met with those of the scarlet girl, Tricia, sitting across the room from her. The scarlet girl dropped her eyes first, peering at the rug just as Joanne had been.

What about her family?

Surely her mother was on the ship with them.

Where is she now?

Joanne resumed staring at her shadow on the rug. Andris was still there.

The sound of horses' hooves upon stone and the wheels of a cart resonated through the windows and into the sitting room.

Joanne moved her eyes towards the lady in green, but only her arm was visible to the girl. It tensed, gripping the end of the armrest tightly as they heard the foyer doors opening.

Footsteps made their way across the castle's entry and to the arch leading into the sitting room, where they halted. Joanne saw one guard, a man dressed from head to toe in a dark uniform, standing beneath the arch.

"Excuse me, Mistress," he called. "Your guest has arrived."

"Show her in," the lady in green replied with no emotion.

The young girl sensed something behind the cool façade.

Excitement.

The man disappeared back to the main doors of the foyer. Before long, he was standing back under the arch.

"Mistress," he called. "The White Mistress."

He stepped aside to allow a young blonde woman into the room.

Joanne instinctively stood to her feet, a sign of respect. She had never met this woman and didn't know what type of person she was. It didn't matter. Her mother and father had always taught her to show respect to older people. That might mean giving up your seat for them, offering your assistance, and even standing as they entered the room.

The other girls noticed Joanne's actions and followed suit, hoping the Green Mistress did not notice them for delaying their response.

They were.

The White Mistress moved her eyes straight to Joanne as she walked through the room towards the fire. The young girl kept her hood high and her eyes low. She didn't want to lock eyes with this woman. Something about her didn't sit right in her stomach.

She couldn't help wondering why they called this one the White Mistress. There wasn't an ounce of white on her.

She wore something that more resembled a patchwork quilt with earthy colours and poor stitching. Her long, whitish hair was untidy and her skin was a little dirty. The majestic appearance of the Green Mistress far surpassed the form of this one.

The lady in green, hooded in her own cloak, lifted herself gracefully from her seat and moved around the chair. She spread her arms wide and embraced the other woman lovingly. The White Mistress cried, wrapping her own arms around the lady in green.

"You're home," she said. "They can't get to you here."

"I missed you," the White Mistress said, pulling away a little.

"I know," the other replied. "The first thing we shall do is get you out of these wretched clothes, and then burn them. The bath is filled with hot water and your room has been prepared."

"I think it worked," the blonde woman told her.

The lady in green appeared very interested in this piece of information.

"I took one of them," she continued. "I took his seed and blood."

"What makes you think it worked?"

"I feel weak," she replied. "It grows. *He* grows."

The lady in green put her hand against the other's abdomen. She looked off into the distance as she held her hand in place.

Her eyes darted back to those of the blonde woman.

"Something is growing," she told her. "It could be the Maji."

The Maji?

Joanne wondered what they referred to. She felt as if she had stepped into a very strange world.

From an abusive ship voyage to a castle with manservants, women of different coloured outfits and now a *Maji*.

What is a Maji?

How she wished she was back with her father, mother and sister, living the simplest kind of life that she could imagine.

"They chased me," the White Mistress informed the lady in green. "They almost beat me."

"They didn't though," the lady replied.

"They have protection."

"Protection?"

"Some warrior women hold power," the White Mistress told her, "but there was another who hasn't yet tapped into what she possesses. An auburn girl."

"Auburn!" the Green Mistress gasped.

Auburn, Joanne thought. Her eyes went wide. The other girls, overhearing the conversation, moved their eyes straight to her. At least one of them had known her and her sister from their village.

Joanne kept her composure, hiding her hair and her features, somewhat similar to her sister's, beneath her hood.

The Green Mistress embraced the blonde woman tightly, "I am so glad to have you back with me."

Still holding the other in a tight embrace, she moved her eyes to Joanne, knowing it was indeed her sister who posed a problem. She also knew that the White Mistress might be in a state of mind to take revenge.

"Girls," she said, "to your rooms until I call for you. I need to discuss a few things with the White Mistress."

The servants led each of the girls by the arms back up the stairs to their rooms. The Green Mistress continued to hold the other woman in place until they were all out of view.

Joanne heard a conversation ensuing, but could not understand the words. They were too far away.

Andris led the girl back into her chamber.

"Thank you, Andris," she said, closing her door before moving across the room to the dresser. She sat down in front of the looking glass and lowered her hood. Her hair was still tidy and held back in a ponytail, but she felt the need to brush it again.

Taking the black lace ribbon from her head, she placed it on the dresser. She ran the fine brush over her scalp and along the length of auburn strands as she thought about the White Mistress' words.

An auburn girl.

Auburn.

Could it be Emily?

Is she still alive?

Is she coming for me?

She hoped and wished for it to be true.

Even with her own chamber, an enormous bed, a dresser and ribbons for her hair, she still felt very much a prisoner. She wasn't in a cage made of iron anymore, and the smell of filth didn't penetrate everything around her.

Her cage was a castle filled with luxuries and manservants. The smells filling her nostrils were of spice and perfume.

Still, she felt like a prisoner.

Oh Emily, she thought. *Please come for me.*

She heard a soft knocking at the door.

"Yes," she said, just loud enough for the person on the other side to hear.

"Forgive me, Miss," Andris whispered through the door. "May I come in and have a word?"

Joanne didn't feel too comfortable allowing him into the room. She has all but lost her trust towards men. Allowing him to take her arm was indeed progress after what had happened to her, but she still felt as if something crawled over her skin every time she brushed against him.

The scarred man had done that to her.

"Yes," she said, defying her instincts.

He entered the room cautiously, head bowed.

"I apologise, Miss. I know you don't like for me to be near you, so I'll stand here. I just need to say something and I beg you to never repeat it. Not to anyone. Please."

He sounded scared.

"I promise." She nodded, urging him to go on.

"You need to be careful," he said. "Don't trust the Green Mistress."

"Why?" she asked.

He looked at the rug near her feet.

"She is responsible for all that has happened," he replied. "I saw the way you tensed when the scarred man appeared at the door. The scarred man serves her and does her bidding."

"She saved me from him."

"No." He looked directly into her eyes, shaking his head. "He delivered you to her. She has done this before. I've heard stories and I know stories can be exaggerated but I've seen things and I believe these to be true."

She felt her face burning. Anger filled her senses as she listened to Andris' words.

"What stories?" Joanne asked, feeling her heart pounding louder.

"That she manipulates girls to become what she is," he answered. "That she can steal your will and then, through your anger, empowers you to do hers."

"Steal my will?" Her brow furrowed. "How could she?"

"By taking your innocence," he told her. His eyes moved back to the floor.

She thought back to her voyage on board the ship. She thought about the times when the scarred man visited her, taking her to his chamber. She thought about the other girls, locked in the cage with her, all of whom were now in this castle, sitting in their own chambers. Each of them had been a victim of the same abuse as she.

"She then promises to keep you safe, Andris continued. "She delivers comfort and luxuries and tells you that *you* have the power here. She told you that no man will touch you, unless you want him to."

"I remember," Joanne said, tears welling in her eyes.

"She has placed me in your charge for that very reason, Miss. It is her will that you and I unite, in time."

Joanne nodded, understanding his words clearly.

"Please don't tell anyone that I told you this," he pleaded.

"I won't," she replied, wiping her eyes.

"I am an innocent, as are all the servants under the charge of the other young ladies," Andris told her. "You are intended to become the one to steal my innocence away from me just as the scarred man stole yours away from you."

"I wouldn't do that." Joanne appeared disgusted by the concept. "I don't want to."

"If she continues to speak her words and show you her ways, you will eventually want to. And you will do so. I have no choice. I am bound. I am a slave and if I don't fulfil my duty to you, I will die," he told her. "But you can choose."

She shook her head. This was too much to take in.

Why was Andris telling her this?

She could order him out of the room and never to speak of it again.

But the look on his face was earnest, and she knew his words held some truth.

"How do you know this?" she asked.

"The stories," he replied. "They all speak of another, like you with great potential but younger, who was taken by the scarred man from her home and set upon by the men of his ship. By the time they brought her here, she was not herself.

"The Green Mistress trained her, just as she is doing with you. Eventually, the young girl gave in to her urges and brought her servant into her chamber and had her way with him.

"Her mind must have been damaged, because she killed him. Some say she stabbed the man in the bed where they lay. Others say she ate part of him.

"That girl is under this roof as we speak."

"The White Mistress?" she questioned.

"So the stories say." He moved into the room a little, holding his hands together, begging. "Please, Miss. Except to clean your room and help with your necessities, I implore you never to ask me into your chamber. I will always do as you command. I am bound to obey you. But, please, I beg, don't ask me to do that."

A lump formed in her throat. More tears streamed down her face.

The man, the boy, was frightened of her.

She frowned and nodded.

"Thank you, Miss," he said, backing away, grabbing the door as he passed through the entry to her chamber. "My apologies for the intrusion."

With that, he closed the door.

She lifted the brush and stroked her hair.

Her vision was blurry from the tears.

Putting the brush down, she rested her elbows on the dresser, placed her face into her hands and sobbed.

Her cage was one of luxury and finer temptations.

Please, Emily. Come.

Eighteen

Patrolling the valley with the other men of Woodmyst, Tomas searched for any horses fatally injured and left lying on the snow during the battle. They walked amongst the dead enemy soldiers peering this way and that as they held their swords loosely in their hands.

Most of the fallen steeds had expired. The ones that still lived received a merciful bite from a blade.

When this act needed his attention, it always weighed heavily on his heart. Putting a man down, one who intended to cause harm, didn't bother him all that much. Sometimes he had wished another solution presented itself, but they chose their own death, in a manner of speaking.

A horse, however, had no say in the matter. It went where its rider willed it. That could mean a lovely amble along the seaside or into the fray of battle.

As he looked into the eye of such an animal, injured with deep gashes along its flanks and spitting blood from its flaring nostrils, he knew the poor beast didn't understand, couldn't understand, what had occurred.

His mind filled with imagery and feelings that he had when he and his brown mare were together. He recalled times when riding across the meadows of his homeland. There were moments where she would follow him like a loyal hound, untethered and free to run. She was a loyal beast, a true friend.

He plunged his blade through the steed's skull, bringing it to rest.

Moving his eyes across the carnage, he looked for the next beast that might need release. Something drew him to woods to the west. Hairs stood on the back of his neck and an icy shiver ran along his spine.

Something lurked beyond his view.

Gathered in the middle of the valley, away from where the skirmish took place, away from the smell of blood and death, the horses stood in a tight mob watching the approaching men.

Tomas had told them to approach naturally as some of the steeds were used to their gait. As they drew near, some of the enemy steeds, including a few from the outpost, moved away. The pack horses and several others from the compound waited in place for the troop to gather them.

They exchanged pats, and nickers as riders reunited with beasts.

The riders gathered the pack animals and the unmanned chargers. Leading them in a wide circle around the battleground, they made their way to the northern ridge.

The men of Woodmyst, now having completed their miserable task, made their way across the snow towards the gathered mob at the base of the elevation.

Tomas made for Emily, who was holding the black gelding. She tossed him the reins before he climbed atop of the beast.

"How are you?" she asked him, noticing his demeanour seemed more solemn than usual.

"I'm all right." He nodded. "I just don't like…"

She looked back towards the horses lying amongst the bodies of men. Knowing Tomas as well as she did, she understood he found it difficult to complete the duty he had just performed.

Reaching her hand over to him, she placed her palm on his thigh. He laid his hand over hers and held it there for a moment.

"Should we burn the bodies?" Gustav called.

"No," David replied. "Let them rot."

"They won't have time," Tomas replied, snapping back out of his pity session.

"What do you mean?" Jeremy asked.

"Our shadows are back," he replied. "In the woods."

"I thought we killed them all," Jeff said, peering towards the woods.

"Maybe they didn't all attack us," Oliver suggested. "Perhaps some of the weaker or younger ones stayed back."

"They are waiting for us to leave," Rhydra told them, her eyes fixed on the shadows beneath the trees.

The others looked at her, wondering how she could know this. She closed her eyes.

"They are hungry," Sharek told them, her eyes closed, her face directed towards the woods.

The troop turned their heads towards her.

"They are frightened," Akasati said.

"They are watching," Karlena breathed.

All Erilian women sat atop of their steeds, eyes closed, faces directed to the western edge of the valley.

"They are many."

The men turned to the owner of the voice.

Emily faced the woods with her eyes closed.

Something had transpired between the women that none of the men could comprehend.

They connected, transfixed.

Tomas sensed a power at work amongst them.

It frightened him a little, even excited him somewhat.

Ever since the time that Emily had mingled with the Erilian warriors, a strange bond had formed between them. A growing energy.

He couldn't say exactly what it was.

But there was something happening.

"How many?" he asked, looking at Emily.

"They do not think like men," Akasati replied.

"They only know that there are others of their kind," Rhydra continued.

"More around them," Sharek added.

"Many," Karlena finished.

"Many." David peered into the woods, simply accepting the strange exchange between the women and moving on. "That could mean two or two-hundred."

The women opened their eyes and looked at one another. They too thought it was a bizarre moment. Confused glances and shaking heads informed the company that the women had no explanation of what had just transpired.

"We should move on," Jeremy told the group. "Leave the creatures to their feast."

Tomas nodded.

It was time to go.

***

The water's heat penetrated her skin and soaked deep into her muscles beneath. It was relaxing, soothing, mollifying.

Thick veils of steam lifted from the surface, reaching to the white marble ceiling and disappearing through tiny vents that took the vapours out of the room.

She rested on a lower stair near a rear corner of the pool to the right; the water sitting just beneath her ears as she tilted her head back, allowing her blond hair to soak beneath the surface. Rubbing her abdomen with one hand, resting her elbow on the other arm on a higher step, she closed her eyes and breathed deeply.

Her memory of this place had not served her too well. With other things on her mind concerning the southern regions, she had forgotten how wonderful it was to be still, immersed in heat.

Allowing her mind to empty, putting matters aside, she tried to focus on rejuvenation. She was here to recuperate and get her strength back.

And now, with the possibility of the life inside her growing into the potential Maji, she needed her energy more than ever.

He was all that mattered.

He took precedence over all other things.

Even the Green Mistress knew this.

There was no time to focus on auburn girls, with prospective powers, following her on the snow. She need not think about the man leading her pursuers and the protection that his women gave him.

She was here.

Blackrock Haven.

The home of the Green Mistress.

Her servants, her slaves, would be enough to stop her trackers.

They had no chance of reaching her here, behind the thick stone walls of the castle.

"Are you comfortable?" A voice reverberated around the chamber.

She opened her eyes, returning to the real world, and saw two servants removing the bathrobe from the Green Mistress.

"Yes, Mistress." She smiled.

The Green Mistress lowered herself into the steamy water as the servants moved away, backing themselves against the walls on either side of the entrance to the room.

Concealing her nakedness beneath the liquid, she moved slowly towards the other, tilting her head to the side, causing her dark red plait to slink over the front of her left shoulder.

She moved around the White Mistress, positioning herself into the corner, pressed against the other's right side. Reaching her right hand across her body, she touched Sumaiyya's stomach gently with an open hand.

"He grows," she breathed. "He's strong."

"He?" the other asked. "You sense it too?"

The Green Mistress smiled.

"I have said it is so." She leant in closer. "Do you doubt me, Sumaiyya?"

"No," she replied as the Green Mistress placed her chin onto her shoulder.

Continuing to rub Sumaiyya's torso with her right hand, she moved her left hand over the blonde strands of hair, pushing them over the White Mistress' ear.

Sumaiyya closed her eyes.

"Now that you're here," the Green Mistress breathed, "you can assist me with training the seven."

"Do you have a favourite, yet?" Sumaiyya asked her, wondering who could take her place.

"None will ever remove you from my heart," the woman told her, deducing the other's thoughts.

Sumaiyya was glad to hear this, leaning her head towards the Green Mistress.

"There is one who shows greater potential than the others," the woman told her.

The White Mistress lifted her head back and opened her eyes.

"Who?"

"Are you jealous?"

"A little," she said. "Who?"

"She dresses in black," the woman answered.

Sumaiyya knew of whom the Green Mistress referred.

"More powerful than I was?"

"You were younger when you were brought to me," she replied, sitting back and pulling her arms to her sides. "There is no comparison."

Rubbing her face with her hand, Sumaiyya wiped some silt from her skin.

"Do you intend to love her as you did me?"

"She hasn't seduced her servant yet," the Green Mistress replied. "None of them have. They've only just arrived."

"Do you intend to?" The White Mistress locked her piercing blue eyes onto those of the other.

"Yes," she admitted. "If she desires it."

Sumaiyya swallowed hard. Her anger was apparent, but she kept control. This was the Green Mistress, and she was entitled to do as she wished.

"I'd like to meet her," the White Mistress said.

"You will," the woman replied, "at dinner."

"What is her name?"

"Joanne. But she should be referred to as the Black Miss if we are to see her converted to our cause."

"I'd like to speak to her." Sumaiyya maintained her stony stare. "Alone."

"No," the Green Mistress told her angrily. "You are never to speak to her without me being present. Ever. Do you understand?"

Sumaiyya lowered her gaze back to the water as she remembered her place.

"Yes, Mistress." She frowned. "Forgive me."

The Green Mistress remained distant for a moment. Eventually, she wrapped her arms gracefully around the other and pulled her into her embrace.

Sumaiyya submitted and rested her head against the woman's neck.

"She is the sister of the auburn girl that you saw on the plains," the Green Mistress informed her.

Sumaiyya tensed and wanted to escape the arms of the woman. Instead, she remained in place.

"Both of them have great potential," the Green Mistress continued. "Together, they could be a formidable force. We need to persuade the Black Miss to become loyal to our cause. The realm lands could finally belong to the Mirikin."

"Should we force her hand concerning her servant?" Sumaiyya asked, putting her personal feelings aside.

"No," the Green Mistress replied as she stroked Sumaiyya's hair with her fingers. "She needs to choose to execute dominance over him. You remember how it works?"

"Yes, Mistress," she replied, remembering all too well when she called her servant into her bedchamber.

She remembered, after having her way with him, his blood and flesh spread across her sheets as she used her abilities to tear him limb from limb.

A small smile spread across her lips as the memory subsided.

She remembered all too well how it worked.

Turning towards the Green Mistress, she ran her hand along the other's thigh and kissed her on the cheek.

"I've missed you, my Mistress," she whispered.

"Have you?" the Green Mistress questioned.

"Yes." She ran her lips over the other's ear.

"Prove it." The woman smiled.

"The guards?"

The Green Mistress gave a quick glance around the room to see the two men by the door and another two against the rear wall, watching over Sumaiyya.

"Leave us," she commanded them.

The men filed out of the room and disappeared through the entrance to the bath, leaving the two Mistresses alone.

Nineteen

The wind had changed direction. It came at them from the north as a gentle breeze, but the build-up of clouds creeping over the mountain peaks told the travellers they were in for some nasty weather. It would only be a matter of time before another snowstorm hit them.

Tomas aimed to make as much ground as they could. There was no way of knowing how far they had to go before they reached the place where the black ship moored. So it only made sense to trek as far as they could before nature's fury unleashed upon them.

"Any sign of our friends from the forest?" he called to Simon, who was riding on the western flank of the group.

"Nothing that I can see," the other replied, scanning the trees carefully.

"Do you…" Tomas looked for the right words as he faced Emily, "*feel* anything?"

"Feel?" she chuckled. "No, I felt nothing. I don't know what that was back there. I can't explain it."

"It was amazing," he told her. "That's what it was."

"You were scared."

"A little," he admitted.

"I'm like her," she said. "Aren't I?"

"Who?"

"The white witch."

Inside, she was struggling with the concept of having this ability, a power that she didn't understand. Something was brewing inside of her that had only manifested in such a way after meeting the Erilian warriors.

She shared a commonality with them. It was beyond tangible. It was within them and surrounding them, a part of them that seemed to live and breathe, consume and digest.

It lived, but it was unlike any living being she had ever come across before. Yet, it was still a part of her, but it connected with similar entities within the other women, joining to become stronger.

She was a witch.

The Erilian warriors were witches, too.

What other explanation could there be?

"You're nothing like her," Tomas stated. "Not at all. She is wicked and evil. She isn't right in the head. You're loving and caring."

She grinned.

"Not to mention much better looking," he continued.

Her grin turned into a broad smile.

Still, the idea of being a witch troubled her.

She hated the word.

Witch.

It sounded evil. To say it, to think it, made her think of delinquent beings, twisted and dark.

Witch.

She didn't want to appear as a detestable being to her friends.

Witch.

She didn't want the people around her to be fearful of her capabilities.

Witch.

She didn't want Tomas to despise her the way he despised Sumaiyya Tarkin, the white witch.

More than that, she didn't want to be corrupted as Sumaiyya had been. She didn't want the power to fill her head and cause her to believe that she could be some kind of overlord.

Witch.

So, she may be one, but she would reject her abilities, denounce her powers if she could just be a normal woman.

Looking at Tomas, she wondered if she had a hand in causing him to fall for her. She recalled Ivo succumbing to the temptations of the white witch, leaving the camp in the middle of the night and venturing deep into the woods to her lair. Her presence had been there before that fateful event. Perhaps she had been luring Ivo for some time prior to that night.

It made sense.

Emily feared she might have been doing the same thing to Tomas. She had fallen for him the very first moment she laid her eyes upon him.

Could it be that she had been manipulating him to fall for her since that moment?

Was she luring him to her will, just as the white witch had done to Ivo?

Was she no better than that evil bitch?

"Do you love me?" she asked him.

He turned his face towards her. Her eyes were both full of worry and sadness. He furrowed his brow and placed his hand on her thigh.

"Of course, I love you," he replied. "What has brought this on?"

"I just wonder if I caused you to love me," she answered. "Or if you love me because you want to."

He smiled.

"If I wasn't on this horse right now, I would kiss you," he told her. "Right here in the middle of this valley, in front of all of these people. Yes, you caused me to love you."

She looked at him, shocked.

"The moment I saw you, I liked you," he told her. "But as I got to know you, and spend time with you, I fell in love. You didn't seduce me, Emily. You didn't get inside my head and make me do anything that I didn't want to do.

"I love you, Emily Grenefeld. And today, I love you more than I did yesterday. Tomorrow, I assume that I will love you even more.

"If we make it through this, I plan to be yours until the end of time, if you'll have me. I would like to be your husband."

She smiled, happy with his answer. Tears streamed down her cheeks.

"I love you, Tomas Warde," she replied. "And I would like to be your wife."

He pulled his horse to a stop. She did the same.

"Hold," Jeremy called, watching the exchange with a wide grin.

The troop pulled to a complete stop as both Tomas and Emily slid from their steeds' backs to the snow on the ground.

He embraced her and kissed her long and deep on the lips.

The company looked on fondly, exchanging smiles. Some nodded as others shook their heads. But all within the group felt only warm thoughts towards the two lovers.

"Should we pitch a tent for you?" David quipped.

Karlena shot him an annoying glare as several men in the company chuckled.

Emily picked up a handful of snow and lobbed it towards the bald man. It exploded on his face, sending the group into a raucous, laughing fit.

"Good shot," he commended her, wiping the cold frost from his eyes.

***

They continued their trek across the snow, northward as the wind picked up and the clouds gathered above them. The sun had started its descent towards the west and the air was feeling chillier than usual at this time of day.

Jeremy noticed the women gripping their cloaks around themselves tighter as the weather bit with frosty teeth. He wasn't sure if they were feeling the cold a little more than the men, or whether the men were putting on a display of bravado, pretending not to feel the cold as much as the women. The truth of the matter was that he was feeling it and donned his own cloak and hood as they pressed on.

Soon after, the clouds opened up and sent a light snow to the ground. The wind whipped the snowflakes directly into the riders' faces. The horses found the experience particularly displeasing, shaking their heads and snorting loudly in protest.

Jeremy knew the worst was yet to come.

He observed the clouds above growing darker and darker as the day drew on. Eventually the glowing orb of the sun, that penetrated the veil of cover in the sky, vanished and a dark shadow crept over the land.

The snow falling became heavier and heavier, collaborating with the northern wind to produce a barrage an onslaught of white.

Pressing onwards, into the blizzard, the riders gathered as closely together as they could. Oliver looked around at the riders close by him. He could see two or three people deep into the white, but no farther. From his place, he could no longer see Tomas and Emily at the forefront of the company.

"Tomas," he called over the din of the gale force winds. "Tomas."

"Oliver," the other replied, barely audible.

"Perhaps we should tether ourselves to one another," he suggested, thinking back to the last snowstorm they had experienced.

"I think that's a good idea," Tomas replied. "But we stay as a group. Not in a line."

"Aye," Jeremy agreed, remembering their loss the last time they tethered together.

They passed reins and straps forwards to the riders in front. Soon, all riders' leads wove their way from rider to rider, eventuating with Emily's and Jeremy's reins being tethered to Tomas' saddle.

Tomas, blinded by the weather, lowered his hood and urged the gelding on. It reluctantly pulled the others forward, towards the north.

The progress was slow, laborious and wearisome.

Climbing yet another rise, where the wind seemed to increase to a ferocious velocity, and then down the other side to cross another wide valley, Tomas wondered if they may need to take rest.

The horses, particularly his steed, were struggling in the volley of snow and wind. His gelding had lowered its head so far that its snout almost dragged against the ground, all to escape being hit in the face with the onslaught.

Tomas understood its plight as he tried to manipulate his hood so he could maintain his vision, but prevent the icy particles from striking his eyes. It was impossible.

His sanity told him it was time to stop. It was time to set up a tent and crowd everyone inside until this storm was over.

His obsession told him to press on. The white witch couldn't be that far ahead of them.

They must have moored the ship with the captive women nearby, somewhere.

He needed to get there.

He needed to fulfil his promise that he made to Antony.

Putting his head down, he urged his horse onward.

Across the plain, the group plodded slowly, slowly. Their cloaks flapped about them like flags caught in the wind.

There was no other sound except the constant howl and whistle that whirled around them, filling their ears.

Simon peered to the west but saw nothing.

Just grey and white.

The trees had disappeared. The mountains were nowhere to be seen.

There was nothing but a wall of snow surrounding them.

Rising again, Tomas risked a glance and saw they had reached the next embankment.

The gelding slowed, wanting to stop. The rider couldn't blame it for trying. He wanted to stop, too.

Perhaps they should, he thought.

Instead, he urged the beast to pull the others on.

They climbed the steep elevation, trudging through thick, wet ground cover. They pushed against the strong northerly winds. The icy snow stung their skin. The deafening roar of the gale hurt their ears.

Reaching the top, Tomas peered into the valley below.

The storm obscured everything like a thick curtain. Dark objects were barely visible through the white.

They could barely see the forest to the west.

There were some shapes near the middle of his view that he couldn't quite determine.

But his breath all but left him when he saw a familiar shape to the right of it all.

Barely visible, behind the blizzard's veil, he saw the tall masts of the black ship.

His eyes grew wide and his heart beat faster.

Nothing else in the valley held his interest at this precise moment.

The hulking mass of the ship they had been chasing, their only reason for heading north, was now before them.

"We found her," Tomas called over the din. "We found the black ship."

Twenty

"Shouldn't we go after them?" one man gathered around the table in the galley asked. A fine hot meal of roast meat and bread sat on plates before them. Most of the nine men congregating for dinner were shovelling the food down as if it was about to disappear or be taken from them.

The stench of unclean, sweaty men surpassed the thick smell of salt. The sound of creaking boards was barely audible over the scraping of cutlery on porcelain and the slapping of lips closing around the feast.

At the head of the table sat the scarred man, a mug of mead pressed against his lips as he watched his head-crewmen acting more like pigs at the trough than men at a table. He moved his eyes to the one who had asked and lowered his cup back to the table, swallowing loudly.

"We won't be going after them," he answered. "Especially in that mess blowing about outside now."

"But," the other started again, "they should have been back? Right?"

The scarred man shook his head.

"They may have had to travel all the way to the outpost," he replied, picking up his fork and knife. "With this weather, they could be held up there and may not be able to return immediately. Give them time, Refal." With that, he shoved a large portion of meat into his mouth.

"They could be dead," Refal stated, cutting a small portion of his meal with his cutlery before placing it delicately over his lips.

The scarred man nodded.

"Maybe so," he replied with a mouthful. "Who cares? Eat your food before it goes cold."

Refal looked to his plate and cut another portion of meat from the fat steak that sat steaming before him. That something to be feared was making its way towards them consumed him.

News had reached them at the port about how someone pursued the White Mistress. After seeing her with his own eyes, he could tell that she was afraid. The White Mistress instilled fear on behalf of the Sovereign into the hearts of men and women wherever she went. If she could be afraid of something, then surely so should he.

He swallowed his food and lifted his mug to help wash it down.

The thought of men, good fighting men, leaving the relative safety of Blackrock Haven to face an unseen enemy, and not yet returning, made him feel uneasy. Khabar, the scarred one, could be right. Perhaps the weather kept them from returning. Maybe they sheltered somewhere waiting for the storm to disperse.

But Refal didn't think so.

He believed they were more likely to be lying in the snow, pierced with blades and arrows.

Some of them were his friends, ordered to their deaths.

All for the cause.

All for the Sovereign.

"Why?"

"Why what?" another, seated across from him, grumbled as he chewed on a thick slice of fat.

Refal didn't realise he'd said the word out loud.

"Nothing," he replied.

Khabar glared at him.

"You said *why*," the scarred man informed him. "What is it that would make you ask *why*? Why are we eating steak? Why are we still inside this putrid ship instead of a warm inn? Why are all the other crewmen enjoying the roaring fires inside the huts around us and possibly the feel of a fucking woman or two inside the pens? Is that why you ask *why*?"

"Why did you order those men to go south?"

The table suddenly fell silent. All eyes moved between Khabar and Refal, sensing a growing tension.

Khabar picked up his mug and relieved it of its contents. Placing the vessel back upon the table, he kept his eyes fixed upon Refal as he gave a command to another sitting by him.

"Fill this." He slid the mug across the table to the man on his right. The man complied, lifting a large pitcher from the table and pouring it into the scarred man's cup.

"I don't need to justify my actions to you, Refal," he said coldly. "But you need to understand that I am given commands to undertake, just as I give commands to you."

He reached for his mug and took another swig.

"She commanded me," Khabar continued. "When she commands me, I must follow. You know what happens to those who disobey."

"We feign loyalty," Refal replied, "you feign loyalty to her, to all of them, because you are afraid. We are all afraid. If we were to unite, we could—"

"Be careful with your words," the scarred man instructed him. "The Green Mistress has ears everywhere. You should have learnt that by now."

"I miss farming," Refal blurted. "I've never enjoyed hurting children."

Khabar kept his eyes on the Refal as the other men lowered their heads, ashamed of their deeds.

"Do you know how much I need to drink before I..." Khabar took another mouthful of mead. "I can never return to farming. I couldn't be a peddler or a fisher. Not anymore.

"This is what we are, Refal. This is what the Sovereign has made us. We can't think about what was and what we could have been and ask *why*.

"We are the Prophets of the Sovereign. We are the voice that goes before. We bring the fear. We testify of the things to come. That is who we are now.

"Forget your farming," he said to all the men gathered about the table. "Forget your happy lives that could have been. Forget any possibility that you could have had with wives and children. Most of all, forget that we had this conversation.

"We serve the Sovereign and that means obeying the will of all the Mistresses." He picked up his knife and fork and cut a portion of meat, placing it into his mouth. "Now eat before your food gets cold."

***

Joanne stared at the empty plate sitting on the table. Sparkling clean silverware sat on either side, napkins neatly folded and a glass of water before her.

She had pulled her hood over her head once again, to narrow her vision to what lay directly in front of her, avoiding the eye contact of the others gathered about. Her concern wasn't the other girls, her fellow-travellers, now wearing their beautifully coloured garments. It was the one sitting at the end of the table, closest to the fireplace.

Even now, with her black hood concealing the other from her view, she could feel those piercing blue eyes digging into her, penetrating with a spiteful stare. She tried her best to ignore it, to will it away, but it was there, boring, drilling into her skin near her temples.

The approaching footfalls of three people approaching made her look up, over the head of the White Mistress to the lady in green being followed by two servants. She followed the woman with her eyes, continuing to avoid those of the blonde visitor.

"Black Miss," the Green Mistress called her as she approached her seat at the head of the table, "your hood, please."

Joanne lowered her covering, revealing her auburn hair to the White Mistress. The digging sensation in her head seemed to intensify. The younger girl was not enjoying the experience and grew tired of the other's staring.

Finally, as the Green Mistress took her seat, Joanne moved her eyes to lock with those of the White Mistress. The other girls observed, afraid. If the ability to cause harm through looking could occur, and they had no doubt that it could after what they had witnessed in the throne room, then this was indeed a dangerous moment.

The cutlery shuddered. Clinking sounds emitted across the table moved like a wave from one end to the other, intensifying when they reached the White Mistress. Her plate moved. Her knife and fork lifted slightly from their places.

The girls' eyes grew wide with fear as they watched the strange occurrence.

"Enough," the Green Mistress said. Her voice was calm and in control.

The cutlery fell back on the table with a loud clunk.

"I thought we had an understanding, Sumaiyya." The lady in green peered along the table at the blonde girl at the far end.

"That wasn't me," she replied. Her eyes displayed concern. "It was her."

"I know," the woman replied. "But you instigated the exchange."

"She might have hurt me," the White Mistress suggested. "She could have damaged the..." She rubbed her belly.

"Yes," the lady in green replied. "She might have even killed you and what you carry inside. Be careful, Sumaiyya."

"I need protection from her," the White Mistress argued.

"You need to remember your place, Sumaiyya," the other reminded her. "If this one is exhibiting such power now, just what do you think she may do to you once she reaches her full potential? You are meant to work together. You are meant to be sisters."

"I have a sister," Joanne blurted.

"Yes," Sumaiyya spat. "We know all about her."

"Silence," the Green Mistress commanded the blonde girl.

"So," Joanne looked from the White Mistress to the lady in green. "She is coming. She will come for all of us."

"She won't last, child," the Green Mistress told her. "It's a wonder she has lasted this long. The weather works against her even now. She is out in this blizzard and it is ferocious.

"If she somehow manages to endure, she will then have all of my servants to contest with. She is only one little girl and my men are many.

"After that, she will need to face the power of the Mistresses, servants of the Sovereign. She cannot survive. She will not survive.

"And what will she take you to, if she does? Can she give you a castle to live in? Does she have manservants to attend to your every need and desire? What can she give you that I cannot?

"You're better here. Safer here. Loved here," the Green Mistress told her, but her words were for all gathered around the table.

"Now," she finished, "we will have no more talk of this. No more display of abilities. It's time to eat."

***

The steeds grouped tightly at the base of the northern ridge. It offered a little protection from the winds that swept over them as it continued towards the south at a high speed.

Near to them were three tents set in a taut circle, their openings facing each other and another canvas sheet tethered over the top. The travellers had effectively created one big shelter with three separate rooms.

They sat together eating a meal of bread they had confiscated from the outpost. Pressing against one another, they attempted to keep warm as they tried to make conversation over the din.

The wind howled over the canvas covers. Loud flapping sounds filled their ears as snow and sleet smacked against the northern facing walls and roof of their shelter.

It was going to be a long night, Tomas thought as he risked a look outside.

Peering towards the coast, a wall of dark grey and white confronted him as the blizzard continued to thrust its fury upon the world around them.

The horses, just a pace or two from the tents, were barely visible as both a thick haze of white separated the campers from their steeds and the light diminished because of thick clouds and a sinking sun.

"We're here for the night," Tomas called over the noise.

Jeremy, seated not too far from him, raised a hand to his ear. He couldn't quite catch the other's words.

"We are here for the night," Tomas yelled a little louder.

Jeremy nodded and passed the word on to those around him.

Tomas stepped and navigated over and around others in his shared tent, eventually finding his place by Emily's side.

She snuggled against him, passing a sizeable chunk of bread for him to eat. He took it gladly, breaking off smaller pieces.

They scarcely spoke during the night, many choosing to try to sleep through the storm just to pass the time. But even this proved difficult with the sound of the wind roaring about them.

They weren't able to light a fire as they simply couldn't risk exposing themselves to the abysmal conditions just to fetch kindling. This meant they couldn't enjoy a hot cup of tea and a deplorable bowl of porridge.

Perhaps there are positives to a snowstorm after all, David thought as the idea of hot, wet oats entered his mind.

He, like many others, decided to simply lie down and close his eyes. The blaring drone of the wind and unpredictable flapping of the canvas made it difficult to drift into slumber. Still, he persisted, keeping his eyes closed, attempting to block the noise out of his mind.

Snoring joined the annoying sounds of the blizzard. Simon's eyes flickered open and bored angrily into the form of David lying on the floor beside him.

How can he do that? Simon thought. *How can he just fall asleep within moments of putting his head down?*

He closed his eyes again, his senses filling with the noise of wind, sleet and rustling canvas.

This is ridiculous.

Over it all, David continued with his loud, rattly snorting.

Simon pulled his hood farther over his head and placed his hands over his ears.

It didn't help.

Twenty-One

The wind had stopped its assault, but the snow continued to drift towards the ground. The steeds had shaken what frost had collected upon them onto the ground. Still feeling the cold, the steeds pressed together to keep warm.

Tomas woke each of the other men of Woodmyst. Stealthily, they left the confines of the crowded tents. Moving past the horses, the men crept along the southern face of the ridge towards the sound of crashing waves.

The sky was still black, and no star was to be seen in the sky. The moon's silver glow barely penetrated the clouds above the mountains and, although it was near, the signs of dawn were non-existent.

Rising to the crest of the ridge, the men lay upon the snow and scanned the terrain to the north carefully. The ship moored securely on the wharf sat quiet and dark. There were no lanterns or signs of life on her deck.

Tomas surmised that the inhabitants of the ship were sleeping, waiting out the storm as they had been, and continued to slumber through the early hours of the morning.

The dock area, like the ship, revealed no movement. No one was guarding, no one was working, no one was there. He expected to see some activity in a port town, but there was nothing.

"What do you think?" Simon whispered.

"I don't see anyone down there," Oliver said.

"Could be they're all still inside after that storm," David put in. "I know I would still be sleeping if you hadn't woken me."

175

Tomas nodded.

With the ability to see much more of the township and beyond now that the storm had subsided, even with the absence of the sun, Tomas gauged the size of the village more clearly.

It appeared to be a neat hamlet with many steep-roofed buildings clustered about the wharves. To the north, five large warehouses stood above the height of the surrounding structures. They were similar in form to the warehouses the men had seen in Oakbeach; large, firm structures made of timber.

Beyond them, high upon a hill to the north-western region of the valley, stood another extensive structure. It was dark and hard to discern in the limited light, but Tomas believed it to be a castle or another fort, like the outpost they had stayed in.

The presence of such a building told the men there were guards and other armed men nearby.

"We need to get down there and take a closer look," Tomas told the others.

"We should see what is in those warehouses," said a soft voice to their left.

They all turned their faces to see Emily and Erilian women lying in the snow beside them. The men were awestruck. They made no sound as they approached and positioned themselves in the snow.

It was the most outstanding display of stealth Tomas had ever seen in his life.

"How did you get there?" Simon gasped, looking at the women beside him.

Emily replied with a wry grin as she continued to scan the ground below them.

"Why the warehouses?" Tomas asked.

"I don't know exactly why," Emily responded. "But we need to get to them."

Tomas nodded as he moved his gaze from the women to the township.

He wanted to ask more questions, but was learning to just go along with certain things Emily suggested. She, and the Erilian women, had tapped into something powerful. He needed to either accept it or go against it.

Considering that he had witnessed the dark powers that opposed them, Tomas considered perhaps there were other powers that might ally to their side. Perhaps the women beside him represented such a thing.

He had listened to Emily's words and decided.

They would go to the warehouses and see what it hid inside.

**

"How long do you think you will be?" Jeremy asked them.

The men of Woodmyst and the women of the company gathered their weapons and prepared to leave under the cover of darkness.

"We should return by nightfall," Tomas replied. "If we aren't back by midnight, assume the worst. In which case, Jeremy, take the men and ride those horses south as fast as you can. Get back to Oakbeach and muster a force. Don't return without numbers behind you."

"I'll bring an armada," Jeremy replied, gripping Tomas by the shoulder. "But I won't leave here without you. We all leave, or none."

Tomas nodded, placing his hand upon the other's shoulder, returning the gesture before embracing as brothers.

The four men and five women moved away from their camp tucked against the southern slope of the ridge, climbing to its peak and keeping low as they crossed to the other side. Moving to the western edge of the town, the spies made a beat for the shadows of some small structures near the edge of the community.

Some small shacks and animals' lean-to shelters sat against neat rows of picket fences. With their knees bent and backs low, they sneaked along the boundaries of the farthest yards, intending to circle the entire township before arriving at the large warehouses way across on the other side.

Pausing behind each structure they encountered, the group took every opportunity to assess the buildings and the streets nearby. If there was any movement outside, they didn't see it. Occasionally, they passed a henhouse or two that were sealed up tight to protect the fowls from the previous night's snowstorm.

Most of the other animals usually occupying the yards had moved to warmer locations such as barns or perhaps even inside the dwellings where the people of the town lived. Tomas was glad for the storm providing the opportunity for them to sneak into the village. There were no dogs to warn guards of their approach. Occasionally, a deep growl came from behind a closed door, followed by some profanity called by an angry master in order to convince the animal to be silent.

As they moved on, carefully, quietly, a few lights flickered to life from the surrounding windows. A candle here, or a poker at a fireplace there, caused a faint orange illumination, partially startling the spies as they crept around the edge of town.

***

"Good morning, Miss," Andris said, peering from his bed to the open door of Joanne's chamber. He sat up, sliding his legs over the side and placing his feet on the floor as he wiped the sleep from his eyes. "I apologise. I wasn't expecting you to be awake so early."

"It's all right, Andris," she told him. "I didn't sleep very well after what happened last night at dinner. I wanted to talk to you."

"Of course, Miss." He rose to his feet, his long nightshirt dropping to his knees and his bed trousers ruffling around his ankles.

"They look too long for you," she commented.

"Miss?" The man was still half asleep. He followed her eyes to his feet and realised what she meant. "It's the way I prefer them, Miss. No one sees how I sleep."

"Come into my room," she instructed him.

"Miss, I thought we..." He lowered his head ashamedly.

"I have seats to sit in," she told him. "Either that, or I sit on your bed or you make me stand here."

"Your chamber it is, Miss." He walked towards her.

Joanne hurried back inside and directed him with a gesture to a seat by the door. He waited for her to sit in one at the base of her bed before lowering himself upon the cushion.

"What would you like to discuss, Miss?"

"I want to know what you do about the manservants," she told him. "I want to know how you came to be here. They slaughtered all the males in my village. None are here as slaves. As far as I know, there were no men on board that ship who were captives."

***

The nine spies came to the first warehouse, the furthest from the wharves where the black ship sat. They huddled against the giant, grey, weatherworn structure, keeping out of view.

It sat upon wooden pillars, elevated off the ground. The group moved to underneath the building, searching for a way in.

Tomas knew they wouldn't find an entry here and signalled for them to move on towards the east, to make their way to the next building.

They crossed the ground beneath the first structure and paused between the two warehouses. They stood in a gap not much wider than a man's shoulder width.

Tomas peered up into the gap, moving his eyes from the front of the structures facing the town to the rear that faced an open plain.

High on the walls, dotted at intervals along the length of the warehouses, were six square windows.

Ventilation hatches.

***

"All the men on that ship are slaves," Andris told the girl. He looked uncomfortable sitting upon the soft cushioned chair that was intended for the female inhabitants of the castle. "All the men in this village are slaves."

"I don't understand." Joanne creased her forehead. "They carry swords and whips. What they did to us on that ship. They captured us and tortured us. How can they be slaves?"

"They do as she commands, Miss." His eyes showed concern, worry. "I shouldn't be talking about this."

"Where do the men come from, Andris?"

"Here," he replied. "We are all from here."

***

"Go to the next building," Tomas instructed David and Oliver. "Climb the walls, quietly, by pressing with your legs against one and your back against the other. Do you understand?"

"Yes," Oliver replied. "That's easy."

"Good," Tomas said. "Get to the top and see what's inside by looking through the hatches near the top. You may need to stay up there for a while to wait for the light. Can you do it?"

David nodded.

"We'll do our best," he replied.

"That's all I ask." Tomas smiled.

The men moved off as he turned to the Erilian women.

"We heard," Karlena informed him.

"Good," he replied. "Split yourselves into two groups. Meet back here as soon as you are sure of what's inside."

The four Erilian warriors disappeared into the shadows beneath the warehouses.

"What about us?" Simon asked, crouching beside Emily.

"Emily will climb with me," Tomas told him. "You will keep watch. Do what you must to keep our location safe. If you think we are about to be discovered, signal us, and get our attention."

"Understood," Simon replied, thankful that they did not require him to climb the walls.

"Are you able to do this?" he asked Emily.

"We keep quiet?" she asked.

He nodded.

"We don't make a sound?"

He looked at her curiously.

"I still think I can beat you to the top," she said, pushing her back against the western wall and pushing her legs against the eastern. Before Tomas realised, she was already several feet off the ground.

"She's one amazing woman that you've got there, Tomas," Simon said admiringly as he watched her climb.

"I heard that," she whispered back down to him. "And avert your eyes."

Tomas shook his head and smiled at Simon as he climbed after her.

***

"You're from here?"

"We were born here," he replied, lowering his head. "We are here for one reason. To serve the Sovereign."

"I don't understand." She shook her head.

"The Green Mistress killed my mother when she first claimed this place, Blackrock Haven, as her own. Until then, we were a port town with many anglers and farmers." Andris moved his eyes across the white rugs on the floor and to Joanne's feet curled up on the cushion beneath her.

"She killed all the women and some men in an open display of power. I was only a small child, maybe two or three, but I remember it so clearly. We gathered where the markets are now. She lined up some important men of the community, one of them the noble who once lived in this castle. One by one, she did to them what you saw her do to that man in the throne room.

"The other men of the village swore their allegiance to her and have served her ever since. The children, myself included, were trained for whatever she had in mind for us. My destiny was to always serve you or another like you."

Joanne thought about Andris' words for a moment. She felt sorry for him and for many in his situation. But she couldn't imagine that the scarred man was being held in his position against his will. He seemed to enjoy his role too much, in her opinion.

Then she thought of something else. All the men in her village were killed, but all the women, except for her mother and her sister, were brought here.

"But why did they take the women and the girls?" Joanne asked. "It makes little sense."

"It actually makes perfect sense in how the Sovereign works," he told her. "She sought you out. You and the other potentials were tracked and brought here. The others from your communities will serve in other ways."

"In what ways?" she asked, fearing she already had the answer in her head.

"I don't think you want to know, Miss," Andris replied.

"Tell me," she commanded.

"They are here foremost to pleasure the men," he replied, embarrassed. "They will become fit rewards for dutiful servants."

"And the other reason?" Joanne asked.

"Miss?"

"You said *foremost*," she told him. "That must mean there is one other reason, if not more."

"They are brought here to breed more servants." He frowned.

She closed her eyes.

So, this is the Sovereign's ideal society, she thought. *Slave women who breed servants who attend to potentials and Mistresses.*

Keeping her eyes closed as she tried to comprehend what she had just been told, she took a deep breath and composed herself, suppressing her anger and sadness.

"Where are the children of these types of... procreation?" she asked.

"She keeps them with their mothers until they no longer suckle," he replied. "She then usually sends them to live with their fathers where they are raised and educated in the service they will provide to the Sovereign."

Her memory raced back to when she had first arrived at the port, when she and the other girls were taken from the ship and onto the wharf. Every face she saw belonged to a man. She had no recollection of seeing any women in the town until she ran into the Green Mistress.

"And the mothers?" She opened her eyes and looked at him. Her eyes felt hot with anger.

He must have seen something more, she surmised, as he gasped in fear and sat up straight with his body pushing into the back of his seat.

"Where are they kept?"

***

Sitting at the top of the warehouse wall, Tomas peered through the dark space inside the hatches of the western warehouse. The sun was sending her light across the sky, but the forms inside were still too dark to discern.

A chill breeze funnelled through the narrow gap between the buildings, causing his skin to form goose bumps all over. His hood still pulled over his head, he wrapped his cloak around his chest as best as he could as he looked to Emily, facing towards him.

"Emily," he whispered, noticing that she was deep in thought, peering into the dark portal beside his head.

"I can't see anything yet," she told him.

"Are you cold?" he asked her. "Are you all right?"

She faced him and smiled, feeling invigorated.

"I'm fine, Tomas," she replied. "There are people in this one."

She tilted her head towards the nearest window.

"How do you know?"

"I can hear some murmurings," she told him. "Some are crying. I think there may be children inside."

"We will need to free them," he said.

"Can you hear anything coming from that hatch?"

"No," he replied. "I think it might be straw and feed. It smells like a stable, but without the manure."

She smiled again, cocking her head towards the ventilation hatch beside her.

"Mama," a soft voice called from the darkness.

Her smile turned quickly into pursed lips.

"There *are* young children inside," she said, a tear in her eye. "One is calling for her mother."

Twenty-Two

There was some movement on the docks as several men made their way to the market area near the wharf. Here they shovelled snow away from the stalls and off the surface of the wooden walkways. Others gathered by the docks before moving towards the warehouses at the far end of town.

"There are some men on the ground," Jeremy said to the men beside him as he panned his spyglass across the township. "I don't see our people anywhere."

The sun had crept above the horizon but, covered by thick clouds that stretched as far as the eye could see from the east to the west. The land below was still dark but discernible.

"Where are they going?" Baldwyn asked, lying in the snow to his captain's right, pointing to the men approaching the warehouses.

"One of them is moving to the right," Jeremy replied after moving his telescope to watch them. "I think the others are going to the left."

He moved his spyglass to the man on the right.

The man, a thin individual, walked to the farthest warehouse on the right, the closest to the water's edge.

Jeremy moved the lens to the others, who were continuing along a road to the left. Thick snow covered the ground, making it difficult to determine alley ways, access lanes and yards from this distance.

The five men Jeremy watched must have had a better sense of their town and its physical organisation. They seemed to follow a particular route past the enormous doors of the other warehouses towards the structure to the far left.

Moving his telescope to the right again, Jeremy saw the lone man sitting upon a platform in front of the warehouse near the water, staring out towards the sea as if in deep thought.

Back to the others, he saw they had reached the far warehouse to the left and were opening the doors.

Jeremy thought he saw something as he moved the spyglass into place to watch the men. As they disappeared inside, he scanned the thin area between the warehouses.

"I found them," he told the others. "Two of them, anyway. They're between the warehouses, high off the ground. Almost near the top. One woman, one man."

"Who?" Jeff asked.

"I'm not sure," the captain replied. "They're too far to see that clearly."

"I wonder why they're up there," Baldwyn said as he rubbed his thigh.

***

"Breakfast time ladies," a voice boomed from inside the warehouse.

Tomas moved his head to the side to find the owner, but could see only rows of large box-shaped objects lining the wall on the far side of the room. The man who had spoken was just below his vision.

He signalled for Emily to find him from her position.

She turned her head, craning her neck. Finally, her head stopped moving, and she held her gaze.

The sound of the main doors of the warehouse sliding closed and flint striking flint resonated through the portal, followed by a faint orange glow. A torch had been lit.

Emily held up five fingers. There were five men inside.

Looking past her and into the room through the small ventilation hatch, Tomas saw that the large boxes along the far wall weren't crates as he had first thought. There were bars on the front and people inside.

It was a prison.

He watched as one man, holding a lit torch in one hand and a ring of keys in the other, approached the first prison cell. The flame, held inches away from the bars, let the man see inside.

A young woman cowered against the back wall, crouching with her hands over her face. Even with nowhere to go, she was so desperately trying to hide.

"Ready for breakfast, my love," the man said to her as he reached forward with a key at the ready to unlock the cage.

Tomas felt anger rising. He wanted to leap through the portal and tear the man limb from limb before the key unlocked the door.

The young woman cried uncontrollably. It was clear, to the man from Woodmyst, that this poor girl had been subjected to such treatment for a very long time.

She was broken.

The man entered the cage as the four others gathered around the open door.

Tomas couldn't watch anymore. He turned his face away, keeping his eyes upon Emily, who watched intently.

A deep frown formed and water built in her eyes. He didn't need special abilities to sense her anger.

Hearing the sounds coming from within the building made his stomach tie into a knot. He didn't want to be here any longer.

Tomas touched her ankle with his hand to get her attention. She snapped her face towards him, and her look was of sheer rage. It frightened him a little.

He signalled to her he was about to descend, and she nodded.

Tomas started making his way down, silently, slowly.

Emily took one last look through the ventilation hatch and wiped her eyes before following Tomas back to the ground.

***

"They are moving back to the ground," Jeremy told the others beside him. "Those men are still inside the warehouse. I wonder what's in there."

"What of the lone man to the right?" Jeff reminded his commander.

Jeremy moved the lens quickly into place.

The platform was empty.

"He's gone," Jeremy replied, moving the spyglass in a frantic attempt to find the missing person. He moved the sight along the street back to the black ship, up and down spaces between the many buildings, but could not find the individual from the warehouse anywhere. "I don't see him."

"Perhaps he went inside the warehouse near the water," Jeff suggested.

"Maybe he jumped in and went for a swim," Baldwyn added.

"The door is shut," Jeremy informed them after moving the spyglass back to the warehouse. "If he is in there, then I can't tell."

Baldwyn looked to the sky.

Covered in black clouds, it promised unfriendly weather.

"Even with this mess blocking the sun," he started, "there is too much light for them to make it back to us safely. They're going to need either another blizzard to cover their tracks or a safe place to hole up."

"We had better pray for a blizzard," Jeremy said, lowering the spyglass. "Because, I see little in the way of safe places. More men are filling the streets."

**

Finding Simon crouching on the ground underneath the westernmost warehouse, they approached quietly as the noise of abuse made its way through the floorboards of the structure above them. Simon shook his head as he watched the other two approach.

"I want to kill them all," he told them when they were close to him.

Tomas nodded.

The sound stopped.

"Please be over," Simon whispered.

But it wasn't.

"There are five of them," Emily told him.

"Bastards." Simon frowned, looking to the ground.

"Six," said Karlena as she sneaked to their side. "We could hear this lot from down there. We need to go in there and kill them now, Tomas."

"We can't," he replied. "We have no cover and they will bring everything they have against us. We won't survive."

"But that poor woman," she protested, gesturing to the building above. "Can you not hear this?"

Tomas looked at her sadly. He wanted to end what was happening above them as much as she did.

"We need to free the prisoners," Simon told them. "And we need to do it under the cover of darkness. Then we need to sneak around and knife every bastard in this village while they sleep."

The noise above them stopped again. They didn't need to wait long before it resumed.

Tomas closed his eyes.

Perhaps they wouldn't miss these men. Perhaps he could sneak in and slit their throats with no one noticing.

He wanted so much to.

"You said six." Emily looked at Karlena.

"Yes," she replied. "There are five in here and we found another near the water. David and Oliver are bringing him."

Tomas felt a slight panic attack in his chest.

"What?"

"They captured one?" Simon asked, peering under the other structures towards the east.

"What are they thinking?"

Five forms crept towards them.

"No, no, no, no," Tomas hissed as they drew closer and closer.

David held the captive tightly by the back of the neck. A black leather strap that held his hands together, snaked around his arms and passed over his mouth, holding a cloth inside to prevent sound escaping.

Forcing the man onto his knees, David pushed the captive into the snow, pressing his face against the icy surface. The man didn't protest, complying with the giant's manipulations.

"What do you think you are doing?" Tomas glared at the others. "We can't take prisoners."

"I honestly don't know what we were thinking," Oliver said. "We saw him standing at the edge of the platform and we just felt it was the right thing to do. So we took him and bound him with his own whip."

"If it's any consolation," David put in, "he has been very compliant."

"Consolation?" Tomas raised his eyebrows as he moved his eyes from the two men to the Erilian women. "What are we going to do with him?"

The sounds emitting through the floor boards ceased.

"Shhh." Simon held up a finger to the other eight spies.

Their eyes instinctively moved to the underside of the warehouse as they waited.

It wasn't long before the sounds started again.

Tomas noticed the captive shaking his head from side to side, closing his eyes and shedding a tear.

"They're going to notice him missing when they've finished in there," he said. "If we keep him or kill him, they will come looking for him. We can't let him go, or he'll tell them."

The captive man moved his eyes to Tomas and moaned through his gag, trying to gain the other's attention.

Tomas looked at him, pulling his dagger from his belt. He could see the man was willing to negotiate. Tomas couldn't see any alternative but to kill him and then kill the others inside the warehouse.

What did he have to lose from listening to this man's plea?

"You will speak softly," Tomas commanded him, "or I will knife you so that you experience pain until you bleed out. Understand?"

The man nodded.

He placed his blade against the captive's throat and nodded to David, who still held the man on the ground. David moved the leather lash from the man's lips and pulled the cloth from his mouth.

"Where are all the guards?" Tomas asked.

"At the castle," he replied. "In the servants' quarters just inside the walls."

"What of the men in this village?

"Most live here and work here," he answered. "Many are loyal to serving the Sovereign. Some serve out of fear."

"Fear of what?" Tomas asked.

"Fear of the Mistresses."

"The Mistresses?" Tomas recalled men at the outpost with the beacon tower, that they had burnt to the ground, referring to the Mistress. He assumed they were talking of the white witch. "There is more than one?"

"There are many," he replied. "They reside all over, waiting for something."

"Waiting for what?"

"I don't know," he told Tomas. "I really don't. But they are every-where and just like the one here, they have servants who are loyal and others who serve out of fear."

"You speak of the white witch?" Emily asked him.

"She is here," the man answered. "But she is not the Mistress of these lands. We serve the Green Mistress. Yasmeen Svoboda."

"And which are you?" Tomas questioned.

"I don't understand," he stated, his voice trembling.

"Do you serve out of loyalty or fear?"

The man wept.

"I am always afraid," he blubbered. "I don't want to die. Not the way that she..."

Tomas took pity on the man.

The noise stopped again.

"Gag," Tomas hissed. David immediately shoved the cloth back into the captive's mouth and slid the leather whip back over his lips. He then applied some weight to the back of the man's head, forcing his face into the snow.

The sound of the cage door clunking shut resonated through the floorboards, followed by footfalls that moved towards the main doors of the warehouse above.

The spies listened intently as the large wooden panels slid loudly to the side, allowing the men to exit the building before sliding shut again.

"Refal," one man called. "Refal."

There was no answer. Tomas moved his eyes to those of their captive. The man nodded to him, *yes, he is calling for me.*

"He's probably gone inside for warm cider," another mentioned.

"Let him," the first voice replied. "I'm hungry."

With that, the men dropped from the platform in front of the warehouse and wandered into the village out of view.

Fresh sobs from above them filled their ears.

"Your friends did that." Simon glowered at the man on the ground. "What a great bunch of men."

The captive, Refal, shook his head.

"Gag," Tomas commanded as he pressed the blade against the man's neck.

"Not my friends," Refal told them.

"But they called for you," Akasati said. "They called for you."

"I am their supervisor," he informed them.

"You let them rape women?" Oliver felt his face growing hot.

"She will kill me if I don't," he replied, sobbing. "She may still because I won't do so myself."

"But why?" Karlena asked. "Why would she want you to treat women like this? Is she not a woman herself?"

The man blubbered. He had no answer for her.

"Power," Emily told them. "It's all about power. She controls them through fear. The women are the reward."

"They are more," he finally said. "They bear our sons. That is their purpose."

Tomas absorbed the words. *They bear our sons.*

He thought of something horrific and had to know.

"What of the daughters?"

Refal looked to him, confused.

"What do they do to the girls who are conceived this way?" he elaborated.

"They are killed." He paused as a lump built in his throat. "*We* kill them."

"Like cattle," David said with disgust. "They breed men by bringing in new female stock."

"What happens to the women once they have given birth?" Akasati asked.

"If they are older," he replied, "they are kept until the infant is weaned. Afterwards, they are slaughtered. The younger ones are kept until they reach a certain age or no longer deliver boys. It is, as you say, like cattle.

"I can't do this any longer. This place is driving me mad. You must kill me. Make it quick." He locked his sad eyes with those of Tomas.

"What about the young girls from the ship?" Emily asked him. "Are they in this warehouse, too? Are they subject to abuse also?"

"We are all subject to abuse here, Mistress," he replied.

"I'm not one of your Mistresses," Emily replied angrily.

"My apologies," he said, and lowered his eyes.

"The girls," she reminded him. "Tell me."

"There are girls inside, yes," he answered. "The men have touched them all. We have taken other girls that the Mistresses call the *potentials* to the castle to receive the teachings."

"Teachings?" Akasati asked.

"They are to become Mistresses of the Sovereign also," he replied.

"And have they been…" Simon didn't know how to ask his question, but Refal seemed to know what answer he was seeking.

"There are none that have kept their innocence here," the captive replied. "All, men and women, have had their purity stolen from them. All."

The nine spies stared at the man in disbelief.

How could such a thing exist?

"We have stumbled into the realms of hell," Simon said, falling upon his rump into the snow.

"By the gods!" David shook his head. "What kind of place is this?"

"There are no gods," Tomas told them. "This place is proof of that."

Refal wept, overwhelmed by the guilt of the things he had once done.

"Will you kill me now?" he asked. "Please."

"Other prisoners?" Tomas demanded to know. "Where are they kept?"

"Will you kill me?" Refal asked again.

"Yes," Tomas told him.

The others looked at the man from Woodmyst with worried faces.

"Quickly?" pressed the captive.

"Yes," he replied. "You won't feel a thing. Now tell me. Where are all the other prisoners kept?"

"In this warehouse," he replied. "This one is reserved for the prisoners. The others are full of supplies."

Tomas plunged his blade into Refal's temple, instantly killing the man.

The sudden motion shocked the others.

"He hurt children," Tomas told them, his face turning into a scowl. "They have all hurt children."

Twenty-Three

Standing on a wide balcony that overlooked the port township of Blackrock Haven, the Green Mistress searched from one end to the other for the presence that irritated and penetrated her mind. Someone was down there. Someone that didn't belong.

Snow gently fell over the township as she closed her eyes and tried to focus, to pinpoint exactly where this new aura was located. Something drew her towards the town; but she couldn't define a specific position of the power's source.

She glared across the snow-covered rooftops to the black ship moored to the wharf. The visitor had followed the vessel.

Could it be that the auburn girl's sister had arrived?

She thought so, but there were more with her. Others with power.

Sometimes in the past where her ships had ventured to locations that drew her attention. Places where others with such power lived. Many times, the ships had returned with her potentials. Many times, she had trained the young girls, selecting the best, choosing the most loyal before sending them to their places of service.

The others, the unsuccessful ones, became the prey of the chosen; a chance for the selected ones to exercise their powerful abilities, a chance to prove their loyalty to the Sovereign.

Sumaiyya was one such as this.

She had come to the Green Mistress ten years earlier. The youngest of twelve girls, aged only nine, she showed prowess and loyalty very early on.

Her power had reached its full potential before she turned ten. They held the ceremony to commemorate her transition from Miss to Mistress in the throne room, as per tradition. There, using her abilities, she slaughtered each of the other potentials, breaking bone and snapping sinew until all eleven girls died an agonising death.

Being the youngest of all the Mistresses, the Green Mistress kept her close, positioned in the lands just to the south. It was the intention of Yasmeen Svoboda to protect the White Mistress, but it was, in fact, more or less the other way around.

Sumaiyya had grown into a force to be reckoned with and had become a guardian of the south. Through her influence, her power, she prevented many intruders from making their way to the northern realm. By disguising her abilities as forces of nature, a snowstorm in winter, a brush fire in the warmer seasons, she deterred the northward advances of men and persuaded others to leave their homes and move south.

As she advanced, both in age and power, she also grew upon the Green Mistress' heart. Both women made several visits, finding comfort with one another.

Yasmeen would never allow Sumaiyya to venture any farther from her realm to the south. Sumaiyya didn't intend to leave her Green Mistress and the sincere love they had. Instead, the White Mistress regarded Blackrock Castle as her home and her realm to the south as her duty.

There had never been a more successful transition, the Green Mistress pondered. *Not one other potential had ever demonstrated such power.*

Not until now.

Her mind moved to the Black Miss, Joanne. She contained more energy, more power than Yasmeen had ever seen in all the potentials, in all the Mistresses.

But she has not yet turned, the Green Mistress thought. *Her servant remains an innocent.*

Scanning the township of Blackrock Haven, sensing power emitting from below, Yasmeen Svoboda considered that the younger sister would need to be swayed to fulfil her destiny before the visitor found her, rescued her.

But she cannot be forced, she thought. *She must choose to do so.*

Time was running out.

These others, hiding in the community, emanated strength. Something in her knew that those present were some that escaped her ships. Other potentials that hid from her servants.

Now, they were uniting.

They were finding their power.

Feeding it.

Building it together.

She felt a twinge of fear creep across her heart.

What if they find Joanne before she submits? Yasmeen considered. *What if they unite with her before she gives in to her temptations?*

The Green Mistress understood that the alliance of such power, the union of such abilities could be too much to stand against. Perhaps too much for both her and Sumaiyya to defeat.

She needed to consider her options.

She needed to make a plan.

She turned away from the view, lowering her hood from her head, and entered her bedchamber, closing the door to the balcony behind her. It was a large room with green tapestries decorated with golden floral embroidery hanging from the walls.

At the far end of the room from her, resting with its head against the wall, sat a large four-poster bed. Curled up beneath the thick covers lay Sumaiyya, sleeping soundly.

She stirred awake as the Green Mistress approached the bed, following her with her piercing blue eyes until the other sat on the edge of the bed beside her.

"Good morning, Mistress." The blonde girl smiled.

198 | ROBERT E KREIG

"Good morning, my love." Yasmeen leant in and kissed her on the forehead. "Get dressed. We have much to discuss before breakfast."

***

The gentle snow had fallen thickly, creating a veil of sorts that obscured the surroundings.

"I'm finding it hard to see anything," Jeremy told his two companions. "I hope they're all right."

"Surely," Baldwyn said, "we should have seen a bit more movement down there if they had been found."

"We are dealing with a witch," Jeff reminded him. "Who knows how they think?"

Captain Jeremy Schoenbach felt his chest tighten as he thought about his friends in the town below. Jeff's words pierced him; they were dealing with a witch.

From his experience, the white witch was someone to be feared. She was unpredictable. She was dangerous and his comrades were in a place that sheltered her.

He thought the worst, but hoped for the best.

Silently praying that the spies were lying low in a place that was safe, Jeremy kept moving the glass across the view below them.

"There." Jeff pointed with his gloved hand.

"Where?" Jeremy asked, moving the telescope.

"Left of the warehouses," the other informed him. "A little towards us where the houses cluster."

The captain opened both eyes. He searched for the place that Jeff referred to with the one without the lens.

Nine dark blobs moved slowly along a fence line to the western edge of the village.

Jeremy closed his eye and focused with the other through the spyglass. Finding the place where the moving objects were located, he spotted the spies. Recognising their gait as they moved to the west, he felt relieved and happy that they were alive. Sudden anxiety overwhelmed him when he considered the enemy wasn't too far from them.

He opened his other eye to gauge where all the other people moving about the town were located. He saw most of them congregating near the wharves where the markets were located.

"Please be careful," he whispered as he noticed a man leaving a house near to the nine. The door to the house was on the other side of a building from the spies. The fence that they crouched behind was part of the yard belonging to the structure.

The man from the house moved around towards the back where the spies were located.

Jeremy felt his stomach tighten as he watched the nine disappear behind a smaller structure, possibly a shed or workshop of some kind.

The man continued towards the shed and opened a door at its front.

The captain saw the nine crouching behind the structure to which the man had entered.

"By the gods," Jeremy hissed.

"What is it?" Baldwyn asked.

"They're hiding behind a tool shed or something like it," he explained. "But a man just went inside."

"Can they move?" Jeff asked.

Jeremy opened his other eye and looked to what lay to the west of the nine spies.

There was nothing but open ground for a long distance before they could reach the forest beneath the mountains.

"No," he replied. "They're stuck in the open. Let's just hope no one else comes upon them."

***

David pointed to the shed and then slid a finger along his throat. *Let's kill him.*

Tomas shook his head and pressed a finger to his lips.

No. Shut up and wait.

Some fumbling, bumping and clattering noises emanated from the small timber shed as the man inside searched for something. Eventually, the sound of the door closing and crunching footsteps moving away in the snow urged Tomas to take a peek.

The man, draped in a dark robe, held a long-handled shovel in his hand, using it as a walking staff as he walked back around his house and out of view.

"He's gone," Tomas told them.

"Do we head for the ridge?" Oliver asked.

"We could be spotted and lead them to our location," Simon interjected.

"We should run to the forest," Karlena suggested. "The falling snow will cover our prints and if we are spotted, we can lead our pursuers away from our friends."

"I like that idea." David nodded.

"All right," Tomas agreed. "The forest it is. But remember, those creatures might be in there."

They looked silently at one another for an alternative plan.

"Dead either way," Rhydra said, lifting to her feet and starting towards the plain.

Tomas smiled and waved the others on after her.

The nine started across the open ground, moving as hastily as they could. Tomas peered over his shoulder now and then to see if anyone followed.

It appeared that the men within the town were focusing their attention upon the market area or still in bed, avoiding the cold, miserable day for as long as they could.

***

"What are they doing?" Jeff asked, watching the nine blobs racing across the open ground. "They'll be spotted for sure. They've no cover."

"I don't think they have much of an option," Baldwyn stated. "Where can they hide that the inhabitants of that town don't know where to look?"

Jeremy watched on in silence, focusing his scope on Tomas at the rear of the group. He was consistently checking as he ran. Slowing his pace each time, he looked over his shoulder and, still able to keep up with the others easily, Tomas displayed a level of stamina that Jeremy never knew any to possess.

Not only that. The man placed himself between his friends and the very present danger that threatened them.

Tarkin was right, he thought as he watched the group draw nearer to the tree line.

There was something about this man from Woodmyst.

The first of the spies reached the trees and immediately dropped to the ground, facing the village. They waited until all positioned themselves side by side on the ground.

"They made the trees," Jeremy informed the others.

"I don't see any pursuing," Jeff said, watching the village.

"That doesn't mean they weren't seen," Jeremy replied. "Keep watching. We need to be sure."

***

"Now what?" Emily asked, huffing.

"We wait," Tomas told her. "We look to see if they followed us. They could be preparing horses right now."

"How long do we wait?" she asked.

"Perhaps an hour," he told her. "We might move a little more into the woods. Use the trees for cover but stay where we can still see if any approach from the town." He then said to all gathered, "One at a time. Move to a more secure location."

"I'll go first," Simon volunteered. "I think I see such a spot from here."

Tomas nodded.

Within moments, Simon had disappeared into the snow speckled shrubbery behind them.

Tomas ordered the women to go next, followed by Oliver and then David.

He scanned the plain carefully before crawling backwards and vanishing beneath the pines.

***

"They've gone," Jeremy said. "They've vanished into the forest."

"I hope they're all right," Baldwyn said, keeping his eyes on the streets of the town.

"Now what?" Jeff asked.

"We watch," Jeremy told him. "I don't intend to leave this spot until our friends are safely back at the campsite."

"Fair call, Captain." Baldwyn rubbed his leg again.

"I am wondering if you should be out here, though," Jeremy said to him, noticing the attention he gave to his injured thigh.

"It's just itching," he admitted. "I'm all right, Captain."

Jeremy nodded, folding his spyglass, opting to watch the town with both eyes.

"I'll take your word for it," he replied. "Keep watching.

"Aye, Captain," the two crewmen replied.

Twenty-Four

Navigating through the trees, the nine spies made their way through the forest towards the rise to the south of them. They had moved deeper into the woods, keeping clear from the view of anyone in the township.

Tomas believed they had gone unnoticed as they had waited for nearly an hour by his measure. The sun had climbed high in the sky, a golden ring glowing through the thick, dark haze above them. The snow continued to fall quickly and thickly onto the plain just beyond their view.

They felt relieved to have the trees to provide some shelter from the weather as they moved through the undergrowth. The branches of the pines were so thickly entangled in places that the ground almost appeared dry, allowing the grass to grow. It was a welcome sight after riding through the blizzard during the previous day.

As they arrived at the rise in the ground, the trees thinned and the snow cover on the ground became thick. With less shrubbery and shelter around them, they became more exposed to any eyes that looked their way.

Tomas hoped the nine members of the group were far enough away from the town, and the snow was falling too thickly for anyone to notice them.

"We need to move quickly," he called to the others as he followed at the rear of the pack.

Clambering up the steep incline using hands and feet, the nine resembled spiders more than humans as they neared the peak. It was steep, closer to the mountains and higher at the crest.

Finally, on the other side, the group hastily made their way back to the forest floor; all except Tomas and Emily. She had waited for him at the top. He sidled up to her and looked back towards the village far below them.

"Do you see anything?" she asked him.

"No," he said, scanning the plain between the town and the edge of the forest. He glanced over his shoulder to see the rest of the group a fair distance down the southern side of the slope. Descending, for some, proved far too much fun as he watched David, pulling his cloak tightly between his legs and sliding on his back, passing Oliver and the Erilian women.

Emily started after them, but suddenly, Tomas pulled her close to him and stole a kiss. She smiled, then gave him another.

With that, she dropped away, using David's technique of sliding down the slope on her back. She was faster than the giant bald man, almost catching up to Oliver before Tomas started his descent, choosing the slower option of using his legs.

Before long, the spies were at the bottom of the ridge, making their way towards the coast.

Their camp was farther along the base of the elevation, nearer to the water than it was to the forest.

The group moved at a brisk walking speed, conserving what energy they had left. The camp was within view as they left the cover of the trees and entered the open ground of the valley.

Emily and Erilian women paused in their tracks and faced the south. Their eyes moved over the far end of the forest as if something was there, just out of view.

"What is it?" Tomas asked, the men now looking in the same direction.

"They have followed us," Emily told him.

"The creatures?"

She nodded.

"They don't hunt us," Akasati continued. "They are just following. They are expecting to feed."

"I don't understand," David said, dropping his hood from his head and rubbing his scalp.

His eyes moved along the edge of the trees carefully.

"They are too far to see," Oliver told him. "You would need the eyes of a hawk."

"They see us," Rhydra informed them.

"Well," Simon said with a hint of sarcasm. "That makes it all right, then."

"They won't attack," Emily stated. "Their stomachs are full. They expect food wherever we are. I'm not sure how to explain it. It's a feeling that I get. It's not words. I just know."

The Erilian warriors nodded. Emily's description of the transfer between the creatures and the five women seemed apt.

"We supply food for them," Tomas suggested.

"Yes," she replied.

"We're not *feeding* them," Oliver said.

"We did," Tomas told him as he continued towards the camp. "We gave them a mighty feast after our last battle. They probably expect something like that to happen again."

"Well then," David said, and smiled. "They should climb the ridge and wait on the other side. Once we finish with the town over there, they'll be eating like kings."

They approached the camp, seeing a small fire burning on the western side of the tents. The dull day and constant falling snow masked the rising smoke.

Some men noticed their approach and ran towards them eagerly.

"Are you all right?" one called.

"What did you see?" asked another.

Tomas held his hands up, signalling them to stand down.

"Where is Jeremy?" he asked them.

"He is on the ridge watching the town," a man told him.

"Get him," Tomas instructed the man. "We need to make plans."

The crewman ran towards the ridge where Jeremy and the other two men still waited and watched.

"Now what?" Simon asked.

"Now," Tomas told him, "I'm going to sit by the fire and request someone to make me a cup of tea."

***

Sitting in her position closest to the throne on the left side of the room, Joanne stared at the stone floor between her and the occupant of the chair across from her. With her hood pulled low over her head, she wasn't able to see the form of the White Mistress, and she didn't intend to.

With Andris by her side, and the ever-present feeling of fear emitting from him, she felt an uneasiness sweeping over her. It wasn't a feeling of her own. It was coming from those around her.

They were all afraid.

But of what?

She moved her gaze to Tricia, draped in her scarlet cloak with her hood over her head. They were all dressed so.

Andris had told her to dress accordingly at the request of the Green Mistress. It had him concerned. Such attire and such requests usually applied to special events, sacred occasions.

Tricia was watching her. As soon as their eyes met, the other looked away, fearfully.

Joanne furrowed her brow.

They were afraid of her.

Moving her eyes, she locked with the piercing blue stare of the White Mistress and held her gaze.

Sumaiyya kept her eyes on the young girl for a long time before she, too, blinked and looked away.

Moving her eyes back to the stone floor, Joanne didn't know whether to feel glad that she scared the White Mistress or saddened that the other girls felt afraid of her as well.

That hurt her deeply. She had shared a cell with them and held them through the darkest time of their lives. And now, they feared her.

She felt so alone.

She felt so unloved.

She felt so unwanted.

Footfalls of boots on the stone floor gripped her attention.

The White Mistress rose to her feet. The other girls instantly followed suit as the Green Mistress moved briskly, gracefully through the centre of the room and up the platform to her throne. Once seated, the others returned to their cushioned chairs and faced her.

A thick silence fell over the room as she carefully looked at each one of them.

"It seems fitting," she said, "as I look over my girls, to see both white and black at the head." She gestured to Sumaiyya and Joanne with her left, then right hand.

"Two contrasting tones," she continued. "Two contrasting personalities. One cannot exist without the other. Together, they are strong."

Joanne moved her eyes to the White Mistress and measured her. There was indeed something great about the woman, she could tell. And she surmised, the other sensed something similar in her.

Perhaps they would be a formidable force if they were to unite. Perhaps they might rule the world and enslave every man that lived under the sun and the moon.

But Joanne despised her.

Her bond with her sister, Emily, was far too strong to discard.

"That's how we will progress," the Green Mistress continued. "Together.

"There will be no more bickering. There will be no more use of words of abilities against one another. We reserve those things for our enemies."

She is my enemy, Joanne thought.

"We are sisters. We are a family." The woman moved her eyes from Sumaiyya to Emily.

The White Mistress rose to her feet. Not knowing what else to do, Joanne did the same.

"Yes, Mistress." Sumaiyya bowed. Joanne repeated the words and gesture.

Both returned to their seat. The younger girl didn't feel that the animosity had depleted at all. In fact, she sensed more rage from the White Mistress than she had felt before.

"With that out of the way," the Green Mistress said, smiling, "I think it's time to congratulate one of the girls for progressing one step closer to her destiny with the Sovereign."

The girls moved their eyes to one another, wondering what the woman on the throne meant. Even the White Mistress seemed perplexed by the words.

"Stand, Scarlet Miss," the Green Mistress commanded.

The girl seated next to Sumaiyya reluctantly rose to her feet. She bowed her head and wrung her hands nervously in front of her.

"There's nothing to be ashamed of." The woman in green grinned. "You only did what is natural. You showed your place of dominance over a weaker species. Command your servant to stand before me."

Tricia looked to the Green Mistress in confusion.

"He is your servant," she said. "Command him to stand before me."

She moved her eyes to the man standing beside her chair.

"Donald," she squeaked, fear and embarrassment tightening her throat.

"Yes, Miss," he replied.

"Stand before the Green Mistress." She pointed towards the ground at the base of the throne's platform.

"Yes, Miss," Donald replied, stepping forward, passing the girl and moving along the centre of the room.

Before he had made two full strides past Tricia, he fell in a crumpled heap. His bones crunched and snapped loudly as he screamed in agony.

Joanne moved her eyes from the horrific, sickening scene to the woman in green. She sat regally upon the throne, extending a taut fist, twisting her arm as Donald writhed on the floor.

Blood spat from the young man's lips as his ribs imploded, penetrating his organs. Joanne moved her gaze to Sumaiyya, who stared at the sight with a wide grin.

The girls seated around the room cried as the screaming continued. Some looked away, others simply couldn't because of shock.

Joanne noticed Tricia crying uncontrollably and shrieking his name over and over. Her heart broken; her dreams shattered as he was slowly being tortured to death before her eyes.

She noticed from the corner of her eye that Andris' hand shook as the event unfolded upon the floor. This could be him suffering on the stones if she ever gave in to her temptations.

Was this punishment? Joanne thought as she looked from Tricia to the broken mess that screamed before her.

And just who was the punishment for?

Him for touching her?

Her for giving into her desires?

Joanne looked to the Green Mistress, who continued to extend her fist, playing with her victim.

You did this to her.

You made her have these cravings.

This was by your design.

Joanne stood up.

All eyes fell upon her, surprised and in awe.

She locked eyes on poor Donald and made a fist of her own.

The poor man's skull caved in with a loud, moist crunch.

His body fell slump to the floor, lifeless.

The Green Mistress stared at her, silent.

It seemed to last for an eternity until the woman in green rose to her feet and walked out of the room. Her footfalls grew fainter until she reached the stairs to which she ascended, disappearing into her chambers.

Tricia stood blubbering in front of her chair, too upset to move, not knowing what else to do.

Sumaiyya gave Joanne one last glance, fear filling her blue eyes, before racing after the Green Mistress.

"What did you do?" Andris breathed quietly.

"It will be fine," she told him. She walked across the room, past the mess that once was Donald, and over to Tricia, her friend from her home. Wrapping both arms around her, she held her tightly.

"I'm so sorry, Tricia," Joanne whispered. "I'm so sorry."

One by one, the other five girls approached and placed their arms around the two.

It wasn't what the Green Mistress had intended with her words, but unity was arising.

They were sisters.

Twenty-Five

Standing on the deck of the black ship, Khabar crossed his arms and looked towards the village, searching.

"Where is Refal?" he called to other men working on minor maintenance nearby.

One of them, a man who had visited the warehouse earlier, stopped cleaning the rails along the side of the ship and looked over to the scarred commander.

"He was with us this morning," the man told him.

"Where?"

"The warehouse. Well," the man corrected himself, "five of us went to the warehouse to, you know. Refal went to the one near the water to wait for us."

"And where is he now?"

"I don't know," he replied. "He was there when we went in. He was gone when we came out. We thought that he might have gone for some hot cider."

"Maybe he went for a cup of tea instead," Khabar said sarcastically. "Did you bother to look for him?"

"No." The other stood up and dropped his rag to the deck. "I came straight here to get to work."

"Perhaps you should look for him," the scarred man growled as he closed the distance between the man and himself. "After all, he is your supervisor and he should be supervising. It's past midday, and he hasn't checked in with me since last night. Can you understand why I'm a tad cranky?"

"Yes sir," the man replied, quickly moving to the gangplank and alighting from the ship.

As he watched the man run along the wharf towards the market, Khabar thought the worst concerning Refal.

He wondered if the White Mistress' pursuers had finally arrived. Perhaps they were hiding in the village somewhere with their eyes upon him at that very moment.

Scanning the village, he allowed his paranoia to get the better of him. Searching for any unfamiliar faces amongst the crowd, he realised his efforts were pointless as he saw only cloaked figures with hoods over their heads.

He hoped Refal was still breathing. Refal had been displaying some questionable behaviour of late. His devotion towards the Sovereign seemed to wane. Things that he said, questions that he asked, made the scarred man wonder if Refal was loyal any longer.

Perhaps the skinny man had practised his skills with his whip.

Perhaps he had taken his frustrations out on a captive in the warehouse.

Khabar hoped something like that was keeping Refal from his duty. He hoped the man was still breathing so he could beat the living snot out of him when he returned.

He hoped he wasn't dead.

Even if the White Mistress' pursuers weren't here, there was the possibility that the White Mistress may have had her way with him and snuffed him when she was done. She was known to have done it before.

Seeing what she had done to the dockhand when she first arrived in town didn't allow for him to second guess what she might do, simply because she felt like it.

She frightened him. Even more so than the Green Mistress.

She was unpredictable, unstable.

There was every bit of a chance that she could have done something to Refal.

He peered across the township towards the castle on the hill. Thick snow fell over the rooftops, creating a hazy curtain between the large stone structure and the place where he stood.

I bet you are warm in there, you bitch.

His mind pictured the woman in white sitting by a large fire.

If you have hurt Refal...

He took a deep breath.

What could he do?

He was a mere man. She was powerful.

Not only that, there was the Green Mistress to contend with, and her power surpassed that of Sumaiyya.

And now, they had seven little witches that surely would know what they were by now.

They hated him for what he had done to them.

They didn't understand the reasoning behind his actions.

They didn't understand that he did it to help them fulfil their destiny.

They didn't understand that it was the will of the Sovereign. Not yet.

If they did, they would continue to despise him. Sumaiyya's reaction towards him was proof of that.

She would kill him if she the Sovereign gave permission to do so.

Perhaps she should, he thought.

He knew he deserved it.

It was the only way.

He wouldn't stop.

He couldn't stop.

What once was an action that was performed out of fear had become an addiction. Inside, it ate away at him, festered and grew like an organism. An entity with its own will.

Yes, he deserved to die.

Perhaps they all did.

Even Refal.

Turning away from the scenery, he moved back to his quarters below the upper deck.

He desperately needed a drink.

***

"How did she do that?" Sumaiyya asked, standing near the door to the Green Mistress' chamber.

"I don't know," the other replied, pacing before the large windows that ran along the length of the balcony outside.

"She is just a child!" Sumaiyya moved into the room towards a deep-cushioned chair. "She hasn't even started her training."

"I couldn't stop her," the woman in green continued. "She just broke through. She just broke through."

"How?" the other questioned. "How has she gained such strength?"

The Green Mistress shook her head as she paced, lowering her hood from her dark red hair.

"She has tapped into something," she said. "She has found some source. But what?"

"She detests me," the White Mistress told the other. "Loathes me. Could this be her source?"

"Perhaps." She stopped pacing and looked at the woman in white. "No. She showed ability before you arrived."

"But only slightly," Sumaiyya stated. "Remember what happened at the dinner table. That was because of me. She was acting out of her anger towards me."

"You may have been the spark, my love." The Green Mistress strode across the room. She placed her long hands upon the blonde girl's face as she touched foreheads with her. "You were not the foundation. Her power is within her. Her strength comes from somewhere else. Otherwise, you would be responsible for what just occurred."

"Her sister," Sumaiyya said. "She knows about her sister."

The Green Mistress pulled away. That was it. The auburn girl who had escaped.

"She will be coming." The woman in green faced the window. "We need to get you to safety."

"They are still downstairs," Sumaiyya told her. "The potentials. They'll destroy us. They'll destroy me."

Yasmeen Svoboda, the Green Mistress, inhaled a long breath as she watched the snow fall outside her window.

"There is a passage," she told the girl. "It leads from the privy and down a steep stair, to a tunnel deep under the castle. You can follow the tunnel to the stables. Take some guards. Take the horses and flee."

"Me?" Sumaiyya shook her head. "What about you? You will come with me?"

"No," Yasmeen replied, crossing the floor to the woman in white again. She wrapped her arms around Sumaiyya. "I must remain. I will keep them occupied while you make your escape. You are important. More important than me." She touched the blonde woman's belly.

"I don't want to leave you." Sumaiyya sobbed. "I want you to come with me. Don't make me leave you."

"I command it," the Green Mistress whispered.

***

"What do we do now?" asked a girl dressed in white. The garments were like those worn by the White Mistress, but the face was not the same. She had brown eyes and bronze skin. She had not come from the same village as Joanne and Tricia. None of the others had.

"We can't stay here," the jade girl told them, turning her focus to Joanne. "The Green Mistress will surely make it hard for you now."

"If she doesn't try to kill you," the girl in gold put in.

"We don't even know each other's names," the lilac girl stated.

"We don't have time for names," Tricia sniffled, her eyes still locked on the remains of her servant resting upon the floor.

"The Scarlet Miss is right. We know each other by the title given to us," Joanne told them.

"Our colours are our names until we are truly free. Scarlet, White, Gold, Lilac, Olive, Jade and Black."

"She is no longer a *Miss*," Andris informed them, his head bowed.

Joanne faced him. "What was that?"

"The Scarlet Miss is now a Mistress," he told her. "Forgive me for speaking out of place."

"Speak, Andris," she told him. "You are not my slave. In case you haven't noticed, things have changed recently. Now tell me, what do you mean by *she is a Mistress?*"

Andris nodded and lifted his eyes hesitantly to meet those of the girl dressed in black.

"After giving in to her desires," he said, "this ritual is performed to advance her to the same status of the other Mistresses."

"The ritual was incomplete," said another man standing against the wall. "The Scarlet Miss was meant to engage in the ritual. She was meant to perform the kill. But you intervened, Black Miss. You broke the ritual. As far as I know, that has never been done before."

"It hasn't," Andris told them. "This was the first time another potential has ever stepped in. What's more significant, and what frightens me, is that you have not given into your temptations. This kind of magic is reserved only for those who have.

"You shouldn't be able to do what you can do, Miss." He lowered his eyes to the floor. "Not yet."

She moved her eyes through the throne room and stopped when she saw two guards standing on either side of the arch that led to the foyer.

"I forgot about them," she said to the other girls.

They all turned to face the two darkly clad men armed with swords sheathed upon their hips.

"What do we do?" the jade girl asked, her voice shaking with fear.

"I don't know," Joanne replied.

Andris moved his eyes from the girls gathered across the room from him to the two guards.

"Where do your loyalties lie?" he asked them, stepping forward.

"We serve the Green Mistress," one of them answered.

"Do you serve out of devotion," he queried, "or fear?"

"It matters not," the guard replied. "We serve her."

"Will you let the potentials pass?" he asked.

"The Mistress has not commanded us to bring harm to them," the guard replied.

"Not yet," Andris said to Joanne. "But she will."

"You should kill them," said one of the other servants hastily. The lilac girl shot him a quick glare, silently reprimanding him for the outburst. "My apologies, Miss."

She breathed a sigh.

"You're not my slave," she told him. "You're free to speak your mind. But we won't be killing them. Will we?"

She looked at Joanne, as did the others. They were waiting for her to come up with a plan and tell them what to do next.

"No," she replied. "Of course not. We should bind them or lock them away somewhere."

"The guardhouses have cells where they keep prisoners for tribunal," said the lilac girl's servant.

"Tribunal?" Tricia asked, still sobbing.

"What happened in here the other day to that man who was caught stealing from the supplies," Andris told her.

"Are there any prisoners in there now?" asked the lilac girl.

"I don't know, Miss," the servant replied.

Lilac turned to the guards. "Are there prisoners in the cells?"

"No," the other guard answered. The first guard shot him a look of contention. "What?" the second guard asked him.

"We serve the Green Mistress," the first guard reminded the other.

"Yeah," the second replied. "Well, she isn't here right now and there are seven of them that could make me into that." He pointed to Donald's remains on the floor.

The gesture set Tricia into a sobbing fit again.

As the other girls consoled her, Joanne stepped forward to address the two guards.

"I can manage that on my own, gentlemen," she said with a bitter voice like ice. "And I will if you do not lay your weapons on the ground."

The second guard complied immediately, unbuckling his sheath and lowering it onto the stone floor. The first guard shook his head before following suit.

"What do you have planned?" asked the girl in white.

"We remove all the guards from the house and place them in the cells," she replied.

"And then?" Andris questioned.

"And then," she replied, "I intend to take this castle from the Green Mistress and her white lap dog."

Twenty-Six

"We sneak over the ridge after nightfall," Tomas told the group gathered by the fire. "Baldwyn and Jeff will remain behind with the horses, but ready to go at a moment's notice." He looked at the two men.

"Aye," Baldwyn replied.

"We go from house to house," Tomas said. "Quietly. And we take out as many as we can before we they discover us.

"Meanwhile, you lot..." he pointed to the women gathered about, "will return to that warehouse and free all the prisoners. Tell them they will need to fight their way out and get themselves to the ship."

"They aren't warriors," one man stated. "Some of them may have never used a blade for anything but preparing food before."

"Then they can pretend that every man that they come across is a big fish," Akasati suggested. "And they can gut the bastards where they stand."

Some chuckled quietly at her comment.

"It doesn't matter what they can or can't do," Tomas continued. "Their only chance to survive is to fight. They can use knives, swords, wooden planks or stones for all I care. They will need to fight and stick together. But they must get to that ship.

"Once there, they take it over and defend it. There are more cages in that warehouse than there are men on that ship, even with a full crew."

"I'm certain there are more prisoners than cages also," Emily said. "And there are children. They will fight hard to protect their children."

"And we will fight with them," Karlena put in.

"No," Tomas told her. "Once you have freed the prisoners and instructed them of where they are to go, you are all to head for that castle. Your next task is to find those girls and bring them back to the ship."

Karlena nodded.

"And what of you?" Sharek questioned.

"With luck, we will continue with our task of wiping out the inhabitants of that wretched town," he replied. "When we see the prisoners free of the warehouse; David, Oliver, Simon and I will join you. We will be your support at the castle."

"Then we go to the ship?" Jeremy asked.

"Not quite," Tomas answered. "The prisoners don't know who we are. You could be more men from the village as far as they know.

"You wait until they take the ship. Once you are sure they are all there, you move to the wharf and defend the captives from there. No one, except the captives, goes aboard that ship until we have all returned."

"Understood," Jeremy replied.

"If we make it through," Tomas said, "we will raid the other warehouses and take what we need for our journey home. Then we will burn the warehouses and the village to the ground. That will be your signal to bring the horses." He pointed to Baldwyn and Jeff.

"If not, and they pursue us instead, the warehouses won't be on fire and that will be a signal for you two to lose the other horses and run for your lives.

"Your task, gentlemen," he told the two men who were to stay back, "is to spread the word of what you know is occurring here. Let's hope the message will get to someone with a sizable force. Maybe a navy or army can rid us of this wickedness."

Jeff nodded silently, hoping that Tomas' plan worked.

"We leave as soon as it is dark," the man from Woodmyst said.

***

Darkness enveloped her so thickly it almost felt tangible, pressing against her flesh and running its substance through her hair. The only light to guide her was from the flickering flames of two torches being held by the guards she had taken from the Green Mistress' chamber.

The sound of slow dripping moisture reverberated throughout the long tunnel that stretched on forever underneath the castle grounds. It must be a primary conduit where the smaller cavities of the privies met together, as all she could smell was shit and piss.

She hoisted her garments so that they didn't touch the filthy surface beneath her as she and the two guards made their way from the stairs they had descended, to the far end of the passage that was beyond their view.

Their footfalls echoed along the tube loudly. Sometimes a hard tap reverberated as their boots touched stone, at other times it sounded moist with a tone of suction as they walked over areas less solid.

Sumaiyya felt the urge to throw up, tasting bile once or twice as they progressed through the dark passage.

Upon reaching the end, the soldiers flashed their torches around to find a way out.

There was a drain at the base of the tunnel that rose in an arch to knee height, covered with thin iron bars.

That couldn't be the way out, she thought.

Besides being too small for her to fit through, grit and slime covered the bars and there was no way that her beloved Mistress would want her to go through there.

"Over here, Mistress," a guard called. He held his light to an iron ladder that extended from the wall to a grate far above.

"You go first," she commanded the man. "You follow me," she told the other. "Leave the torches."

Hand over hand, rung by rung, they climbed.

The ladder rattled in places and clanged loudly when they tried to move with haste.

"Slowly," she whispered to them. "We don't want to draw attention."

Carefully, they rose towards the grate far above.

It was slow going.

It was laborious work.

But they got there.

Arriving at the top, the guard lifted the grate as quietly as he could. He surveyed the land about and noticed they were outside the castle grounds, just east beyond the giant walls that surrounded the compound.

To the east stood another building with large doors.

The stables.

He slid the grate silently onto the snow nearby and lifted himself from the passage. Reaching back into the dark space, he helped Sumaiyya from the hole.

She lifted herself, stretching her arms above her head as she peered around her. Recognising the stables, she started down a slight embankment towards them.

"Mistress, wait," said the first guard in a hoarse whisper as the other clambered out of the drain.

She turned to face him, annoyed.

"Please wait for us," he told her. "You could be in danger out here and we have been placed in your service. Let us go first to ensure your safety."

Knowing the Green Mistress had commanded them to guard her, and that they had her wellbeing in mind, she still couldn't help feeling slightly frustrated by the overprotective sentiment.

She could take care of herself, to destroy men at a whim.

But it's not the men you need to fear.

She pursed her lips.

"All right." She submitted to the man's words. "Run along and see if it's safe for me to follow."

"Yes, Mistress," he replied, passing by her and heading for the open doors of the stables.

***

The cell door made a loud metallic ring as it slammed shut on the guards. They had all surrendered without hesitation, understanding what power the Black Miss possessed. The word of her abilities had spread swiftly throughout the men in service to Castle Blackrock.

The girls and their servants stood near to the servants' quarters outside the giant stone building that was the castle. The snow continued to fall, and the air was chilly around them.

"That's all of them?" Tricia, the Scarlet Miss, asked.

"No," said the servant to the girl in jade. "She has her own guards posted throughout her quarters. Between the top of those stairs and her chambers, there could be a dozen guards."

"We could burn them out," the olive girl suggested.

"We need to be sure," Joanne told them. "If we set fire to the castle, they could escape and we won't know until they were far away. We need to see both the Green and White Mistresses die with our own eyes."

"They may have already escaped," one of the other servants said. "None of us has had eyes on them since the Green Mistress stormed out of the throne room."

"I think we need to go inside," the lilac girl announced. "I'm freezing."

"She may be waiting for us," the girl in white said.

Joanne thought about that.

It was true that the two Mistresses had more than enough time to manoeuvre themselves to a more suitable location. The woman in green knew her home well and may have positioned herself in a place to trap the girls.

"At least one of them is inside," Joanne told them.

"How do you know?" Andris asked her.

"I know," she replied, sure that she was right.

"There is someone in there," the girl in gold agreed. "Someone with power."

"It's the Green Mistress," Joanne told her.

"What about the White Mistress?" asked another servant.

Joanne shook her head. "She is near, but I don't think she is inside any longer."

"Where could she have got to, then?" Andris queried.

"I need to get inside," the lilac girl said again. Her teeth chattering.

"Here," called her servant, opening the door to the servants' quarter near to where the group gathered.

***

Three horses burst from the stables and galloped across the snow towards the north. The White Mistress gripped her steed's reins as she leant over the animal's shoulders with her hood pulled far over her eyes.

The two guards rode at either side of her, checking over their shoulders for any pursuit, and seeing none.

The sun had lowered past the mountain peaks, casting a great shadow across the land. That, along with the thick falling snow, provided cover as they raced away from the port town of Blackrock Haven.

She placed her hand on her belly, knowing that what she did now was for that which grew inside her.

Some guilt filled her heart as she thought about her love, the Green Mistress, left behind to face her enemies alone.

Her sacrifice was for the cause they followed. The will of the Sovereign. The life of the Maji.

A tear streamed down her cheek as she thought she might never see Yasmeen again.

But, there was a chance.

Yasmeen Svoboda was powerful and still might thwart her adversaries.

She could only hope.

Racing into the wilderness, leaving it all behind, building her future would be her nourishment for now.

If the Green Mistress should fall, it wouldn't mean the end.

When the time was right, the White Mistress would return.

If her offspring were the Maji, then her destiny would be complete. He would rise with unlimited power.

The Maji.

The Heir of Darkness.

Ruler of all.

He would be lord above all dominions, all kingdoms, all realms and all gods.

And she, the White Mistress, the mother of the Maji, would stand by his side.

She smiled as she pictured it all in her head.

The world would burn in flames.

***

"I'm not ready to go back inside," the lilac girl said, standing by a stove to keep warm.

"Me either," said the olive girl.

"We'll wait a little longer," Joanne told them. "But we can't stay here forever. We will need to go back inside eventually and face her."

Some others sat on the edges of bunks gathered around the room or around a crude table in its centre. Joanne leant against the door frame as the others tried to muster their courage.

"You don't need to come back, gentlemen," she said to the servants. "This isn't your fight."

"We swore to serve you," Andris replied.

"I told you; you are free," she replied.

"I choose to serve you." He locked his eyes with hers. "Joanne."

She wiped her eyes and nodded.

"We are armed now," said another servant holding a sword he had appropriated from one of the guards, now locked in the cell at the end of the building in which they sheltered.

"We will protect you from her men, so you can get close to her."

"You are servants," the girl in olive said. "*Were* servants. What do you know of fighting?"

"They trained us to not only meet your every need and want," another servant replied. "They also trained us in the art of battle. Our task is to protect you until our last breath if need be."

"Oh." The girl in olive nodded, impressed.

"I can't promise your survival," Joanne told them.

"We know our duty to you," Andris told her.

"I know," she replied. "But I was also talking to the other girls."

They placed their attention upon Joanne. The looks on their faces told her they understood.

"You were all afraid of me until this day," she said to them. "You believed I had great power."

"*Have* great power," Tricia corrected her.

"But I can't do this without you," Joanne continued as she moved her eyes across the room to each face. "I need you. All of you. And I am afraid too."

Twenty-Seven

With no word yet about his missing man, Khabar took to mead to pass the time. He could feel the effects of the fermented liquid over his body; numbness in his fingers and unstable vision.

He was behaving a little too groggily and needed some air to clear his head.

Upon opening the door to his quarters, he felt the hammer-blow of the frosty night air. It was sudden and alarming, and sobered him somewhat.

He stumbled out of his warm room and put his hands on the rail that encircled the ship's deck. The gentle wind was blowing from the mountains towards the sea. The sun had vanished and night was upon them.

"Has anyone found Refal yet?" he growled to a five men gathered on deck.

"Not yet," one replied. "Ghunlok is still looking. Do you want us to join the search?"

Khabar nodded and waved them off.

The men moved along the wharf towards the abandoned market-place. The scarred man had noticed that the area had been quiet for most of the day. Some had braved the weather to peddle their goods and trade for what they needed, but the constant falling snow kept most away.

Those who had braved the elements had returned to their dwellings, perhaps hoping the next day would provide better weather for their bartering. But with these conditions, and the unpredictable weather of the previous few days, Khabar didn't like their chances.

Feeling the strange sensation of tingling over his face, the scarred man realised he had drunk way too much mead. Much more than he had planned to.

He took a walk to sober up. Steering himself towards the gangplank, he staggered across the deck and onto the steep plank that led to the wharf next to the ship.

Carefully, he moved down the wide board, balancing as if he was walking on a wire with his arms stretched out to his sides. Step by tiny step, he gradually made his way to the steady surface of the wooden walkway below.

Pleased with himself, and realising how silly he must have looked, the big man chuckled as he corrected his posture and headed in the township's direction. The wooden boards rattled beneath his heavy footfalls until he stepped, almost fell, to the snow-covered ground where he planted his feet upon the firm surface.

His mind trailed to his missing crewman, Refal. In particular, he considered recent words and behaviour of the man.

He knew the thin supervisor was struggling with his role, his duty in the Sovereign's service.

Khabar felt similar emotions regarding the actions he had performed for the cause.

Sometimes, he wondered if taking a walk off the side of the ship during a tempest might be the best means of escaping his duty.

He wondered if Refal had done this very thing.

Khabar considered the girls he had hurt over the years. The only reason, he believed, that he could still drink mead and stagger along the streets of Blackrock Haven, was because those girls, the ones still breathing, understood the cause. But he knew that they all held a deep hatred towards him. He knew they all would kill him if they were given the right to do so.

The hatred, the disgust that was reserved for him, wasn't just felt by those he had hurt. He loathed everything that he was. He detested what he had become.

The older he became, the more he detested his role in the scheme of things, the more he wished for death.

It's your duty, he told himself.

If you refuse your duty, the Mistresses will kill you. Painfully. Slowly.

He considered that for a moment. He had allowed his fear to mould him into a monster. A sick, twisted monster that enjoyed what he did when he was doing it.

He winced at the thought.

He wasn't enjoying it now.

Perhaps a slow, painful death was what he deserved.

Perhaps it was time to give up his duty and grasp at what little portion of humanity remained in him.

Perhaps that was what Refal had done.

He stopped walking and looked towards the castle high upon the hill. Wiping his eyes and fighting the temptation to return to the ship, to escape the stiff wind and snow, he changed direction and made his way towards the Green Mistress' lair.

His bravery was probably brought on by his drunken state, but he had decided.

He was going to face her.

He was going to tell her he was finished with it all.

He was going to take whatever punishment she would give him.

He was going, of his own accord, to die a free man.

***

Ghunlok had spent most of the afternoon knocking on doors and talking to those he encountered of the whereabouts of the missing Refal. No one could give him a location of his hiding place, nor had any seen him since the previous day.

It appeared the only men to see Refal all day were those accompanying him to the warehouses in the morning. Not a soul in all the township had laid eyes on him since.

Concerned that his supervisor might have met with foul play, Ghunlok started searching from one side of the town to the other for a body. His targeted locations; tool sheds, wood piles, under raised platforms, and anywhere he would consider stashing a body if he needed to hide one.

Beginning at the southern end of the village, Ghunlok slowly made his way through the streets, going from yard to yard in his search. He quietly called Refal's name, hoping the man had only taken to some excessive drinking and had crawled into a hiding hole to sleep it off.

"Ghunlok," he heard someone call from behind him. He was on his knees with his head poking beneath the raised floor of someone's house when he heard the voice.

His head bumped hard against the beams that supported the floor as he brought himself around to face the one who had summoned him.

Seeing stars as he sat upright in the snow, he rubbed his scalp and looked up.

"Yes?"

"Have you found Refal yet?"

"Yes," he replied sarcastically. "And that is why I'm sticking my head under this bloody house."

"No need to be nasty," the other said, frowning.

"Well!" Ghunlok started to his feet. "Have you found him?"

The other furrowed his brow. "Of course not."

"See?" He pointed to the man, still rubbing his head with the other. "I knew that. Do you know how I knew you hadn't found Refal yet?"

"Because I asked you first?"

"Exactly," Ghunlok replied, angry because he had bumped his head. It throbbed and stung at his touch. "I used my brain to deduce that you hadn't found Refal because of the question you asked me. Surely, you have a brain too. You could see me sticking my head under a house, looking for the man. I rarely stick my head under houses. I don't find the fun in it."

"Sorry, Ghunlok." The other sighed. "Should I knock on some doors?"

"No," he replied. "I've done that already. No one has seen him since this morning. Start looking in other places, like underneath houses. Just make sure not to bump your head when some damn fool calls your name."

The other nodded, his face towards the ground as he shuffled off through the snow.

***

They folded camp.

The fire extinguished.

The horses packed, and weapons checked.

Checking the sky for light, Tomas could see the faint silver glow of the moon trying to push its way through the thick clouds. With limited illumination, the snow-covered ground appeared as a dull grey, presenting a similar tone to their dark cloaks.

With the addition of a consistency in the falling snow, it would seem that the weather was on their side.

Gathering the horses closer to the sea, laden with camping equipment and riding gear, Baldwyn and Jeff prepared for a long wait.

"How will we see the fire from here?" Jeff asked the other, peering towards the ridge that blocked their view of the port town beyond.

"It will be a big fire, Jeffrey," Baldwyn explained. "We'll see the glow of the flames. Even from here."

The other seemed content with the answer as their captain, Jeremy, approached them on foot

"Are you two sure of what you need to do?" he asked them.

"Aye sir," Baldwyn replied.

"Aye, Captain." Jeff nodded.

"Remember," said Jeremy, as he looked at each man squarely. "If the worst should happen, you let these horses go, and ride as fast as you can. Understood?"

"Aye," Baldwyn replied. Jeff simply nodded.

The captain reached into beneath his cloak to his coat pocket, where he retrieved Tarkin's spyglass.

He held it in his hands, delicately, admiring it for a moment.

Stretching his arms towards Baldwyn, he handed over the device.

"Hold on to this," he commanded. "If I don't return to retrieve it from you, you must get it back to the *Adelandria* for me."

Baldwyn frowned as he nodded, realising that this might be the last time he would see his captain.

With his heavy heart still weighing so from the recent loss of their previous captain, Baldwyn took the spyglass and slid it into his coat beneath his own cloak.

"That's your mission," Jeremy told them. "To get that spyglass back to its home."

"Aye sir." Baldwyn nodded, his eyes watering. "We won't let you down."

"I know you won't." Jeremy smiled before turning away and walking back to the mustering group of warriors near the base of the elevation.

***

The three men of Woodmyst lined up upon their bellies at the top of the ridge, watching for movement as they waited for Tomas to arrive. They had been watching six men carefully as the light continued to fade and the land below grew dark. The men were moving through yards, crawling near buildings and lifting objects here and there.

"What do you think they're doing?" Oliver queried.

"They're searching for something," David replied.

"Yeah." Oliver tilted his head to the side. "But what?"

"Maybe that poor bastard we left under the warehouse," Simon offered.

"What was that about the warehouse?" Tomas asked as he plonked himself in the snow beside Simon.

"Nothing." He shook his head.

"So." Tomas moved his eyes over the township. "What's going on down there?"

David pointed to a yard at the western edge of the town. "There are some men looking for something."

"How many?" Tomas asked.

"Six," the big man replied. "No, wait."

He pointed to a figure walking from the market area towards the warehouses.

"Is that one of them," Oliver asked, "or is it some other fellow?"

"It's a new one," David answered. "The other six are to the west. See?"

Sure enough, the other six men were moving through the yards and between buildings on the other side of the township.

"Now there are seven," Simon said. "So what? We can take them out."

"They could raise an alarm if they see us," Oliver told him. "Then we'll have every bastard and his dog on us before we get started."

Tomas weighed up the advantages and disadvantages.

Something inside told him there was urgency towards their intended mission.

He knew there were risks involved if they were to take the village whilst men moved throughout the streets. The entire purpose for attacking at night, when darkness covered all, and the men tucked away in their dwellings, was to utilise the element of stealth.

But he also knew there would probably be guards watching in any case. To him, the risks were worth it and hadn't really changed.

"We go," he told the others.

Turning towards the men gathered below him, Tomas beckoned them with a wave of his hand.

The Erilian warriors and Emily huddled together in a tight circle, arms around one another, near to where the men stood. They stood silently, eyes closed, and breathing deeply. The men didn't know whether it was simply a *woman thing* or something deeper that worked in accordance with the abilities they had recently exhibited.

"All right, lads," Jeremy said, regaining the attention of his men upon seeing Tomas' signal. "This is it. Keep quiet and be quick. We're not here to torture. We're here to claim to town. Most importantly, stay alive."

With that, he started climbing to the crest of the ridge.

Tomas and the men of Woodmyst crossed the ridge and ran noiselessly and swiftly down the other side. They were halfway between the base of the ridge and the nearest building, a small tool shed, when the women hit the level ground not far behind them.

Pressing their backs against the toolshed, the four men watched the women approach them as the nine male crew members of the *Adelandria* descended the slope.

"How did you move so quickly?" David whispered to Karlena as she sidled up to him.

"Shhh!" Tomas hissed as he peered around the corner of the shed.

The crewmen made their way across the open ground, keeping low and watching their surroundings as they approached.

Tomas eyed the dwellings nearby.

There was no movement.

No reaction.

They had arrived unnoticed.

The men crouched before him, using the structure as a barrier between themselves and the village as Tomas surveyed the land ahead.

Eventually, he turned to face them, locking eyes with Jeremy.

He gave his command to engage in the same manner that they wished to fulfil their mission, quickly and silently, with one gesture.

A simple nod of his head.

Twenty-Eight

The crewmen followed Jeremy around the right side of the tool shed and into the yard of the adjoining dwelling as Tomas led the women and the men of Woodmyst along the fence line that bordered the western edge of the village.

"We take out the six men searching the properties," he whispered to them as they sneaked in a northerly direction, tracing the boundary.

"What about the seventh?" Oliver asked, "The one near the warehouse."

"We'll get to him soon enough," Tomas replied. "We need to go there in any case."

Crouching low and moving as stealthily as they could, they embraced the shadows of larger structures and lowered themselves to the level of picket fences and feed troughs that lined the yards of the houses at the edge of town.

They spotted the first of the six men searching the village near a house at the far western point of the community. Three other houses clustered nearby.

Tucking themselves against the snow that had collected by a fence, Tomas watched the man as he ducked under a house, looking for his lost thing.

"We take him here," Tomas told the others. "We also enter these houses and take out anyone inside. Quietly."

The others nodded and waited for him to make his move.

Tomas waited until the man moved from his position, climbing clumsily over the waist-high fence to the neighbouring yard where he placed his head under another hut.

As quick as lightning, Tomas was on his feet and moving, his dagger in his hand. His footfalls were swift and silent as he crossed the first yard.

David was on his feet, running behind his commander. He could not keep up and didn't bother with trying. His efforts would have been in vain.

Tomas, to David's amazement, leapt over the fence effortlessly. He took a few more paces before falling upon the man. With a quick motion, he slid the blade across the man's throat before rising to his feet.

David reached the fence and clambered over it as quietly as he could. As he pulled his leg over the barrier after him, Emily and the other women leapt over the fence silently, landing on their feet and jogging to Tomas' side.

By the gods.

Before the big man could reach his commander, and before the other two men had cleared the yard, Tomas pointed to Rhydra and Sharek and then to the house behind him.

You two will take that house.

He then pointed to Simon and Oliver before jutting a finger at the house in the yard where they stood.

Take down anyone in that dwelling.

David watched as the finger pointed in his direction before turning upon its owner, then towards the third house in the cluster.

We'll take this one.

Tomas then pointed to the three women remaining, pointed to his eyes with two fingers.

Stay and watch.

All nodded. They understood.

Tomas pulled his sword from his sheath, signalling for all to move to their positions, ready to go. He crouched and moved to the nearest door and touched the latch.

Looking about and waiting to make sure the other members of the group were where they needed to be, Tomas lifted the handle to open the door.

There was no resistance.

There was no lock.

The door opened inward with a quiet creak.

A quick look at the others told him they were underway with their tasks. He gave a quick nod to David.

Are you ready?

The big man returned the gesture.

Let's go.

The two men entered the dark dwelling, hearing the soft sound of snoring and feeling the warmth of a fire within.

***

Jeremy crept through the shadows of the house with another crew member. They kept low to the floor and moved precariously, attempting to avoid making a single floorboard squeak as they progressed along a narrow corridor.

There were rooms on either side of them. The captain counted six, three on either side with an open arch at the far end, the door they had entered behind them.

Jeremy signalled the other to close the door, to keep the heat in.

Let's not wake these buggers with cold air before we have time to confront them.

The crewman shut the door quietly, a soft thud signalling the completion of the action.

Jeremy reached for the first door on the left and opened it slowly. A long, loud creak ensued, causing a deep concern that the men sleeping inside might awaken.

Broom, mop, blankets and knick-knacks.

A bloody cupboard.

He reached over to the door on the right, directly across the corridor from the closet.

Upon opening it, the sound of soft breathing reached their ears.

They had found the first bedroom.

Jeremy signalled they were about to enter the room. The other nodded.

Keeping low, daggers in their hands, the two men moved to the side of the bed.

Jeremy watched the sleeping man breathing soundly, oblivious to the captain's presence.

Some trepidation overcame him.

The man was unarmed and sleeping.

He looked just like any other man.

The sleeper could very much be like one of his own crew members.

A man with dreams and aspirations.

He didn't know if this course of action was the right one to take. By all standards, he was about to commit murder.

But so have all the men in this village, he thought.

They took their ships and pillaged, killed and raped, burned and destroyed. All without a second thought.

They are the murderers.

They deserve this.

You'll be saving countless lives, families and communities.

Jeremy closed his eyes as he lifted his blade.

They hurt children; he remembered Tomas telling him. He remembered Meaghan. He remembered the love they had shared, only to have it ripped away by a man just like this one.

They all deserve to die.

He plunged his blade through the sleeping man's throat.

The man's eyes flashed open as gargling and spitting sounds emitted from the wound in his neck.

The crewman stuck his dagger deep into the man's heart, completing the ghastly task.

The sleeper went limp.

The gargling stopped, and the blood stopped spitting from his neck.

Jeremy looked down upon the man lying in his bed, never to wake again.

"Come on, Captain," the crewman whispered softly. "We've started now. We need to finish it."

Jeremy nodded. The crewman was right.

There was no turning back now.

They retraced their steps and made their way to the next door along the corridor.

***

Khabar leant on his shoulder against the platform outside of the western-most warehouse. His head was spinning and walking was more difficult than he thought it would be.

He considered if he should return to the ship and sleep the effects of the fermented drink away, but he didn't think he would make it that far without falling on his face.

The night was still early, but it was freezing in the falling snow and building wind coming from the west. If he fell asleep in the street, he didn't believe he would wake up.

Perhaps that would be all right.

He pondered that for a moment.

No, I must face her.

He turned towards the castle, way, way up on the hill. It was so far away; much farther to get there than it was to turn back to the ship.

And his cot, his nice comfortable cot, was on the ship.

You won't go through with it, he told himself. *You'll wake up sober and your fears will return. You won't see her.*

He took a deep breath as he placed both hands on the platform to steady himself.

Lifting his head to the doors of the warehouse, he considered what they held inside those walls. He thought about the cargo he had brought with him and where most of it ended up.

All those women were inside those walls.

You could go inside, said a familiar voice inside of him. It wasn't the inner voice he usually listened to. It wasn't the voice that urged him to go to the Green Mistress.

It was the monster.

They need you; it told him. *They love it when you come to them.*

He shook his head.

He knew the monster was wrong.

They didn't love him. They feared him. They hated him.

They feel so good; it hissed. *Smooth skin. Soft hair. You need to touch. You need to love them.*

He lowered his forehead against the platform and wept.

The monster was strong. Too strong.

He could feel the urge growing and his desires beating the part of him that wanted to do what was right.

"I don't want to," he blubbered. "I don't want to anymore."

Yes, you do, it hollered back. *Don't deny your needs. Don't deny them your love.*

"Leave me alone," he cried. He tried to stand upright, intending to continue to the castle.

Even if it took him all night, if he had to crawl on hand and knee, he would go to her and tell her he was through.

And if he collapsed on the way, fall asleep in the snow and die, then that would be fine too.

He slipped and fell onto his back.

Staring at the dark sky above and the white spots that drifted to the ground, he smiled for a moment.

Perhaps the crawling will start a little earlier than planned.

He rolled onto his side, towards the warehouse, to get his arms and legs underneath himself, so that he could rise to his feet again.

But something grabbed his attention.

Something under the warehouse, tucked in the shadows.

Something that didn't belong.

On his hands and knees, he crawled, passing beneath the platform and under the floorboards of the structure.

He could hear the sobs of women and girls above him. Sad, frightened sobs.

They need you.

They want you.

He ignored the monster and continued towards the strange shape. The out-of-place shape.

It wasn't smooth like snow, or jagged like rock.

It was the shape of a man.

Reaching the figure, he could see the boots and legs of the individual sticking out from under a dark cloak.

Wrapped around the limbs, along the body and around the arms, which were pulled tightly around his back, was the black leather strapping of a whip.

Refal's whip.

With his enormous paw of a hand, he pulled the body towards him, rolling it over onto its back.

Refal's eyes were closed, appearing as if he was asleep.

Blood clustered at his temple told Khabar what had killed his crewman.

He looked at the body for a long time, wishing he could say the man didn't deserve his wounds. But he knew better.

Like him, Refal had also partaken in some dark deeds.

Khabar considered raising the alarm, but he remained silent.

If someone was here to release him of his torment in the same manner, he welcomed it.

You need to tell her; the monster said.

Khabar shook his head.

They will kill everyone, it persisted. *They will kill you.*

He didn't care. It was time for it to be over.

Do your duty.

"No," he replied.

Twenty-Nine

Gathered in a line with their backs pressed against a small lean-to shelter, the group of nine caught their breath after racing across an open yard to yet another cluster of houses. Tomas scanned the area around the right side of their hiding place and saw two of the searchers checking around the houses right near them.

He signalled the women to go left and make their way to the warehouses. The first of these overshadowed the structure they hid beside.

With Emily and the Erilian warriors creeping off in one direction, he led the three men into the yard and towards the houses.

David moved silently towards a man who was sticking his head into a toolshed behind a house. Simon did the same to another that was on his belly, attempting to see under the hut.

Within moments, blood spilled and two men lay motionless on the snow.

Signalling to the two men, Tomas instructed them to stay in place and keep watch. He then tapped Oliver on the arm and pointed to the nearby house.

Sneaking inside, Tomas and Oliver disappeared into the darkness as David and Simon waited.

They weren't very long, returning within moments with their daggers in their hands. Tomas gestured for the two waiting men to move into the next house nearer to them.

Before long, David and Simon were indoors while Tomas and Oliver moved to the next door and waited for their friends to emerge.

When they stepped out from the building, their commander pointed to the next building as he and Oliver entered the door near them.

And so, it went on.

As one pair of men were inside performing their ghastly deed, the others were keeping watch as they moved to their next target location.

The men of Woodmyst were silent and swift, clearing seven houses within mere minutes.

***

Emily watched the path ahead of them, seeing a clear route to the warehouse where she had heard the child's voice and witnessed the assault upon one of the poor women inside. It was clear, except for the lone figure standing on the platform with a sword in each hand.

The others were looking about, making sure nobody spotted them as they approached their objective. When Emily stopped in her tracks, they weren't expecting it and almost ran into her.

Their eyes flashed forwards and saw the big man.

He didn't move towards them.

He didn't make a sound.

He just waited.

It seemed pointless to try and hide. Instead, they lifted themselves upright and approached the warehouse with their swords drawn.

"I could hit him with an arrow from here," Akasati whispered to them. "Quick and simple."

"No," Karlena told her. "I think he wants a more honourable death."

"None of them deserves one," Rhydra grumbled as they drew nearer to him.

The women ascended a wide set of stairs at the end of the platform, stopping at the top to lock eyes with the fiend.

They saw his scar, stretching across his face from the top of one side to the bottom of the other.

Emily recognised him as the man who had killed her mother. The Erilian women recognised him from the stories their beloved and departed Captain Tarkin had told.

"I am Khabar Faraq Wahil," he growled. "I am captain of the slave vessel, *Frykt.*"

"We don't care who you are," Emily replied, her emotions causing her voice to tremble slightly. "We know what you are and what you did. You are a monster."

He lowered his eyes and frowned, nodding his head.

It was easy to accept her words when he had been saying the same thing about himself for such a long time.

He *was* a monster.

He *still was* a monster.

And no matter what he did, he couldn't change that.

"You are right," he replied, swaggering a little. The mead still affected his equilibrium. "I remember you. Even with your hood up over your auburn hair. I know your face. If you hadn't run off and killed one of my men, I would have raped you myself, just as I did your sister."

Emily grew intensely angry. Her fury filled her so powerfully that her skin grew hot.

"I am Khabar Faraq Wahil," he said again, as tears streamed down his cheek. "And I am a monster. I killed men and boys, even babies. I have raped women and young girls. I deserve to die."

The women stared at him, confused by his words.

I deserve to die.

For what seemed like an eternity, they watched him, swaying back and forth. He moved his eyes across each of them and smiled.

"I deserve to die," he said again. "But I won't go easily."

He ran at them, blades held high.

***

Jeremy moved between two properties on his way to the next house. The crewmen of the *Adelandria* had managed to make it nearly half-way across the town, clearing each dwelling and closing the distance between themselves and the warehouses at the far end of town.

As he moved towards his next target, he heard a scuffle in another house nearby.

First a thud, then a crack of something made of timber. Next was a loud crash, like smashing glass with a last scream of someone calling out but suddenly silenced.

"What was that?" someone called out from the house.

Within moments, the door flung open right near him and a large man armed with an axe stepped on the snow.

Thinking quickly, Jeremy plunged his sword into the man, sending him in a screaming bloodied fit upon the snow.

And now it begins, the captain thought as he heard several other people answering the call of his victim.

Doors flung open and armed men, still half dressed, attempted to come to the rescue of their fallen friend.

Caught by surprise, many of them were planted onto the snow as the crewmen of the *Adelandria* responded with stealth and accuracy. Many men of Blackrock Haven, still half asleep and weary, fell as they stepped from their doors.

Others, in houses still a distance away, saw the carnage and had time to throw on a leather vest and grab their swords.

Now outnumbered, they forced the men of the Adelandria into combat. Silence and stealth were no longer needed.

The enemy knew they had arrived.

***

"What the blazes?" David hissed as the sound of swords clashing echoed across the quiet town from both directions.

"It would seem our friends are having a spot of trouble." Oliver smiled.

Tomas frowned. He heard the many sources of clanging noises from the south where the captain and his men were located. Some calls from men rose above it from time to time.

He was tempted to head over there to offer help, but the sound of conflict to the north had him concerned for Emily and the captives in the warehouse.

Doors of the nearby cottages flung open and several men came rushing out.

"Cut them down," Tomas barked. "Then get over to those warehouses."

The men raced forwards, blades at the ready.

Slashing and hacking, the men of Woodmyst sent most of the warriors to the ground before the enemy realised what had happened. A small few turned and defended themselves against the attack from the four men.

Using sword and fist, Tomas fought relentlessly and aggressively, spilling the blood of his enemy across the clean, white snow.

By the time they had finished, seven bodies lay upon the ground in a pool of thick, dark liquid.

Without time to waste, the four men turned their attention to the noise coming from the warehouse.

Dodging buildings and leaping fences, they ran into view of the platform where the five women were blocking blows from a large man with two swords.

"He's drunk," Simon said. "He's good."

"You admire him?" Oliver asked.

"He's still standing," Simon admitted. "I don't think I could stay alive this long if I was up against those girls."

The big man blocked a blow from Akasati with one hand as he lunged at Emily with the other. She knocked his sword away, causing him to open his arms and expose his chest.

Karlena stepped forward and slashed at him with her curved sword.

He stepped back, just in time, and the blade slid over his belly, leaving a shallow cut across his skin.

Some blood spilled from the wound, but he didn't feel it, didn't notice it. Too intoxicated to care, he stepped towards them again.

A great flurry of sword exchange ensued as the five women surrounded their opponent, looking for a way through his defences.

He was quick, Tomas noted, but he was tiring and his balance was off.

It was only a matter of time.

The scarred man turned, facing each of the warriors in turn as he blocked and parried their blows.

With a quick attack, he struck Rhydra on her thigh and Sharek on the right arm. They both recoiled, allowing the man to focus briefly on the other three.

Emily thought quickly and lifted her boot into the scarred man's crotch.

It was a hard blow, sending the man crashing to his knees, dropping one sword so it fell from the platform so he could grasp the area in pain with his hand.

"This is for my sister," she hollered as she swung her sword with great velocity, cutting through his gripping hand and deep into his groin.

Tomas felt no pity for the man, but he and the men next to him felt that.

"By the gods!" David winced.

The scarred man screamed an ear-piercing scream that broke through the darkness of the night.

Emily slid her sword out of the wound, the sound of bone and flesh scraping along the steel.

The index finger of the grasping hand fell onto the platform as a pool of blood formed around the man's knees.

He dropped his other sword and looked up at Emily and mouthed the words, *thank you.*

Lifting his chin as high as he could, feeling immense pain, he stared directly ahead.

He silently wished the mead had made him more numb than this.

But he knew he deserved what he had got.

"I am Khabar Faraq Wahil," he said, fighting the agony. "Servant of the Sovereign. Slave to the Green Mistress. And I deserve to die."

Servant of the Sovereign? Karlena thought. *This man is only a servant?*

Emily swung her sword wide, bringing the blade across his neck.

His head rolled off the platform and landed in a thick pile of snow.

As she stood there, watching the headless corpse fall, she sobbed.

"That was for Mama."

***

"Anything?" Jeff called, seated upon his steed at the base of the elevation.

"What?" Baldwyn called back from atop of his horse on the crest of the ridge.

"Can you see anything?" the other hollered back.

"Yeah," Baldwyn answered. "Lots of fighting in the middle of the town."

Baldwyn didn't like what he was seeing at all.

There were nine men grouped as others came towards them from the north. The nine were holding their position, but the enemy was approaching from the dwellings that separated them from the warehouses.

He couldn't see the doors of the large buildings on the far side of town, so he did not know how Tomas and the others were coping. He could only hope the captain's bad luck was being exploited by the other nine members of their group, taking the warehouse while others distracted the townsfolk.

The crewmen of the *Adelandria* needed some reinforcements that weren't about to show up anytime soon. He and Jeff were both as useful as a pimple on a boil for the moment.

All he could do was watch.

"No fires?" Jeff called.

"Not yet," he called back.

Not yet.

Thirty

Upon entering the foyer, the manservants surrounded the girls, holding swords at the ready.

Before them stood the grand stairwell. To either side were open arches. One led to the throne room, the other to the sitting room with a great fire blazing against the far wall.

One servant peered into the throne room as another looked through the access to the room across from it.

The first servant turned back to the group and shook his head.

There was no one in the throne room.

The other pointed to the passage at the side that led to the bath on the lower level of the castle.

Is she taking a swim? Joanne thought as the group made their way into the sitting room.

Together, they moved along the corridor, down the extensive set of stairs into the room with the pool in its centre. Their footfalls reverberated from the tiled walls and around the room.

Nothing.

The room was empty.

No guards.

No Green Mistress.

Nobody.

"Maybe she has gone," said one servant.

"No," the jade girl said. "She is here."

"We go back," Andris said. "We keep looking until we find her."

Joanne nodded, turning towards the corridor that led back to the reading room.

Eight armed men stood in their way.

They were silent and quick. Not one in the group had heard their footfalls as they approached from behind.

Joanne felt her heart stop at the sight of the guards.

Before she could react, the six servants jumped between the guards and the girls.

There was no time to size each other up as the guards chose their opponents quickly, leaving two of their men to focus their attention on the unarmed girls.

Joanne watched as Andris blocked and parried, hacked and swung with his blade, all the while monitoring her and the guards that were approaching.

The girls would have to deal with the two guards themselves.

Creeping closer and closer, they grimaced as they drew nearer and nearer.

"Nowhere to go, pretty ones," one of them slurred. "What are you going to do now?"

Joanne reached for Tricia's hand.

The two laced their fingers before reaching to the others on either side of them. A moment later, all the girls were holding hands in a line before the pool. Their eyes bored into the approaching men like long, invisible daggers.

They felt it, stopping a few feet away from the girls, fear spreading on their faces.

Watching, focusing, willing it, the girls saw the guards' eyes melted in their sockets as dark bubbles and blisters formed on their skin over their faces.

Slowly, parts of their flesh melted away and fell to the floor like cinders.

Screaming in pain, the men dropped to their knees, letting go of their blades so they clanged against the hard floor.

The strange sight distracted the other guards, fighting the girls' servants.

Andris used the disruption to his advantage and plunged his sword deep into the chest of his adversary. The other servants saw this as their cue to do the same.

Six guards fell to the clean, white tiles with gaping wounds as two charred men crumpled into a pile of ashes on the floor.

The servants took a quick glance towards the work of the potentials. They had seen nothing like it before.

"You burnt them," one servant said, astonished and in awe. "How?"

Joanne shook her head. She didn't know.

"We just thought *fire*," Tricia told him. "And there was."

All eyes were on the pile of ash that once were two men, except Andris'. He was peering into the corridor to see if any more men approached.

"We need to move," he said. "More will come."

***

After breaking the lock with their swords, Tomas and David slid the large doors of the warehouse wide open.

The stench inside was thick and sickly, comprising sweat, urine and faeces.

Stables smell better than this, Tomas thought as he entered the dark, cavernous building.

Voices and fear-filled groans of women and children filled his ears as he strode into the room. He thought it would have been better to let the women in first.

Emily followed him as David and Simon used flint to light two torches hanging on the wall on either side of the door.

"It's all right," she called softly. "We're here to free you."

"The men," a scared voice called back. "You have men with you."

"They are not from here," Emily replied, not knowing where the voice came from. "They are from Woodmyst."

"Woodmyst?" another called. "Woodmyst is a myth. Destroyed by dragons. None survived."

"We survived," Tomas replied to the woman's voice. "We saw the dragons and their masters. We are here now with a small band of others fighting in the town as we speak. Will you join us?"

"Join you?" another called. "I thought you said you were here to save us?"

"No," Emily corrected the woman. "We are here to free you. You may need to save yourself before this night is through."

The Erilian women and the three men split into two groups and took a side of the warehouse each, breaking locks and opening cage doors.

"Where are we to go?" another called. "We're far to the north in the middle of nowhere."

"You need to take the ship," Emily replied as she opened a cage, letting a young girl and an older woman out of a pen. "Either that, or start walking."

"The ship? I don't ever want to set foot on that thing again."

"I understand," Emily empathised. "But that is our means of getting home. All of us."

David stood in front of the cage where the five men had gathered earlier, holding the flickering torch high in his hand with the cage door open.

"Come on, love," he tried to coax the girl inside. "It's time to go."

The young woman was curled up against the back of the pen, covering her face, cowering away in fear. Her hair was so tangled and dirty that he couldn't tell what colour it really was. Her skin appeared bruised and broken in places.

He felt tears on his cheeks and a tightening in his throat as he reached out to her.

"Sweetie, I'm here to help," the giant tried to reassure her.

"She's scared," Emily told him. "All men are dangerous to her. Allow me."

David nodded. He was sympathetic to the girl's plight, angry towards those who had done this to her. He wanted to hurt all of those who were responsible for what had happened to these captives, but he wanted to help them even more.

Emily entered the pen and touched the girl gently on the arm.

"It's not safe here," the auburn girl told the other. "You need to come. You need to trust us and come."

The girl slowly moved her head towards the light.

Her breathing was shallow and raspy as she looked at Emily.

She had the eyes of a scared, timid animal.

Afraid to move.

Afraid to stay.

Caught somewhere in the middle, expecting to be hurt no matter what she did.

Emily reached out to her.

"Come," she said soothingly.

There was power behind the word.

David could feel it. He took a step backwards, as if knocked off balance.

"Come," she said again. The ring of distant thunder softly rumbled through the room.

The girl reached her arm towards Emily, trustingly.

The auburn girl leant into the timid creature in the cage, allowing her to wrap her arm around Emily's neck.

Lifting to her feet, Emily took the weight of the girl, helping her out of the cage.

"This is David." Emily continued to use her alluring, soothing voice. "He is a friend. Go with him."

The girl moved her scared, wide eyes to the bald giant and hesitated.

"Go with him," Emily repeated.

She reached her bruised arms out to David, wrapping them around his shoulders as he put one of his massive arms around her waist. He used his other arm to sheath his sword over his back before lifting her off the ground in both arms.

"Tell Tomas, I won't be joining you at the castle," he said to Emily. "I need to make sure she gets on board that ship."

Emily nodded.

"I need to," he said again, his eyes filled with water.

"I know David." She placed a hand on his shoulder.

***

Slamming his fist into the face of an enemy fighter over and over, Jeremy struggled to gain the advantage. His sword was blocking the blow from his adversary and he needed to act fast.

The first strategy that came to his mind was to punch the man in the face.

Eventually, the fighter eased up and fell back upon the snow.

Jeremy plunged his sword at the fallen man, digging deep into the other's belly.

There was no time to celebrate as another foe came rushing towards him from his right.

Pulling his sword from the fallen man, still kicking and screaming in pain, Jeremy blocked the oncoming blow from the other by knocking his sword high.

Continuing to grip the hilt of his blade, the new opponent tripped and continued past Jeremy, planting face first into the snow.

The captain was after him, pushing his blade through the back of the man's neck before he had time to regain composure.

He turned his attention back to his original adversary, who held his arms up in defeat.

"I'm dying," he said in protest. "You've killed me already."

"Too slow," the captain replied, thinking of his Meaghan as he stuck the blade into the other's chest.

Noticing more men approaching from the village as his crew fought on an open plot of ground between some clustered houses, Jeremy ran to give aid to his men.

They formed a line of sorts as they confronted the enemy, assisting each other with a kill when they could; fighting two at once when it was necessary.

Spinning, twisting, hacking and stabbing. The captain was feeling tired. The fighting was taking its toll on him.

Chancing a look, he glanced towards the warehouses to the north. He could see the far-right structure had its doors wide open.

At least some things were working in their favour.

Just not here.

***

Surrounded by women, David made his way back into the town, still carrying the young distressed lady in his arms. He had risked the cold by removing his cloak and bundling it around her before leaving the warehouse.

"Are you really from Woodmyst?" asked another young woman, walking briskly by his side. She was pretty in features, but dishevelled and beaten. It was difficult to see what she really looked like beneath the grime and grit all over her.

"Yes," he replied. "We are rebuilding our village."

"Are you with wife and children?" she asked.

He shot her a questionable look.

"No," he replied. "There are none in Woodmyst with children yet. And no, I am not with wife."

"What do you do in Woodmyst?" she asked. "How do you make a living?"

"I'm a farmer," he replied. "Crops and sheep. What is with all the questions?"

"I didn't marry either," she blurted. "I just turned sixteen. We wait until our sixteenth birthday before we are allowed to have someone court us. It's our tradition."

"Uh-huh." David nodded. *Does she ever take a breath?*

"But the Prophets of the Sovereign came and took us away before any of the men in our village could declare his interest. Then the Prophets of the Sovereign killed all the men and burnt my village.

"But if Woodmyst is to be my new home, and if the men are anything like you, I might not die an old maid yet. Are there many like you in Woodmyst?"

"Like me?" David asked, confused by her words. She was talking way too fast for him.

"Big, strapping, strong," she said, looking at his arms.

"No." He smiled. "I'm one of a kind."

She smiled back.

"My name's Martha."

Thirty-One

The girls followed their servants back towards the sitting room. Andris led the team through the wide corridor, stepping slowly, precariously, attempting to dull the sounds of their footfalls.

It was pointless.

Poking his head around the corner, looking towards the foyer, he could see all the guards from the cell near the servant quarters now standing at the end of the room near the large, open arch. There were twelve that they had locked in the pen, but there were more than that standing before him.

He straightened his posture and walked into the middle of the room. The other servants followed.

The guards glowered at the boys as they moved into view.

Andris held his hand up to the girls, signalling for them to wait.

"You may as well come out," one guard called. "We plan to kill you, too. Whether that's now or later, it doesn't matter."

"Oh," said another guard towards the back of the group, "our weapons. We'll be wanting them back."

"She let you out?" Andris asked.

"No," the first guard answered. "Our friends here from her quarters let us out. Brought us some new shiny swords to play with."

Joanne looked at the other girls. They had confidence and believed they could defeat the guards. The Black Miss held her hands out to the others.

They formed a circle in the corridor, and closed their eyes, and their individual willpower became one.

Andris, seeing the bonding occur in the corner of his eye, smiled as he spoke to the first guard.

"You want these swords back?" he said calmly. "Come and take them."

The first guard raced forwards, bringing his blade across his shoulder with both hands in a downward striking motion towards Andris.

The servant stepped into the blow and blocked it with his own sword, smashing into the iron with a loud ringing sound that echoed throughout the castle.

Several other guards stepped in to join the attack. The other servants of the girls blocked and parried blows as the enemy soldiers moved on into the room towards them.

Blocking blow after heavy blow, the gold servant tussled with an individual who hacked his heavy blade downwards over and over with ferocity. His actions were so fast that the boy had no chance of turning the tables in order to make a strike of his own.

The girls focused their attention, sensing the plight of the gold servant.

Hacking, hacking, hacking.

The guard was relentless, pushing the boy backwards, forcing him to his knees.

CRACK!

The guard stopped; his sword held high, ready to hack at the gold servant again.

CRACK!

Blood trickled from the guard's nose, dripping onto the rug lying on the floor.

CRACK!

His eyes rolled into his head so that they could see only the whites.

Falling to his knees, the man moaned, opening his mouth wide to allow a flow of blood and saliva to drain.

He fell to the floor in front of the gold servant, lifeless.

The boy surmised that this was the doing of the *potentials*. There was no time to be thankful as another guard came towards him.

Back on his feet, swinging his blade, the gold guard entered the fight once again. As he exchanged blows with his opponent, he saw another guard fall away to his side, chest and head smoking and charred.

The girls had struck again.

The guards seemed undeterred this time, though previously most of them had expressed fear towards the potentials and were willing to be locked in the cell.

Something had changed.

It must be the Green Mistress, Andris thought as he plunged his sword into a guard's chest. *They fear her even more.*

Swinging his blade at a new adversary, he saw the head of another to his right explode. Accepting that it was the girls and silently thanking them for joining the fight, he focused his attention on his immediate enemy.

More men moved into the room.

A quick count, more of an estimate, told him there were around twenty armed men between the arch and themselves.

Screaming, falling to his knees, another guard closer to the foyer writhed in pain as his skin bubbled and charred.

It distracted Andris' foe long enough for the Black Miss's servant to swipe his blade across the other's belly, spilling entrails onto the green rug.

The boy moved to the next guard, sword high above his head, stained with the blood of the fallen guards around him.

The guard squealed, sounding like a little girl as both of his knees bent awkwardly, snapping ligament and tissue before he crumpled to the ground.

Before Andris stuck his blade into the fallen guard, another across the room collapsed as his head imploded, as though a giant hand had squished it like a grape.

The girls are getting stronger, he thought. *And quicker.*

Iron collided loudly in the sitting room as the servants continued to beat their enemies down.

The girls remained in their circle, united as one.

All the while, she watched, observed.

Waiting.

Waiting.

***

Reaching the outer gates, Emily, the Erilian warriors, and three men surveyed the land before them. Rhydra repositioned the cloth she had wrapped around her thigh, slowing the bleeding from her wound sustained from the scarred man's blade. Sharek rubbed her arm; the wound was not much more than a scratch. Emily had bandaged it as best as she could before they left the warehouse.

Tomas peered around the entrance to the yard. There were no guards at the gatehouse. The gates were wide open. It was as if the witch was expecting them, inviting them in.

Perhaps she is, Tomas thought suspiciously.

"Over there." Simon pointed to a building that rested outside the walls to the castle grounds.

It was large, similar to a barn, with its doors wide open and lantern light emitting from within.

"Should we investigate?" Oliver asked.

Tomas thought about it for a moment.

Clanging and ringing made its way across the wind into his ears.

There was a battle nearby.

He looked to the castle, then to the other building outside the walls.

"You two look into that building," he commanded Simon and Oliver. "We'll go after the girls."

The two men nodded and ran over the thick, snow-covered ground towards the lonely building that stood a short distance from the wall.

Tomas turned his attention to the castle standing menacingly before them. The sounds of swords clashing were coming from within.

He turned to face Emily.

"Are you ready?"

She nodded.

Together, the six warriors crossed the ground between the gatehouse and the main doors of the castle.

Keeping their eyes peeled for guards or hidden assailants, swords held tightly in their hands, they drew nearer to the doors.

Tomas wondered who could be fighting inside and why.

He considered that a faction may have formed a resistance amongst the guards.

Perhaps the white witch was putting in her bid to gain control.

Perhaps the slaves were revolting.

Perhaps there were potential allies inside.

He was sure there would be a means to exploit whatever was happening inside and use it to their advantage.

The din of battle grew louder.

The cries of men joined the sounds of iron.

They grouped by the doors, both open wide, revealing a large room with a giant stairwell to the rear.

Surveying each of the women near him, Tomas saw their fear and anxiety. Most of all, he saw their eagerness to get inside.

For the Erilians, this was a revenge mission.

They were here to avenge their home that the Sovereign had destroyed through his servants.

They were here for the white witch, to treat her with the edges of their swords for what she had done to their commander and lover, Captain Dakmel Tarkin.

They were here to help their friend, their sister Emily, with retrieving her sibling.

They were ready; Tomas could see it in their eyes.

He looked over to Emily, who was taking deep breaths, keeping calm as she prepared to fight.

Reaching out to her, wrapping his arm around her waist, he pulled her towards him. His lips touched hers, holding her for an eternity.

"Just in case," he told her.

"We need to win, now," Karlena said to the other women.

Tomas smiled as he released Emily from his grasp.

Tightening their grip on the hilts of the swords, they moved through the open doorway into the castle of the witch.

***

Gustav dropped another of the townsmen into the snow at the far right of the line. They were inching towards the docks where the black ship waited.

He risked a glance along the road that led from the wharves to the warehouses and saw a mass of people heading in their direction.

Before having time to discern if they were friend or foe, he was engaged in another exchange of swordplay with yet another man from the village.

He blocked the first blow, but was a little slow with his parry on the second.

The enemy's sword cut into his forearm, forcing him to drop his sword into the snow.

His reaction time was slow.

He reached with his good arm for his dagger still on his belt, but he knew it was useless.

The assailant brought his sword down fast, directing it towards Gustav's head.

The crewman of the *Adelandria* closed his eyes.

There was nothing he could do to prevent it.

CLANG!

The sound rang in his ears.

Perhaps that's what it sounds like from the inside when your skull gets split by a sword, he thought, keeping his eyes shut.

CLANG! CLANG!

He opened his eyes to see another crewmen skirmishing with his would-be killer.

Gustav reached for his sword. Retrieving it with his good arm, he stood up. He tried to grip with his wounded arm, but it hurt too much.

A slow flow of blood dribbled down his glove and onto the snow.

Ignoring the pain, the throbbing pain, he moved towards the two fighters near to him.

As the crewmen fought the assailant, keeping him distracted, Gustav slid his blade deep into the enemy's ribs from behind.

The man fell to the ground.

"Thank you," said the crewman.

Gustav shook his head and held his wounded arm up. "Thank you. I was done for."

"Can you fight?" the other asked.

Gustav shook his head.

"I think it will be all right," the man told him. "They are starting to thin. I haven't seen any more coming from the houses to fight us. You should help with the women and girls." The crewman pointed with his sword towards the mob approaching from the warehouses.

Gustav turned his head to see David towering above those who surrounded him. He was carrying someone in his arms.

Holding his sword in his good arm, Gustav jogged across the snow towards the group.

"One of them comes for us," a woman screamed shrilly.

"It's all right, Martha," David told her. "This is Gustav."

David smiled as the other drew near, changing his countenance when he saw the blood dripping from Gustav's arm.

"You're wounded," the big man stated.

"I can't fight," Gustav replied. "Not very well. But I can help you."

"All right," David nodded. "Then you can help us take the ship."

"I think all the crew of the black ship are over there," said Gustav.

"Then this won't take too long." He smiled, stepping up some steps that led to the wharves.

"We should help," said a woman near to David. She was looking over at the skirmish on the ground not too far from them.

"We don't have weapons for you," the big man replied.

"There are some on the ground," she replied, referring to the dead men who had no need for their blades any longer.

"What about the ship?" David asked.

"You take the ship," the woman told him. "I have to do this."

David wanted to stop her, but the girl in his arms needed to be cared for.

"Who will come with me?" the woman called.

There were twenty that didn't hesitate, following the woman into the fray.

David watched them move behind the line to where several bodies lay in the snow.

Turning back to the dock, he led the remaining thirty women to the gangplank of the black ship.

"You go ahead," he said to Gustav. "My arms are full."

The other man nodded and took the lead. He strode up the steep board to the deck of the vessel.

Besides the slow, deep creaking of timber rubbing against timber, there were no other sounds.

He signalled for the others to come aboard. Eventually, they all gathered on the deck, standing in the open.

"The captain's quarters are in there." Martha pointed to a place just up some steps, on a smaller deck above where they stood. "We should take her there. The bed is soft."

David didn't want to know how she knew that the bed was soft, but it wasn't hard to guess.

He hated what the crewmen of this ship had done to these women. He hated bringing them back to the vessel that held so many terrible memories for them.

Following Martha to the upper deck, he carried the traumatised girl to the captain's quarters.

Martha opened the door for him and led him inside.

It stank of mead and sweat.

Carefully, he placed the girl on the bed. She breathed rapidly, emitting small moans with each exhale as she rolled onto her side, reaching for David.

"I'll stay with her." Martha crawled onto the bed beside her, lying behind her and stoking her hair.

The girl's breathing eased, and she relaxed.

"She'll be all right," Martha told him.

David nodded and returned the way he had come, closing the door behind him.

He didn't want to leave the girl and Martha alone. Both of them had suffered much.

Too much.

Still, there were others on board that needed help.

He descended the steps back to the lower deck and saw all the women engaged in various tasks.

Some were opening storage compartments and retrieving ropes and tackle, while others were descending to the lower decks.

"What's going on?" David asked Gustav, who was giving instructions to the women and girls.

"I'm preparing the ship for departure," he replied. "And giving them something to do."

They told me they couldn't just sit here waiting. I said, *do you want to help get the ship ready to go?* They said, *yes.* So now they are getting the ship ready to go."

"What's down below?" David pointed to a set of stairs that descended to below the deck.

"There is a cargo hold, I think," Gustav told him. "There are big doors that open on the side of the ship to load and unload supplies. I'm hoping they kept the sails down there. The women are looking everywhere at the moment."

"Good thinking. I'll go and help," David said. "You keep watch for visitors. We don't need any unwanted guests."

Gustav nodded and turned his face towards the marketplace as David descended the stairs.

Thirty-Two

Twenty women came racing in with blades held aloft. They swiftly executed their fury and rage upon the enemy soldiers. The sheer will and determination that they displayed as they ganged up on the townsmen stunned Jeremy, outnumbering them, surrounding them as they joined the crewmen of the *Adelandria* in their fight.

Eventually, there were six remaining, all petrified as they glanced from the mob surrounding them to the many bodies of their comrades lying dead in the snow.

One man put his sword on the ground, raising his hands in surrender.

"Pick it up, you bastard," a woman called. "We don't intend to let you live. You may as well try to fight back."

He did so reluctantly.

"Why so scared?" called another. "You didn't seem so frightened when you came to see me the other night."

"Are you afraid that we'll do to you what you did to us?" taunted another. "We're not sick in the head like you lot."

A townsman swung his blade at one woman standing beside the captain.

Jeremy blocked the blow, stopping the blade inches from her face.

She lunged forwards and stuck her sword into his belly, poking it all the way through his back.

The other women would not wait for the others to build the courage to attack, choosing to cut down the remaining five townsmen instead.

The crew of the *Adelandria* stood back, watching, staring, awestruck, as the women continued blow after blow, even after their enemy had fallen to the ground.

Some of them cried as they hacked into the dead men. Others wore blank faces, showing no emotion whatsoever.

Jeremy quietly summoned his men to his side, leaving the women to vent their frustrations, and moved towards the wharves.

"Go to the warehouses," he commanded them. "Grab as much food as you can. See if there are barrels of fresh water and bring those, too. You know the drill."

"Aye, Captain," they replied before racing off to fulfil their new orders.

He watched the men jog past the market area before moving his eyes to the black ship. There, he saw movement on board as others looked to be preparing the ship for travel.

Sails were in place, ready to be hoisted. All they needed to do now was load the ship and get on board.

He turned back to the women to see that a few had moved away, filled with emotion as they fell to their knees, sobbing. Others moved towards him, intent to return to the ship.

A couple continued to hit into the bodies, not much left to strike but bloodied pulps upon the ground.

He wanted to stop them. He wanted to console the others and tell them it was all right.

But he didn't know what they had been through.

His experience with these men differed from theirs.

He lowered his eyes and turned away, sheathing his sword as he moved off towards the black ship moored to the wharf.

***

"Joanne," Emily called as they entered the foyer of the castle.

Tomas raised his sword as several men inside an archway to his left turned to see where the call had come from.

With the Erilian warriors by his side, they cut down the guards within their vicinity immediately.

Moving into the fray, the six warriors hacked and swung their blades, connecting with iron and flesh as Emily continued to call.

"Joanne," she cried. "Joanne."

The voice penetrated deep into her being.

She opened her eyes and broke contact with the other girls.

They all faced the sitting room, towards the sound of the calling voice. They glanced at one another, confused, befuddled.

Was it the Green Mistress?

Was it a trick to make them lose concentration?

Joanne wanted to risk a look. The voice was familiar.

It sounds like Emily.

She moved her eyes to Andris, hoping he might have seen who the caller was.

"Don't go out there," Tricia told her. "She'll kill you."

"I think it's my sister," Joanne told her.

"Joanne," the voice called again. "Are you in there?"

The Black Miss lowered her eyes.

It was worth the risk.

"I'm here," she called back as she stepped into the sitting room.

Emily almost dropped her sword as she watched a girl, clothed in black from head to toe, step from a passage at the side of the room. Even beneath the cloak and hood, she recognised her sister's gait.

It was her.

She had found Joanne.

Emily grinned and allowed an uncontrollable giggle to escape her lips. She placed her hand against her mouth as tears streamed down her cheeks.

My sister, she thought. *I found my sister.*

She wanted to run to her, pick her up, and squeeze her in her arms. But twenty men blocked the space between them.

"I'm coming," Emily called. "Wait there. I'm coming."

More girls, dressed in similar apparel to Joanne's but in different colours, moved into the room behind her.

Joanne reached for Tricia's hand.

Within moments, the seven girls had formed a line behind their six servants, joining as one.

Andris, in the middle of a tussle with a guard, watched his opponent fall suddenly to the ground.

There were no marks, no wounds, no smoke or bone crunching noises.

He simply dropped to the floor.

As did the next one and the next one.

It was sudden.

Five of the guards fell with no warning sign of doing so.

He turned to see the seven girls focusing their attention on the guards, stepping forwards slowly.

"Move ahead," Andris called to the other servants. "The Black Miss advances."

The other servants turned to see the united potentials stepping towards them. Swinging their blades at their enemies, they pushed the guards back, back, back towards the arch.

It dumbfounded Tomas as he saw the guards backing away from the fight inside the room, edging towards the arch. They continue to face the others inside and ignored the six in the foyer.

We have swords too, Tomas thought. *Are we not as dangerous?*

"It's the girls," Karlena announced. "They frighten the men."

One guard closer to the foyer stiffened. Something suddenly flayed his back open as if the air carried a blade.

"They frighten me," Tomas said as he watched the man fall to the floor.

The Erilian women plunged their blades into the guards as they backed out of the room. Even then, they didn't turn. Their eyes never left the seven girls approaching through the room.

With the room cleared of enemy soldiers, the six warriors faced the six servants who stood before the seven potentials.

Andris locked eyes with Tomas, sword ready to strike.

"Joanne," Emily called softly.

The girls were still connected. They had stopped their advance but seemed oblivious to their surroundings.

"What do you want with the Black Miss?" Andris asked her, keeping his eyes on Tomas.

"She is my sister," Emily sobbed, stepping forward.

The gold servant moved in her way and raised his sword.

"Hey," Tomas barked.

"No one approaches the potentials," the gold servant told them. "Not without their permission."

The girls lowered their hands and broke the connection.

"It's all right," Joanne told the servants, stepping past them to approach her sister.

"Joanne," Emily whispered as they embraced. "I've come to take you home."

The Black Miss sobbed, "They burnt our home and murdered Mama."

"We have a new home," Emily told her before looking to each of the six girls. "All of us. We will go to Woodmyst."

"Woodmyst," boomed a slurring voice from behind them.

They turned, peering past the foyer into the archway beyond.

At the far end of the room, upon her throne, sat the Green Mistress.

"She's here," Joanne hissed.

"Who is she?" Emily asked.

"Who am I?" the Green Mistress called. "I am Yasmeen Svoboda. Ruler of these lands. Chief Sorceress of the Coven of Mirikin. The Green Mistress."

She rose to her feet, glaring at them as they crossed the foyer to enter the throne room.

"Or perhaps you know me better by my other title," she said with a grimace. "The Sovereign."

Thirty-Three

"You?" Karlena glared at the woman in green. "You're responsible for all of this?"

"For this," the Green Mistress replied, "and so much more."

Akasati shook her head. "Why?"

"Why?" the woman repeated. "For power. That's why."

"You attacked our villages," Emily said. "How does that give you power?"

"Your villages were just in the way," she replied. "What I truly wanted was you. All of you." She pointed to the women.

"My men," she continued. "My prophets spread the word of my coming. I took what I needed to build my kingdom. I guided those who would serve under my authority. My Mistresses rule in my strongholds throughout all the lands. And soon, very soon, they will strike."

The servants of the girls positioned themselves between the Green Mistress and the others.

"You think you can stop me from getting to your beloved women?" She scowled. "I made you what you are. I can destroy you like that." The click of her fingers resonated loudly through the room.

Andris moved his head slightly as he struggled against pressure being applied against his chest. He dropped his sword as he attempted to suck air into his lungs, but something prevented him.

He heard five more blades falling to the stone floor as the other servants beside him struggled with the same difficulty.

His heart raced as genuine fear overwhelmed him.

Dying wasn't what he was afraid of. He faced that fear when he was a child. He knew one day that he would die and nothing would change that. It was the fate of every man.

His fear was for the Black Miss. His task was to protect her, yet he couldn't protect himself.

"Stop it," Tomas ordered her.

"Who are you to make demands of me, man of Woodmyst?" she slurred. "When I am through here, I will travel to your village and take your men as my slaves. I will use them to breed sons like these pitiful creatures.

"I will force them to take my ships, steal the females and murder the men before burning their homes into dust, all on my behalf. All for the Sovereign.

"And if they refuse..." she scowled. "If they choose to defy me. I will destroy them like this. Or perhaps something more spectacular like this."

Suddenly, gold servant's head exploded into a puff of vapour.

The Green Mistress chuckled as the headless body fell to the floor.

"Stop it now," Tomas barked.

"Before I'm through with your home, man of Woodmyst," she told him, "I will finish the task that the dragons did not. I will destroy them all. Everyone you love will die."

"Words," Tomas spat. "You have taken the coast. We own the mountains. We hunt in the forests. We survived the Night Demons and their pet dragons' fire. We rise from the ash and you are nothing compared to that. You putrid excuse of a dog."

Her eyes grew wide with anger. She thrust the five remaining servants out of the way with a wave of her hand.

They crashed against the left wall in a heap.

The men gasped noisily as the Sovereign moved her focus from them to the man of Woodmyst.

"Tell me, bitch." He glared at her. "Where is the white witch?"

"You won't find her," the Green Mistress told him, fury building in her eyes. "She has departed. But one day, if you somehow survive me, she will come for you."

"I'll count the days, whore," he coaxed her, taunted her, made her focus all her attention on him.

Her eyes grew dark, webs of black spreading like tendrils across her face.

She screamed at him.

"COME ON," he hollered at her.

She raised her hands, stretching her fingers towards him, the corners of her mouth rising into a mad grin as she squeezed her hands into a fist.

He felt his chest tighten.

He felt his face compress.

He felt as if he was being crushed by a giant vice.

A sudden, inhuman scream penetrated his ears.

The room seemed to shake upon its foundations as the Green Mistress suddenly flung through the air, smashing into her throne and thudding high against the stone wall.

Tomas felt a release. The compression ceased, and he could breathe again.

He turned to see women forming a circle with the girls in coloured garments. They held hands, eyes closed, united together as one.

Except Joanne, the Black Miss.

She was beside Tomas, her feet inches off the ground.

Her mouth was wide open, emitting an awful shriek.

Tomas felt as if his heart was going to stop as he looked at the young girl, fear filling every part of his being.

Black mist had formed around her eyes, expanding out to the side like vines.

She reached her hands towards the Green Mistress, fingers curved like claws.

She stretched her digits as wide as they could go.

The woman in green screamed in pain as her body stretched unnaturally.

Tomas thought he heard a few loud moist crunching sounds coming from the witch hanging high upon the wall.

"You can't kill me," she managed. "If you kill me, another will rise in my place. This will bring death. This will mean war."

Joanne fell silent.

Darkness enveloping her eyes.

Her fingers still stretched apart.

"If the Sovereign's demise brings war," the Black Miss said in a monotone, emotionless voice, "then so be it."

She clenched her fingers tightly, making two fists.

The Green Mistress, the Sovereign, suddenly imploded, splattering her insides across the wall and falling to a pile of bloodied mess upon the floor behind the throne.

Joanne relaxed and dropped to the floor, almost falling to her knees.

Tomas stepped in and caught her before she hit the ground.

He glanced over at the circle. They appeared as if they had just fought an amazing battle, weary in body.

"How did you know to do that?" he asked Emily.

"I don't know," she replied, lowering herself to the floor. "We just did."

He moved his eyes down to the face of the girl in his arms. Some auburn hair stuck out from beneath her black hood. It amazed him at how similar her features were to Emily's.

They shared a commonality, he deduced, that ventured beyond physicality.

He had just seen it.

They were both able to motivate, encourage, and inspire others with similar abilities.

He saw it with Emily on the plains when the women could sense the creatures nearby.

He saw it with the sister when she led the other girls during the squabble in the other room.

He saw it now when they united to defeat the Sovereign.

It was all beyond his understanding, but he knew there was something special about both of them.

He looked at the others; the Erilian warriors and the other girls in colourful cloaks.

There was something special about all of them.

Thirty-Four

The five servant boys helped the girls to their feet as Tomas held Joanne in his arms, carrying her to the foyer and away from the Green Mistress' throne room.

"You," he called to Andris, who watched Tomas like a hawk. "Torch the castle."

"Would you prefer me to carry her so you can do it yourself?"

"What have I done to you, boy?"

"She is the Black Miss," Andris replied, "and I have sworn to protect and serve her."

"And what a wonderful job you are doing," Tomas told him. "In case you haven't noticed, she has just saved us. Now, instead of worrying about whether I am a threat, how about you torch the bloody building." He turned to the other boys nearby. "And you lot help him. Meet us by the gatehouse."

Tomas carried Joanne through the main doors of the foyer, followed by Emily, the Erilian women and the six other girls as the servants rushed into the sitting room.

They scampered over the bodies of the guards, crossing the room to the fireplace still alight at the far end of the room.

They used their swords to pike burning pieces of wood before moving around the room to set tapestries, curtains, and the rug alight. Quickly moving through the rooms behind the giant stairwell, they set fire to anything flammable before returning to the foyer. There, they flung their burning wood high upon the stairs where they divided to ascend to the Green Mistress' quarters to the left and the potentials' rooms to the right.

With haste, they ran outside, making a beat for the gate where the others were waiting. Tomas, still holding Joanne in his arms, pointed with his chin towards the stables.

Heading their way were Simon and Oliver on horseback and leading a team of twenty steeds behind them.

"Look what we found," Simon called. "Do you think we can fit them on the ship with the other horses?"

"We'll try," Tomas told him as they drew near.

"We bridled them," Oliver told him. "But we didn't bother with saddles."

"Good enough." Tomas lifted Joanne to Simon, who positioned her in front of him so that she leant against his body.

Andris gave Tomas a disapproving look.

"She's my sister, boy," Emily said to him. "And I know that man and trust him. I don't know who you are. Until I do, eyes off her."

Andris lowered his eyes. "Yes, Mistress."

"What did you call me?" Emily sounded annoyed.

"I'm sorry," he replied. "You're like them. You all are."

"We are nothing like them." Karlena shook her head at him. "Make no mistake, boy. We might have power. But we are nothing like that bitch and her white witch dog."

"I'm sorry," he repeated, lowering his eyes still more.

"Leave him alone," Joanne groaned. They all turned to her. She looked down to Andris, her eyes full of pity for him. "He's a victim too. They all are. They don't know anything outside of fear and subjugation. They need to be shown how to live."

Emily felt her sister's words bite deep into her heart. She looked at Andris with fresh eyes, compassionate and remorseful.

"I apologise," she said to him.

"I understand, Miss..." He corrected himself. "My lady."

"Well, that really tugged at the heartstrings," Simon grunted. "Can we go now?"

Tomas allowed a wry smile to creep over his face.

"Mount up," he called to the others. He helped Sharek and Rhydra, both injured from the fight with the scarred man, onto their steeds by offering a boost.

When all climbed upon horseback, they galloped down the hill towards the warehouses at the northern end of the township below them.

The castle's windows filled in flames as the interior transformed into a furnace.

The snow continued to fall, drifting to the south because of strong northerly winds as they drew closer to the warehouses. There, they saw several crewmen taking stock from the stores and lugging it back to the ship farther down the road.

"Hey lads," Oliver called.

The small group of men let out a cheer.

"Will we have room for these horses on board?" Simon asked.

"Should do," one crewman answered. "We're just finished loading food stores and water."

"What are you getting now?" Akasati questioned.

"Blankets, and we were considering taking a couple of barrels of mead."

"Did Captain Shoenbach permit the mead to be brought on board?" Karlena asked the crewmen.

They were silent for some time before one of them spoke.

"No," he said, sounding like a disappointed child.

"Then take the blankets and get back to the ship," she ordered.

"Aye," they chorused, gathering the covers and leaving the barrels behind with the other stores they didn't need.

Simon peered into the open doors of the warehouses.

"Tomas," he called. "They could have tea in there."

"Forget it," he said. "We need to get to the ship."

"Not yet," Akasati said as she dropped to the ground. She climbed to the platform of the first warehouse on the left and reached around the door for the torch hanging on the wall.

"Flint," she called to Simon.

He reached under his cloak and into his pocket for the small stones. He tossed them to the Erilian warrior one at a time, and she struck them together to spark a flame.

With the torch lit, she tossed the flint back to its owner and grabbed the other torch from the opposite side of the door and ignited it. Once it was well lit, she tossed it into a cell nearby.

Some bedding inside the pen caught alight immediately and spread its flames along the floor, finding straw and blankets to feed its hunger as it grew.

She ran along the warehouse's platform, leaping across to the platform of the next storehouse. There she reached into the door and found another torch to light.

She repeated the process, and the contents of the warehouse were ablaze within seconds. She continued on to the next building and the next until she had thrown a flame into all structures.

Once she mounted her steed, they resumed their heading to the ship.

The flames of the warehouses stretched high into the air. The heat was intense and caused some of the nearby houses to smoulder. Before long, they too were burning, spreading the fire to the next house, and the next.

***

"Any sign?" Jeff called.

Baldwyn watched as the fire spread across the town at the far end of the community.

"We need to move," he called.

"What?" Jeff hollered back. The wind drowned out his friend's voice.

"We need to move now," Baldwyn shouted back to him.

"Oh." Jeff held onto the leads tightly as he urged his steed forward.

Reluctantly, the horses followed the man as he climbed the embankment.

***

Leading the captive horses and their riders along a ramp, Tomas ascended to the top of the wooden walkway and rode along the wharf to the black ship moored to its side.

Jeremy stood on deck waving to the approaching group, happy to see his friends.

Tomas let a smile grow on his face as he waved back. He was glad to see the other living and well.

"Bring them into the cargo hold," the captain called out, pointing to the open hatches on the starboard side of the ship. "Plenty of room."

Tomas nodded as he passed Jeremy's position and directed his horse up a wide, shallow ramp. Inside the cargo hold, he could see supplies of bread, salted pork, eggs, and barrels of water to his right at the bow. Next to them were a dozen chickens in a pen, some feed for them in sacks piled upon shelves above the pen.

At the other end, the stern, a high stack of bundled straw reached from ceiling to floor. Some more barrels of water lined the walls on either side for a short distance. Between the barrels and the door to the cargo hold were several roped areas to house the horses.

He could see from the outside that the ship was large, but nowhere near as large as the *Adelandria*. Inside, it appeared larger than Tomas thought it would be. It reminded him of the stable house he had visited as a boy, where he first encountered his brown mare.

Wooden beams supporting the ship's structure, positioned at regular intervals along the length of the vessel, had bright lanterns hanging from them, brightly lighting the cavernous area.

"This way, sir." A crewman directed him to the farthest stall towards the back of the ship. Before long, they roped in all the captive horses before the riders made their way up a set of steps to the deck above.

"How's it looking?" Tomas called to Jeremy, who was standing on deck with David.

"We'll be underway as soon as Baldwyn and Jeff arrive with the horses," he replied. "As soon as we stow the equipment, we'll set sail.

We might want to grab our bedding for our stay on board and make up a few places."

"Why is that?"

"This is a cargo ship," Jeremy told him. "They refit it with cages on the lowest level, but they are far from suitable accommodation. I've barred any from venturing down there. Totally off limits.

"Apart from that, there is limited bedding for the regular crew, so I've offered the crew's accommodation to the women. Even then, some of them will need to sleep on the floor, which is why I asked the men to gather as many blankets as they could.

"This will not be a comfortable trip home, I'm afraid."

"At least we're going home," Tomas replied.

"Good answer." Jeremy clasped a hand on the other's shoulder. "I trust your task was a success."

"The Sovereign is dead," Karlena announced as she crossed the deck with the rest of the group in tow. "This one killed her." The Erilian woman gestured to the young girl in black, leaning against Emily as they ascended the stairs.

"A girl?" David gasped.

"*We* killed her," Joanne corrected the other. "Together."

"This is Joanne," Emily told the others. "My sister."

"You found her." David smiled. "Thank the gods you found her."

"Gods!" Tomas shook his head as he peered towards the southern end of the town. "Who is that?"

They turned to see a large mob approaching through the darkness. Tomas tensed, fearing the worst.

Perhaps the witch had sent the dead after them.

The white bitch had done it before. Who knew what the Sovereign was capable of?

Jeremy reached for his spyglass. Patting his pocket, he remembered he had given it to Baldwyn.

The mob drew nearer and nearer, their image becoming more discernible through the falling snow.

There were horses. Many horses.

Tomas felt too tired to fight anymore. He could see on the faces around him that everyone felt the same.

"Hello," called a familiar voice.

"Hello," came a reply from the gangplank below.

It was Baldwyn and Jeremy, bringing up the horses and supplies.

***

The horses went into their pens, and they stowed the supplies. They brought bedding and blankets to the upper decks as passengers claimed places all over the ship to sleep.

When the crew shut the doors to the cargo hold and everyone ready to go, Captain Jeremy Schoenbach gave the order.

"Cast off."

The northerly wind filled the sails and pushed the black ship away from the docks towards the open sea.

Steering to the south, the vessel started its long journey to Oakbeach.

They were going home.

***

The vessel grew smaller and smaller as it pulled away from the shore. The fire drew nearer and nearer as it crept across the rooftops towards the southern end of town.

Flames brought fear.

But hunger brought desperation.

The smell of blood was too inviting.

The creatures raced across the ground, keeping to the southern edge of the town. They circled to a patch of ground where many bodies lay and dragged them away from the human dwellings, far out onto the snow.

As the flames engulfed the town and structures crumbled to ash, the creatures feasted.

Thirty-Five

For five full days and nights, the wind blew constant and true, pushing the black ship to the south at a great speed.

With full supplies being rationed well and those who could pitch in where they could, the ship could continue its voyage day and night.

"The gods are on our side," David would say now and then, mainly to get on Tomas' nerves as there wasn't much else to do for fun.

Sometimes, Tomas would bite back with a growly, "There are no gods.

It became such an expected reaction that whenever David made the call, the girls in colourful robes would reply before Tomas had the chance.

"There are no gods," they would chorus before exploding into a giggling fit.

"You bastard," Tomas would often say in jest to the bald giant, who would react by falling into a giggling fit of his own.

The crew smiled at these minor exchanges between the girls and the men, not because they found it humorous, but because they were glad the children were being children again.

Passing the first outpost made of wood was exciting, enabling Emily and Erilian warriors to share their story of their journey with the younger passengers on board.

As they moved by the many plains before the next iconic landmark, they considered the battles on the snow against man and beast. The Erilian women mourned Rhyodia again. Tomas wept for his mare.

Sailing by the giant mountain with its arm falling into the sea was a monumental moment for the crew and the men of Woodmyst. It was here where they had lost their beloved Captain Tarkin and their friend Ivo to the murderous white witch, Sumaiyya Tarkin.

All who knew the men made a silent and solemn vow to avenge them. They would search for her and one day remove her from the world.

Jeremy used the spyglass to look towards the shore. Snow-covered the place where they had set a pyre. The smoke from the white witch's lair had vanished.

He hoped she had vanished too, perhaps dead in the ice lands to the north.

But he knew better.

During one night, they sailed by the ruins of the stone watchtower and the fire pit. Tomas and Emily stood on deck, peering towards the shore.

There was no more orange glow from the pit where they had burnt the remains of enemy soldiers and straw men. It appeared lifeless. Dead.

Abandoned.

The young woman lying in the captain's quarters brought herself onto the deck. She sat on the steps near the door to the room for most of the day, just resting silently and looking at the scenery as it passed by.

David wanted to approach her and talk to her, but knew better than to try. He could see it in her eyes. She wasn't ready to receive male company.

She might never again.

Martha stayed with her, silently consoling her with hugs and cradling arms. For now, that was enough.

It was only another day and a half after seeing the fallen tower they spotted the seaside port of Oakbeach.

The crewmen dropped to their knees and cried tears of joy when they saw her. Her tall masts standing high and strong. Her broad hull and cannon ports lining the side of her bulk.

The *Adelandria*.

"She is beautiful," Jeremy said as he steered the ship towards the port.

Tomas didn't see it. He found the vessel to be an admirable construction, but it was just a ship to him.

"Must be a seafarer thing," he said to Oliver.

"Mmm," the other agreed with a nod. "Give me a farm any day."

"I always thought you paid too much attention to your goats," David quipped. "Farmboy."

Oliver punched him in the arm, hard.

Jeremy ordered the ship to slow as they neared the dock.

Soon after, they were alongside the wharf. Reynard Merys, the wharf owner, was there to greet them, tying off the lines at the dock.

"Welcome back," he called as the gangplank lowered. "I see you found a ship."

"We'll be scuttling her as soon as we offload our cargo," Jeremy told him.

"Why?" he asked. "She looks seaworthy enough."

"She was used for evil, my friend," the captain replied. "There are too many bad memories on board."

Sure enough, after all cargo and belongings removed from the ship, and as the sun sank behind the mountains, they took away her from the shore and her anchor dropped a little distance away.

The men on board took a rowing boat back to the dock as Akasati lit an arrow before firing it from the end of the wharf into the deck of the large black vessel.

Gathered on the shore with all that had been on board, as well as most of the folk from Oakbeach, they watched her burn. Her masts creaked and cracked loudly as the wood splintered and ripped apart from the heat. With a loud groan, the main mast smashed to the deck, followed shortly thereafter by the lesser two posts.

Soon the frame of the ship was ablaze, the flames weakening the hull so that sea water seeped into the lower decks.

She started to sink gradually as flames engulfed the captain's and crew's quarters.

Slowly, slowly, she vanished beneath the waves, smoke and steam drifting across the water's surface as the only sign that she was ever there. Before long, it too vanished, brushed away in the wind.

***

Innkeeper James Halle was more than happy to open his establishment to the returning travellers. He offered the rooms to the men of Woodmyst again, but they declined, giving them to the seven girls instead, as the men opted to stay in the barn and set up tents in the yard if the innkeeper would allow it.

The Halles were happy to oblige, allowing a fire to be built in the yard and for the younger of the rescued women to bed on the floor with Joanne and the six girls in coloured garments.

Emily and the men of Woodmyst gathered with the crewmen of the *Adelandria* and the Erilian women in the main room of the inn to share a last civilised meal in a manner to say their farewells to one another.

"We will see each other again," Jeremy told them. "It's inevitable."

"You're talking about the white witch," Oliver said.

"The Sovereign said there will be war coming." He looked at Tomas. "Correct?"

"That's what she said," Tomas replied.

"And it would appear that we have many of these *Mistresses* out there," he continued.

"We know from what those boys told us that the intention was for your little sister and her friends to be a part of that."

Emily nodded.

"Then I think her war is coming." Jeremy frowned. "I think we'll encounter these Mistresses, eventually. We can't be complacent. We can't ever forget. We won't be safe on the coast and you won't be safe far inland at Woodmyst. This war will spread across all lands."

"How do we fight such a war?" Baldwyn asked. "We are only a small band of people. If they have resources and men to successfully wage a war so big, how can we ever believe we can win?"

"They have resources," Jeremy told him. "They have fear on their side. They have burnt villages and raided towns. They've raped and stolen women and children and wiped out entire populations along the coast.

"All they need to do is mention the *Sovereign* in certain places and word will spread like wildfire. Fear will spread with it.

"And while people scurry and hide, they will move in and gain control, seize power. They've already done the groundwork for the past ten years. They found their potentials for her. They grew into her Mistresses, and like disciples, they expanded her kingdom.

"They have set the pattern. This isn't over. By killing the Sovereign, we may have strengthened her, more than she already was."

"What do you mean?" Tomas questioned him. "She's dead. I saw it. There's no coming back from that."

"She doesn't need to," Jeremy told him. "She will now become an ideal. She's a way of life. A god."

Tomas sat in silence as he moved his eyes to the fire in the corner of the room. Watching the flames as he thought of the captain's words, he never felt more like drinking a mug of mead in his life.

***

Anya, James' wife, doted on the girls personally, mothering each and every one of them while they were under her roof. She practically tucked them all into bed before she retired for the evening and cradled any who she heard crying in the night. It was no wonder all the young girls hugged the innkeeper's wife before they mounted their horses to leave.

They exchanged friendly embraces and handshakes with the crewmen of *Adelandria*. Emily formed a circle with the Erilian women, touching foreheads with each of them as they said their farewells.

David waited to the side until they were finished with their tearful exchanges. When Emily moved away, he stepped in and gave each one of them a great big hug.

Back upon their horses, Emily, the men of Woodmyst, the girls in coloured cloaks, and the five boys of Castle Blackrock directed their steeds towards the mountains. A mob comprising twenty women followed them, including Martha and the silent girl, as well as several who had come from the village in the mountains. The rest of the women that were rescued from the warehouse in Blackrock Haven had remained in Oakbeach, where they would start a new life or seek transport to find surviving members of their families.

Before long, they had entered the forest and were climbing familiar slopes towards the mountain peaks.

***

It was four days' journey, over the peak and through the Forest of Khun, before they arrived at the place where Emily's and Joanne's mother was buried. They stayed for a little while to pay their respects, allowing a chance for the two girls and those present who knew the family to grieve together.

Moving on, they camped for the night near the stream where they first encountered Emily after her escape. With supplies of salted pork, bread and tea still plenty, their journey wasn't one of desperation. Still, some women asked how much farther.

The men couldn't blame them. After all, they had spent days on board the black ship locked in cages, only to be moved to other cages to spend the rest of their lives in.

Tomas sympathised with them. They were eager to see their new home, to get as far away from the memory that the scarred man and his kind had instilled in them. They hoped Woodmyst might offer such an escape. A new life.

"We may still have three more days of journey," Tomas told them honestly.

He hoped for less, but calculated for the worst-case scenario such as a blizzard.

"Will we visit the village?" asked Tricia. "My father and bothers were..."

"We will," Tomas told her. He looked at her for a long time. A question had been brewing in his mind for some time since meeting the girl. He knew she had come from the same village as Emily and her sister, Joanne. But he had not seen her recognise any of the other women they had rescued as a relative or close friend.

Not willing to ask her directly, he waited until the girls were asleep and all the others had retired for the night, when he and Emily were alone by the fire.

"Does Tricia have a mother or sisters?" he asked.

"Her mother died before they moved to the settlement," Emily told him. "I don't know the entire story. Just that she grew ill and passed. There were two boys, no other girls. My guess is that they were all murdered during the raid."

Tomas held her close to him.

"The other girls didn't find their families either," he said. "No mothers. No sisters."

"They are all sisters now, Tomas," she replied. "After what they have been through, we couldn't expect them to ever separate again."

He nodded.

"They all look to your sister," he said after a while. "She leads them."

"She has a great power inside her," Emily said, her voice sounding weary.

"She looks to you," Tomas continued. "And you have a great power in you too."

"Are you afraid of us?" she asked, pulling away slightly to look into his eyes. Hers appeared heavy to him. She was tired. He guessed she was sitting up for his sake, not for her own.

He shook his head.

"I love you, Emily," he told her. "I'm just trying to understand."

She knew his words were true and leant against him again.

"Me too," she admitted, closing her eyes.

"I don't possess power," he said as he hugged her tightly. "But I want to help you and the girls comprehend what you can do."

"You have power, Tomas," she told him. "I've seen it."

"What do you mean?" he asked.

She was silent.

Her breathing eased, and her body relaxed.

Power? he thought as he held her against his body. *I hope I have enough to carry you to bed.*

Thirty-Six

An early start the next morning saw them reach the mountain village, Emily's home, by mid-afternoon.

Some women from the settlement spent their time weeping as they remembered fond times and terrible times in the small community.

It was a strange thing when Tomas considered it. Their enemies, those responsible for the surrounding desolation, destroyed, yet they still managed, even now, to torment these women to the point of tears.

The men had considered camping at the site again, just as they had done when they first set out on their journey.

"We should find a clearing to stay the night," Simon told them. "We can't camp here. This is hallowed ground."

David felt a knot in his belly as Simon spoke his words.

"He's right," the big man put in. "We can't stay here."

Tomas nodded as he observed both Emily and Joanne standing in what was once their home, embracing each other, sobbing uncontrollably.

"Tomas?" Oliver nudged the other, bringing him back to the conversation. "What do you say?"

"We won't pitch camp here," he replied. "We can't."

***

They rode on a short distance and in the first clearing they came upon; they pitched their tents and made a fire. Setting up camp had become a speedy process, with the additional help of the five boys from Castle Blackrock. They were quick learners and proficient workers.

Andris explained to the men of Woodmyst that their training started when they were still infants. They were taught the required skills for basic survival and defence so they could be an efficient protection for their allotted potential.

"That's kind of upsetting," David told him as they sat about the fire, drinking tea and eating salted pork.

"What do you mean?" said one of the other boys.

"That you are expected, from birth, to do this one task," the big man replied. "And only that one task."

"Isn't that the way it is in many places?" Martha said to David, the silent girl leaning against her as they sat upon a log near the bald giant. "If your father is a farmer, then you will be a farmer. If your father is a blacksmith, then you will be a blacksmith."

"That is true for many places," Tomas told her. "But most of the villages near us recognise individual choice. Redwood Pass, for example, is a logging town on the other side of the Lunkhul Forest from our home. We trade with them and pass by it on our way to Old Castle.

"You would think, it being a logging town, that their sons would be loggers. But some of their sons have moved on to be scholars in Kailibard, or merchants in Old Castle or many other forms of occupation.

"We embrace difference and individuality," Tomas finished.

"And your women?" Emily asked.

"You have your individuality too," he said. "Let's see. There's the cooking and the cleaning and the..."

She smacked him on the shoulder playfully.

"We don't hold women back from what it is they want to do," Oliver told them. "You could apply to study with the scholars just the same as any man. You could pick up a sword and shield and fight in any army. Most choose not to, but the ways of the west are not like most places. Not since the Night Demons."

"How did that change things?" Andris asked.

"The men," Oliver told him. "The *wise* ones, that is, realised that life is too short for traditionalism. Someone or something could wipe us out at any time, so we may as well enjoy life and be what we want to be while we can."

"Given that it doesn't harm anyone," Simon put in.

"Right," Oliver agreed. "There are laws. So, if a woman doesn't want to marry and bear children, as tradition expects her to do, she doesn't have to."

"And the men?" Martha asked. "Are they expected to fight or join armies?"

"All men fight in times of desperation," Tomas told her. "So do the women. We have armies throughout the western realms. You can join the military if you wish, or sew with needle and thread if you desire. It's your choice. But if needed, we will answer the call to fight. We must protect our right to be free."

***

The next day, they descended most of the mountain range as they navigated through the Forest of Khun. Tomas sheltered in the caves where the Night Demons took him and the other men as children.

"One more night," he told them.

They tethered together the horses deeper inside the cavern as the campers set up a fire just inside the mouth of the cave. Tents were erected and some large stones and logs moved into place around the hearth to sit upon.

It seemed odd to have a campsite that wasn't completely encompassed by white, Emily thought, as she looked at the dark soil on the ground beneath the shelters. She was glad to be out of the wind and snowdrifts, but the chill of winter still ventured deep into the cave, penetrating through her thick clothing.

Emily noticed the men were uncharacteristically quiet during the night. Even Tomas, who still held her and kissed her, remained silent.

She could tell it was the place in which they sheltered. There was something, a memory, that occupied their thoughts for the time being.

"This place holds memories," she said to him.

He nodded.

"We were brought here as children," he told her. "Taken from our home by the Night Demons."

She looked around at the faces by the fire. All eyes were on Tomas, except for the other men of Woodmyst, who stared into the flames of the fire.

"They bound us with ropes and gagged some of us," he continued. "They put a bag over my head and sat me down, way down the other end of this cave."

He pointed past the horses, into the darkness.

"They gave us water, and fed us and took care of us with gentle hands." Tears built in his eyes as he recalled the events. "All the while, their warriors were attacking our walls and slaying our fathers. If that wasn't enough, they sent dragons to burn our mothers and elderly who were gathered in the Great Hall.

"When they had finished with our village," he said as he wiped his eyes, "they put us on horseback and took us home. The only adult survivor was Richard, who has been our father to all of us.

"Now we are rebuilding."

"You visit this place often," Joanne perceived.

He looked over to her, meeting her eyes.

"Yes," he replied. The other men of Woodmyst moved their eyes to him. "I come every summer and spend one night here. It helps me to remember their faces sometimes."

"Your mother and father?" Emily asked.

He nodded.

"Although," he said, "the last few times, I've been remembering what they looked like less and less."

"I didn't know." David frowned. "I thought you went away hunting."

"That's what I told everyone," he admitted.

"I could come with you next time, Tomas," the big man offered.

"We could," Simon added.

Tomas shook his head.

"I think this will be my last visit to these caves for a long time," he said as he looked at Emily. "I think it's time to leave the past and look to the future."

She reached to his face and wiped his tears with her fingers before leaning into him.

***

"The gods are on our side," David said as they rode during the next day.

The sun was shining, and the birds were singing. He took a deep breath and feigned a cough, setting the girls into giggles again.

"Smells like home," he sang.

They climbed a slight incline for a short distance to the crest. Below them stood an all-familiar sight to the men.

Woodmyst.

The river flowed quietly to their left, and the grove sat to their right. They looked down from the hill to the small village with several neat huts with smoking chimneys. A few people moved about between the dwellings, braving the cold.

Two riders approached, armed.

Tomas wasn't concerned. It was the practice of the town to send an armed welcoming party if any visitors showed up.

"We're home, Tomas." Simon smiled. "What do you miss the most?"

"My bed," he admitted, not needing to think of an answer.

"Tomas," called a rider, smiling ear to ear. It was Lor, his closest friend.

"You haven't married my sister yet, have you?"

"No." He laughed. "Of course not. She wouldn't have it."

"So, you tried?" Tomas asked as he moved to his friend's side to clasp hands.

"I won't lie to you." Lor smiled more widely. "Yes. I love her more than you. Why should I have to wait?"

"We have much to talk about, Lor," Tomas told him. "But we would also like to rest. We need to find accommodation for these people."

"I think we can manage," Lor replied.

"This is Emily." He introduced the auburn woman to his friend. "She is Antony's daughter and, with his blessing, she will be my wife."

Lor punched Tomas in the arm as he let out a delighted laugh.

"Good for you," he said. "About bloody time."

"I'll say," murmured David.

"This is Joanne." He pointed to the girl in black. "She is Emily's sister."

"A pleasure, my lady," he said as he looked at the other six girls in colourful garments. "And what's with the rainbow?"

"That is a long story," Tomas replied.

Lor moved his eyes to the five other men riding with his friends.

"I am guessing the women came from the village?"

"No," Oliver said. "There's more to it."

"And the pretty boys?"

"Still part of the same story," Oliver replied.

"I'm intrigued." Lor frowned. "You must tell us all about it. But first, let's get you home. Where's Ivo?"

***

Moments later, they penned the horses in the stable and the community had been called together by the large fireplace in the centre of the village.

Richard exchanged hugs with the boys upon seeing them and shed tears when he heard about Ivo.

Antony wouldn't let his daughters go.

Oliver attempted inconspicuously to make his way to Agnes Fysher's side where, under the watchful eye of her sister Jane, he made her smile with words that he whispered in her ear. Simon and David chuckled quietly as they observed their friend's eyes continuously wandering from the young woman's face to a particular area that he favoured below her neck.

The rescued women were all standing together timidly, afraid. After greeting her brother with an embrace, Linet approached the women with the other daughters of Woodmyst. Some verbal exchange was occurring between the ladies as Richard took to a makeshift platform by the edge of the fire. Becka held his hand as he addressed the crowd.

"People of Woodmyst," he began. "We have lost a valuable and well-loved member of our community. We need to take a moment to remember a good man, Ivo Hamond, lost on a perilous mission to rescue these women from cruelty and slavery. He was a son to me, and a brother to you. May he live on in our memories."

The gathering fell silent as they took time to pay their respects to the fallen member of their community. They all shed some tears as others mourned. Some formed smiles as fond memories flooded the minds of those who knew Ivo best.

After some time had passed, Richard spoke again.

"We have a desperate need to meet. These ladies and boys have been rescued from tyranny and oppression. They now need our help. Who would be willing to take some of these women under their roof until we can build suitable dwellings after the winter has passed?"

"All done," Linet called.

"Oh." Richard frowned. "What about the boys?"

"I've sorted that." Lor raised his hands. "They'll share with some of us lads."

"And," Richard said as he turned to the girls in colours. "And the girls?"

"I'll look after them," Tomas told him.

"You have one bedroom," Richard reminded him. "And one bed. Right now, Antony is using it."

Tomas nodded.

"Antony can continue to use my bed," Tomas replied. "I'll need some help to clear my sitting room of all my furniture so I can put bedding down for the girls. I hope you don't mind, Antony."

"No," the old man replied, holding his daughters in his arms. "It's your house, Tomas. I'm just grateful to have my girls back."

Emily kissed her father and made her way over to Tomas. After all he had been through to rescue people he didn't even know, he was still willing to sacrifice more.

"And where will you sleep, Tomas?" David smiled.

Tomas pursed his lips.

The barn could be warm enough, he thought.

Perhaps I could bunk with David or Oliver.

"We'll pitch the tent by the house," Emily replied as she placed her arms around him. "He has me to keep him warm."

Richard felt his heart grow warm as he watched the two embrace. They all did.

The old man was more than convinced that Woodmyst's future rested upon Tomas.

A natural leader that others followed willingly, including himself.

A respected man who put others before himself.

One that he considered as a son.

The only one that he felt could take the responsibility and weight of his community with the dignity, temperament and love that it required.

Even with his aversion towards the gods, Tomas was the guiding light for many of them.

People listened to him, and he listened to them.

He was the true chief of the village.

The torch-bearer that they needed.

The heir of Woodmyst.

Epilogue

She had watched from a pint high upon the mountains as fire destroyed the castle, her home.

Inside, she knew that her lover, her Mistress, was gone and that they would never have the chance to hold one another again. No longer would she feel her touch, her presence, her power.

She felt lost, alone, and heartbroken.

Weeping as the flames burst through the windows of the upstairs rooms, she imagined the bed-chamber of the Green Mistress with its beautiful tapestries and adornments suddenly engulfed in flame. She saw the dresser with brushes laced with fire. The long curtains ablaze with bright flames. The bed that she had lain upon so many times, where she had felt loved, turning to ash.

A fury built within her.

A fire deep within her kindled and grew until a furnace burned against the back of her eyes.

She wanted to return to the town below.

She wanted to destroy them all.

But they were too strong.

They had too much power, even for her to overthrow. For now.

The little Black Miss and her followers.

The auburn girl with her man from Woodmyst.

They were all there.

She couldn't risk it, she thought as she rubbed her belly, sensing the life within.

Her task was to protect *him* now.

Watching the warehouses ignite, she pondered where she should go. The other Mistresses dwelt strategically throughout the coastal realms, and the closest resided far to the south.

But she couldn't go that way.

The enemy would watch for her.

They would be prepared.

Those who were still in the town below her would see to that.

West was her only option. She would find refuge with one of the Mistresses in the west.

It would be a long journey.

She needed to cross the mountain range and travel over the vast plains that spanned the realms between Blackrock Haven and the western sea.

The rooftops of the houses to the northern side of the town caught fire as she turned her horse away.

With the guards flanking her, she rode slowly, ascending the steep slope of the mountain, heading for the lower ridge to the right of the peak.

As they drove their horses, plodding through the thick snow and shielding themselves from the weather with their cloaks, she considered the future for the Coven of Mirikin. Without the Green Mistress, there was no definitive leader within the group.

She thought of the others and didn't see any prospective Prime Sorceress for the Coven of Mirikin.

None, except for herself.

She questioned why she shouldn't be considered for the position.

Yes, she was the youngest of them. But she had been serving the Sovereign longer than some.

The others who had been with the coven longer than her were nowhere near as powerful as she. Her skills surpassed them all.

She was stronger.

She was worthy.

She could be the new Sovereign.

If they opposed her, she would crush them all and wipe them out.

With intent to take leadership of the coven by force, if necessary, she rode over the ridge and into the highlands of the mountain range.

Steep hills and jagged crests spanned the landscape before her.

Strong winds from the north blew across their path, bringing with it icy snow and stinging sleet.

She wrapped her cloak tightly around her, hunching her shoulders forwards as she felt a deep chill. Shivering slightly, she urged her horse forwards.

Reaching behind him, one guard undid his bedroll and retrieved a blanket, offering it to the White Mistress.

She took it without a word and wrapped the thick drab grey material around her body.

It smelled of horse; she thought as they pushed on, into the dark night, into the bitter alps before them.

Sheltering in shallow caves as they crossed the range and growing desperate for food, the three travellers resorted to approaching the small settlements and farmhouses that dotted the land in order to raid stores for supplies. There, they would torture, molest, and slaughter those who dwelt within before enjoying the spoils of feasting and bedding together.

And so it was, for all the miles that they travelled upon the border of the ice lands to the north. The two guards had eventually developed a taste for it, an addiction.

A light in the distance would draw them like a moth to the flame. She found it thrilling to watch them in action as they raided properties, and performed their lewd acts, partaking when she wished.

But, while it became her guards' focus to find the next farm or the next tiny village to raid, she remained fixated on the cause. For every step their steeds took, for the many, many miles and the countless days that they trekked, her mind consumed with the end goal.

I will become the Chief Sorceress, she told herself.

I will continue the cause.

The legacy of the Green Mistress must be protected.

The Sovereign will live on through me.

I will unite the Coven of Mirikin once again.

We must make the preparations for my son.

She rubbed her belly whenever she thought of him. There was no sign of a bump yet, but she could feel him inside her.

Growing.

Developing.

His power will be absolute.

His rule will surpass all.

They will all bow.

They will all worship him.

They will fear his name.

All will know the Maji and tremble.

And then, she grimaced, *there must be war.*

About the Author

Robert E Kreig was born in Newcastle, Australia and grew up in its outer suburbs.

He has always had a love for books, particularly well-told stories involving action, adventure and fear.

Some of Robert's favourite authors as a young reader included J. R. R. Tolkien, Stephen King, Orson Scott Card, Ray Bradbury and Frank Herbert. As he grew into adulthood, the list continued to lengthen, adding more influential writers such as George R. R. Martin, Matthew Reilly, Nathan M. Farrugia, Dan Brown, James Patterson, Michael Connelly and Lee Child just to name a few.

Inspired by movies like Star Wars, King Kong, Jaws, Jason and the Argonauts and other great adventure pieces, Robert listened to the voices in his head and entertained the strange visions dancing through his mind to assist him with writing his fantasy series The Woodmyst Chronicles.

Robert has penned ten books for the series which follow the lives of many characters, particularly focussing upon a family who must face many trials before the epic conclusion. Clashing swords, strange creatures, flying dragons and sorcery inhabit the world surrounding Woodmyst.

Robert is always working on something new and has also written a standalone book, Long Valley.

Robert currently lives in Canberra where he dreams of one day becoming a full-time writer.

Other Books By This Author

THE WOODMYST CHRONICLES

From a faraway land...
...comes a new adventure.
The Woodmyst Chronicles is the story of a small community that faces the hardest of trials in a world filled with darkness, violence and magic.

Books In This Series...
THE WALLS OF WOODMYST
THE SONS OF WOODMYST
THE HEIR OF WOODMYST
THE WARLORDS OF WOODMYST
THE HUNTRESS OF WOODMYST
THE SHADOW OF WOODMYST
THE BRIDES OF WOODMYST
THE GODS OF WOODMYST
THE WEAPONS OF WOODMYST
A FAREWELL TO WOODMYST

LONG VALLEY

In the small community of Long Valley, nestled comfortably beneath snow-capped mountains, people quietly go about their business. Everybody knows everybody and there are no worries to give mind to.

But something has awakened.

A tragic accident near the valley's army base sparks a number of terrifying events, placing the local civilians in mortal danger.

A contagion is subsequently released into Long Valley, infecting pets, livestock, wildlife and people.

It's up to the local law enforcement and a small band of citizens to try to keep the town safe.

In the end, it becomes a struggle for survival as the people of Long Valley are overcome by the urge to feed.

www.whitekeepbooks.com

www.robertekreig.com